Captain Hawkes

ISBN: 978-1522959885

First Published in 2016 by Blossom Spring Publishing.

Captain Hawkes Copyright © 2016 Claire Voet.

Claire Voet has asserted her right under the Copyright,
Designs and Patents
Act, 1988, to be identified as Author of this Work.
British Library Cataloguing in Publication Data.
A catalogue record for this book is
available from the British Library.

Also by Claire Voet

WHITTINGTON MANOR

WHITTINGTON MANOR II – THE POPPY SUNSET

THE GHOST OF BLUEBELL COTTAGE

THE OTHER DADDY – A WORLD AWAY

A HELPING HAND (SHORT STORY)

"CAPTAIN HAWKES"

Claire Voet

1911-1912
WHITBY
North Yorkshire

Chapter One

The pale sky was shredded by occasional clouds, which partially covered the sun. The abbey stood tall, a monument to Whitby. It seemed that, from almost every angle of Whitby, you could not fail to notice its captivating outline looming on top of the east cliff. Close to the abbey stood St. Mary's church. The wind whistled around the graveyard, and the steps leading down into the town were scattered with blown and rustling leaves. The locals thought nothing of climbing these prominent one hundred and ninety nine steps at times of worship. The congregation, known as the *church parade*, had been photographed many times over the years while they made their way up and down the narrow, uneven steps in their Sunday best, showing off their finery; women in particular, with their long flowing silk or cotton dresses with button detailing, braid and lace trim and, of course, elaborate hats and parasols to match.

Below the abbey, in the harbour, scaffolding stretched far and wide while men worked. A steel framework had been erected, used to advance along the sea bed and out to sea as the work progressed. It had two large parts to it that resembled legs, and so the locals had nick- named it *the walking man*. The laughing shrieks of seagulls could be heard loudly against the clanking of timber, fishermen selling their catch down at the quayside, and the sounding horns of boats and trawlers coming in and out of a busy little harbour.

Captain James Hawkes stood on dry land for the first time in many months after a long voyage around Europe. He inhaled the air. 'Whitby at its best,' he mumbled under his breath. He threw his heavy sea bag over his shoulder. Still swaying a little from the sensation of being on high seas for so long, his eyes darted urgently between folk as they went about their business. He searched eagerly for Victoria. Why was she not there to meet him? He checked his watch. He had written to her to say he was on his way, giving her his expected arrival date and time. Perhaps she had not received his letter; it was the only explanation he could think of. He had missed her so much. He could still smell her perfume and remember the feel of her soft lips against his. Victoria Crawford, he could hardly wait to see her and hold her in his arms again.

He made his way past numerous busy shops. James Hawkes knew the streets of Whitby like the back of his hand. Although born in Hull, he had grown up in Whitby as a young boy, and then as a teenager the Hawkes family had moved to Ruswarp, a neighbouring village on the outskirts. Now at twenty eight, James had matured into a fine figure of a man; tall, broad, with fair tousled hair and sun-kissed skin, a little weather-beaten from his days at sea, but handsome nevertheless.

In some ways it felt like he had not been away for any time at all as he walked down the familiar streets of a secretive, busy, little town located on the north east coast of England.

Walking into a jewellery shop, a bell over the door chimed and James removed his hat. He was soon greeted by a gentleman with thinning, grey hair and an almost toothless grin. 'Ayup! If it isn't our very own Captain 'Awkes.'

'Mr Spence!' He gave the shopkeeper a firm handshake. 'I hardly recognised the harbour, what's happening?'

'Oh that monstrosity, it's an extension t' pier,' Mr Spence rolled his eyes. 'Don't see why they 'ave to change things. Nowt wrong with it - stood there good and proper for many a year.'

'They'll have their reasons, no doubt,' James replied, tactfully, knowing full well that the pier was in desperate need of restoration and had not come a day too soon. However, Mr Spence obviously thought otherwise.

'Any'ow, you're back. 'Ow was your trip?'

'Same as always, Mr Spence. Same as always.' James perused the shelves, hoping to find something suitably eye-catching.

'Miss 'Awkes's birthday is it?' Mr Spence put on his spectacles, ready to get down to business.

'No. My sister's birthday is later in the year,' James informed him. 'I wish to buy a gift for Miss Crawford.' He peered into a glass case in front of him at a fine display of hand-crafted jet jewellery.

An instant look of concern swept over Mr Spence's face at the very mention of Miss Crawford's name. He had heard the rumours, but they were yet to be confirmed. Obviously Captain Hawkes had no idea, what with him being at sea for many months. But was it

- 3 -

Mr Spence's place to tell? Before he had a chance to decide, James had picked out a heart-shaped pendant and handed it to him. 'I'll take this one please.'

Mr Spence, seizing the opportunity of a sale, and brushing his deliberating thoughts to one side, decided to say nothing and took the money instead, thanking James and bidding him farewell, leaving no chance of the conversation developing further and his knowledge getting the better of his guilty conscience.

James was back on his way, pleased with his purchase and looking forward to seeing Victoria's eyes light up at the sight of the pendant, he knew she would love it. She had a passion for jet jewellery.

He inhaled the fresh air. It was nippy, but that was quite usual for the north east of England in spring. It was good to be back in Yorkshire where he belonged. If truth be told, he was getting tired of being away at sea. After months of missing Victoria, he had realised just how much she meant to him, the only woman he had truly loved and wished to spend the rest of his life with. She would need a husband to be close to home, not one that was away at sea for months on end.

He envied his brother, Robert, inheriting the family corn mill in Ruswarp after their father's death. The mill would have been the answer to his problem. He quite fancied the idea of running a mill. Joseph Hawkes, a hardnosed businessman, had rarely shown his emotions, but it had been Robert, who he had clearly favoured, while for James he had no real purpose. His daughter Lillian, he tolerated, but he had not much to do with her. Other than a shared portion of money, Joseph Hawkes had left his youngest son nothing else, not even prized possessions, they had been shared between Robert and Lillian; Robert inheriting the most.

Pursuing a life in the navy had seemed the perfect solution for James and, after his mother had died, the decision to leave had been easy. She was the only person that had understood him implicitly. James had inherited his easy-going nature from her. She and James had talked about their dreams of travel over and over, and she had made him promise her he would travel the world before he settled down. James had worked hard in his chosen profession, travelled far and wide but even now, as a respected Captain, he suspected, had his father still been alive, it would have made no difference to him. He wondered why his father had never found it in his heart to be proud of him.

The wind had picked up as he marched on down cobbled streets with squat houses, some with bow windows and lace curtains that twitched as they watched the captain walk past. He turned into Sandgate Lane, and then walked up to the market square. He needed to cross the square to get to old Tom, the blacksmith, whom he knew would have a spare horse for him. Feeling slightly jaded after his long journey, and not having a carriage to meet him on arrival, thanks to Victoria not showing up, he decided he would sooner ride home than wait around to catch the train, or walk.

The market was busy as usual. James was greeted by a number of familiar faces and shook hands with many. Stall holders went about their business shouting out their produce, and some folk browsed, while others purchased.

The wind, picking up even stronger now, knocked over a stall taking those standing nearby quite by surprise. A girl, who looked to be in her early twenties, scrambled to pick up the fruit and vegetables before they bruised. A bare-footed urchin seized the opportune moment to stuff apples into his pocket and make off with them. The girl hurled a string of abuse at the offender, but it was too late for he had already scarpered.

James, acting on impulse, threw down his bag next to her and charged after the lad. The boy led him on a merry chase through winding alleys and cobbled lanes, but finally James caught up with him, pinning him up against the wall. The apples fell from the boy's pockets, and he trembled from head to toe from fear of being caught. Much to his amazement, James made no comment, only took back the fruit and handed the boy one apple to keep. James knew full well hunger had been what drove the lad to steal in the first place. He slipped him a coin and put the boy back down carefully on his feet. The boy stared at the shiny coin in his grubby little palm, and then back at James with eyes full of gratitude.

James arrived back at the stall and handed the apples to the girl, who was still battling against the vexing wind. 'Thank you, kind Sir, take one for your troubles.' She handed him a bright red apple. She was a pretty girl with fair hair, tied neatly up in a bun at the back of her head, and wispy strands that had come loose in the wind, whipped against her face. She wore a bright, sunny smile and a twinkle of amusement in her pale blue eyes.

'It was no trouble.' He handed the apple back to her.

James looked familiar to her but she couldn't quite place him. He was a handsome gentleman; she couldn't deny that.

'Captain Hawkes is my name,' he called out to her, as if reading her questioning mind, as he walked away, and in a flash he was gone. She smiled coyly. 'Captain 'Awkes, of course,' she muttered under her breath, impressed by the good-looking captain who had gone out of his way to help her.

Old Tom had loaned him a silver-grey mare, having agreed that Bill Sanders, James's servant, would return her by the following morning. James rode through the low fields towards Ruswarp. The wind grew stronger, even more so now that he was out in open country.

Ruswarp could be seen nestled in the fold of glorious countryside. The River Esk flowed through it, passing the old mill that had stood the test of time. "Risewarp" was the old name given to it back in 1146, meaning 'silted land overgrown with brushwood.' Now it no longer was overgrown with brushwood, far from it. It was well maintained and people often came to visit to row along the river. There was no hustle and bustle like Whitby, but there were workers coming and going to the mill, and farmers bringing their livestock to auction, walking their animals across fields, or sometimes using the railway's cattle trucks.

The mare plodded on, then turned into a dusty narrow lane. The steeple of St. Bartholomew's church could be seen clearly now, and behind the church, just a little further up on the right hand side, stood *Crawford House*. Its turrets and architecture gave the impression of a small castle. It was indeed a grand property.

The lights burned brightly through the windows of the early eighteenth Century manor house, boasting fourteen elaborate rooms with elevated views over the River Esk. In the front courtyard stood a number of horses and carriages and also one Ford T motor car. Inside of the welcoming lit house, the Crawfords hosted one of their famous dinner parties.

The highly polished mahogany dining table sparkled from so much silver, coupled with the finest china and crystal cut glasses. At least twenty guests, a mix of different backgrounds, but all equally as important, sat at the table. Amongst the guests were Robert Hawkes, James's brother, and Lillian Hawkes, James's sister. Lillian sat next to Domenico Cifaldi, an Italian fellow who was internationally acclaimed as a pioneering photographer, and had managed to develop photography as an art form. His reputation stemmed from his ability to take such natural photographs of locals and places of interest; they included many of Whitby harbour, fishing and fisher-folk. Lillian found him to be positively fascinating.

The Crawfords were well respected for owning many of the small businesses in Whitby since the early part of the eighteenth Century, having pushed their way up from humble beginnings on the wave of new industries. The Crawfords were the employers of many locals, not just in Whitby but in neighbouring villages too, and it had been they who had sold the mill to Joseph Hawkes, James's late father, back in 1869.

John Crawford, now at the age of forty nine, took life a little easier these days, spending more time than he had in previous years with his wife Rose, and daughters Victoria and Violet. John, a distinguished gentleman with a thatch of grey hair that seemed a vast contrast to his dark eyebrows, stood up straight with his shoulders pushed back and a glass of wine in hand. And now that everyone else had a glass of wine in their hand, John smiled at his eldest daughter Victoria and she gave a small, gracious bow of the head. Rose, as any proud mother would be, smiled broadly, knowing what was about to happen. Violet, recently turned nineteen, was oblivious to her sister's news, having been away at her grandmother's house in York and returning only an hour ago, just in time for the dinner party.

'Ladies and gentlemen…' John, Crawford began. The table fell silent. All eyes were on him, waiting for what he was about to say. But before he had the chance to say another word, the first footman opened the large double doors, announcing the arrival of Captain James Hawkes.

All heads turned. James found himself amongst company quite unprepared for his arrival. 'Forgive me for turning up unannounced.' He flashed an apologetic smile at John and Rose Crawford, before noticing Victoria amongst the many faces staring back at him, bemused by his entrance. She looked beautiful. Her dark curls framed her pretty face. Her midnight-blue dress, edged in cream lace, complemented her dark blue eyes perfectly. But there was something different in the way she looked at him. She appeared uncomfortable by his presence, almost embarrassed.

'Nonsense,' replied John. 'James, how wonderful of you to join us. I'll have a place set for you at once.' He waved to the footman who was straight on the case of organising a place at the table.

'Oh I could not possibly intrude,' James protested.

'Intrude? Why, it would be our pleasure. It's not every day we get the honour of a sea captain to grace us with his presence at our dining table.' There were sniggers and chuckles around the table. It was hard to tell if they were mocking or actually honoured. Nevertheless, James soon found himself sitting down at the table.

'Dear brother, we were unaware of your arrival,' Lillian said, apologetically from across the table, having not bothered to get up and greet him properly. At the age of almost thirty, Lillian was still single. Her fine looks were somewhat spoilt by her large nose. On first impressions one felt almost shocked that her beauty had been marred in such an unfortunate way.

'I wrote to Victoria.' He glanced at Victoria across the table, who appeared embarrassed, her cheeks coloured a soft shade of pink.

Robert stepped in. 'Victoria received your letter James, but we didn't feel it appropriate for her to come and greet you as you so kindly suggested.'

'Why ever not?' James looked utterly baffled.

Robert did not answer.

'Forgive me, but what has my letter to Victoria got to do with you?' James pressed with urgency.

'Well, given the circumstances,' Robert replied indignantly. 'I'd say, everything.'

'I think it's time I continued where we left off.' John Crawford rose to his feet once more. 'I was about to make an announcement when Captain Hawkes arrived.'

'I apologise once more Sir, for my awfully bad timing,' James said, still staring at Robert with indignation.

John continued. 'I am delighted to announce that my beautiful daughter, Miss Victoria Crawford, and Mr Robert Hawkes,' he pointed to Robert, smiling from ear to ear, 'Are engaged to be married.'

It was only then that James noticed the platinum sapphire ring on Victoria's finger. He sat speechless, totally flabbergasted, while a toast was made and everyone offered their congratulations to the couple. He could never have seen this coming, never. He and Victoria had been close for years and not once had she shown the slightest interest in Robert, or Robert in her. What was Robert thinking? Why take the girl he knew James loved?

In the silence that followed, once everyone had piped down, Mrs Crawford said 'How nice it must be to be back home again Captain Hawkes. I never go away, well not any further than York to visit my mother. What is America like Captain Hawkes?'

He noticed how she had called him by his title instead of his first name. Was it because they were amongst company? 'I am not well acquainted with America, having only visited a couple of times, Mrs Crawford. I travel mainly in Europe,' James replied, struggling to keep his emotions in check. Talk broke out once more at another part of the table, relieving the tension.

They were served a fine array of fish, poultry and meat, and everyone ate well, while chatter covered a number of topics. Victoria did her best to make no eye contact with James, aware that on many occasions he was watching her closely.

Eventually the party dispersed into a large drawing-room. Guests mingled, giving Victoria the opportunity to slip away from her fiancé and find James, she owed him an explanation if nothing else. He stood alone nursing a large brandy, staring out of the window, lost in thought.

'James…I'

At first he did not turn around to face her. She stood at his side looking out of the window with him. He blinked away the sting of his tears then looked into her troubled eyes. 'Why?' It was the only question he had for her.

She opened her mouth to answer but could not find the right words to follow.

'I thought you felt the same way as I.' He continued. 'The night before I left, you said you loved me. God, did I mean nothing to you?'

'Yes of course you do, did.' She composed herself, trying hard not to release the tears now appearing in her own eyes. 'James I… something happened when you were away…'

'Ah, there you are darling, Robert is looking for you.' Rose Crawford appeared at her daughter's side. 'Captain Hawkes,' she gave a courteous bow, and before another word could be exchanged, she whisked Victoria away.

James took another swig of his brandy, his expression full of anguish. Lillian spotted him on the other side of the room and made a beeline towards him. 'James!'

'And I suppose you knew of this? Didn't think to mention it in your letters?' His anger was brewing as much as his heartache.

'I honestly had no knowledge of such a match between them both. You know what Robert is like. Do you really think he would confide in me?'

James slammed his brandy glass down and walked away. The room felt stuffy, he needed some air. Robert, so far, had kept his distance, watching with interest from afar and then he followed him outside into the courtyard.

Tethered at the entrance, Tom's old mare gave a greeting - a guttural sound, its breath forming a cloud of mist in the cold night air.

'Leaving so soon James?' Robert called out. 'You know you really should get yourself a motor car. Far more comfortable and they are all the rage these days.' He paused, contemplating what he had just said, looking at the horses and carriages surrounding them. 'Well at least they will be when Yorkshire finally catches up with London, and the rest of the world. I'll show you my beauty if you like, she's parked over there.' He pointed at a black, highly polished Ford T.

James stood with his back to him, not rising to his bait and not caring a jot about a motor car.

Robert continued. 'I do hope you will be able to make the wedding, or does the sea beckon you so soon?'

James turned to face him this time. 'Are you not satisfied with taking the mill from me that you now have to steal Victoria from under my very nose?'

'Such accusations brother, I'm truly hurt. 'You know full well the mill was bequeathed to me. Furthermore, Victoria is not yours to steal. She is not promised to you. I don't see your ring on her finger, do you?' Robert stood defiant, with an evil glint in his eye. Their stare locked challengingly which seemed to go on far too long. James had the patience of a saint; had it been the other way around, Robert for sure would have retaliated with violence, but James, keeping his cool, did not flinch. He knew his not rising to the bait would irritate Robert far more. Punching him there and then would have given James great satisfaction, but he knew that was precisely what Robert wanted him to do, and he refused to play right into his hands.

'You know my feelings for Victoria perfectly well,' he replied, his voice low and precise.

Robert gave a sinister chuckle. 'She does not want a sea captain for a husband, never at home to escort her to social events or look after her properly.'

'Oh and I suppose a miller would make a far better suit.'

'I am not just a miller. I own the mill. It is my business. As well as my land and property,' he bragged.

James regretted his words the moment he spoke them. Of course Robert was better for her. He was an eligible bachelor, he had much to offer and, more importantly, he never went away for months on end. But why Victoria? Out of all the single women in Whitby and the surrounding villages, why had he chosen Victoria?

Lillian ran out into the courtyard, worried and clutching her shawl tightly over her shoulders. She had noticed them both from the drawing-room window and did not want any trouble to take place at *Crawford House*, especially in front of so many guests.

'It seems Victoria has made her choice,' Robert answered smugly.

James turned around, unable to look at his brother any longer, and untied his borrowed mare.

'James!' Lillian's footsteps sounded across the cobbled courtyard towards them. 'James!' she called out again. 'Where are you going?'

'Home… if I still have one that is. Or have you taken my house too?' He gave a sideways glare at Robert from his saddle. Robert laughed out loud, highly amused.

James gave a nudge of his foot and he was off. The clatter of hooves as the mare side-stepped back down the long drive, petered out into the darkness of the night.

'Must you be quite so impertinent?' Lillian sighed.

Robert shrugged, untouched by her frustration. They walked back across the courtyard together.

'Is it my fault father left me the mill? What business sense does James have? One could hardly blame father for his reasoning.'

Lillian sighed heavily again. 'I think James is more upset about Victoria at this moment in time,' she pointed out, feeling sorry for her youngest brother.

'Which makes it all the more fun.'

'Fun?' Lillian's hazel eyes searched Robert's face, now that she had pulled him back to look at her. 'Is this all it is to you… fun?' A deep frown creased her forehead. 'You do love Victoria, don't you?'

Robert, still amused, replied, 'Love is a very strong word, dear Lillian.' He walked away, leaving Lillian utterly speechless.

Chapter Two

Soon he would be on his own land. The day had started with so much promise, and the prospect of returning home had filled him with great excitement, but now that had all diminished. He would be relieved when his journey had come to an end, and glad of the chance to rest.

The wind had died down a little now. The trickle of a stream as he passed over it, under a small uneven stone bridge, brought the comforting feel of home again. They were all familiar sounds and smells he had thought about and missed, while away at sea.

An owl hooted and flapped into the night. And there, under partially cloaked moonlight, stood *Heron House* in the distance. It was built in a square, compact, courtyard. The house was in good repair for its age, built in 1709, but the surrounding land was in desperate need of attention, knee high in weeds. In reality, *Heron House* was too big for James alone. It looked bigger than he had remembered as he came closer to it.

There were no lights burning from the old house as he headed down the dusty lane towards his home. He led the weary mare into the stables around the back.

Eleanor, standing in nothing more than a sheet wrapped around her slight frame, hurried from the window back to the bed, demanding that George get up at once. 'It's Captain 'Awkes, 'e's back!' George Tanner grabbed at his clothes frantically from the heap on the floor, getting dressed as quickly as he possibly could. His dark hair was ruffled, and his deep brown eyes looked up at her apologetically, coupled with the fear of getting caught.

Eleanor, now dressed, but dishevelled, smoothed out the creases from the bed, plumped up the pillows and placed the thick heavy blanket back where it belonged.

George crept out of the back entrance of the house without another word. He could see James's silhouette in the moonlight, heading towards the front entrance.

Suddenly *Heron House* lit up, as Eleanor went about lighting the lamps. It would have been better if it had stayed dark. Now that James had entered, he could see the dreadful mess. Unwashed dishes and cups scattered the oak table; garments of female clothing, strewn all over the chairs. A mouse scurried from underneath a piece of mouldy bread and James wrinkled his nose with disgust. He then stepped into a sticky substance on the floor.

'What in heaven's name do I pay you for?' He looked up from his boot, his glare descending on Eleanor's worried face. She swallowed hard and pushed a loose strand of fair hair back behind her ear. She possessed mousey features and looked younger than her twenty two years. 'I beg your pardon Sir. I 'ad no idea of your return.' James soon realised he had forgotten to notify her, but it still gave no excuse for the state of the place. 'Whether I'm present, or not, is neither here nor there,' he said precisely. He took off his hat and threw it down with his bag on a chair. Eleanor picked it up at once. This room was the main living area, being the largest room of the house. It was panelled with oak beams, and on the far side of the room stood a broad fireplace, and on the other, a large oven and cooking area. Unlike the parlour, which was only used for receiving guests, it was an ideal family room which could be lived in quite easily without having to use much of the rest of the house, other than the bedrooms of course. Its cosy corners and stylish furniture made it warm and inviting even on the coldest of nights; but not tonight, for it was dirty, cold and far from welcoming.

'I don't pay you good money, Eleanor Jones, to have my home left in such a state.' He made his way to the drinks cabinet and poured himself a much needed large brandy. It had been a long and eventful day. 'Where's Bill?' James enquired, enjoying the harshness of the brandy still tingling in the back of his throat while watching Eleanor light the fire in front of him.

'Gone Sir.'

'Gone where?' He found himself talking to her back as she busied with the fire in front of him.

'Don't know Sir - 'e upped and left one day.'

'Well who has been doing the heavy work, attending to the horses and so forth?' He looked at the chopped pile of firewood next to the open fire, Eleanor would not have managed to chop so much wood.

'Me, well not entirely me,' she admitted. 'George 'elped me.' Two little dots of pink appeared on either side of her cheeks at the mention of his name.

'And who is George?' James asked, now with his boots off, relaxing in the chair with his brandy.

'George is…' she groped for the right words. 'We're in love, Sir.' There, she had said it. She knew how fond George was of her, and it would only be a matter of time before the locals found out anyway. She was sure he would soon propose to her, so what would be the point of keeping it from Captain Hawkes? She did not like to tell lies, especially as he was always so good to her.

'I see. How delightful.' James hated his bitter tone but couldn't help it. After his evening at the Crawfords, love was a sore topic.

'So Bill has gone and you thought you would play happy families in my home with George?' James continued, while Eleanor topped up his glass with more brandy.

'No Sir, it weren't like that at all. He 'elps me a lot, does George. What was I supposed to do? I couldn't manage all this alone.' Her eyes pleaded with his for forgiveness.

'Clearly not,' James replied, sounding a little more forgiving this time.

'I shall inspect George's work in the morning, and if he has done a good job, I may offer him employment,' he said. 'Seeing as I am going to need a replacement for Bill.' His anger never lasted long with Eleanor. She was still just a child in his eyes, a child he had saved from a very poor background. She had come to him one night in a storm, no shoes on her feet, her hair matted, and the only dress she possessed in tatters, begging for work. He had just moved into *Heron House* and word on the street was Captain Hawkes would be looking for servants. As much as he hated to, he had disappointed many. His simple lifestyle did not require him to employ more than three people at a time. One maid had recently left to get married, leaving Eleanor and Bill, and now Bill had gone too.

'That's most kind Captain 'Awkes, but I'm afraid George 'as employment now with t'other Mr 'Awkes. 'E only 'elped me out before 'e started at mill.'

James looked baffled, was Robert taking on more staff again? He must be doing well. He took a swig of his brandy.

'To be 'onest, I think that's where Bill went too.' George had mentioned to her of his being there the day before. Bill had been talking with old Jim, who hired staff, and rumour had it Bill was due to start work at the mill that day, but George had failed to mention it that evening, their passion had got the better of them and they had had no time for talking. She didn't see it her place to tell James, after all, it could have been idle gossip, the village was full of it.

'Well that does not surprise me.' James sighed heavily, was there no end to his brother taking from him? 'Are you sure you wouldn't like to seek employment with Mr Hawkes too?' he asked sarcastically.

'Oh no Sir. I would not dream of leavin' your service.' Eleanor managed a reassuring smile and a small curtsy.

'Well you had better pull your weight then,' he replied harshly, but with a trace of humour to his tone. She gave a small curtsy again and made her way to the door, then stopped and turned around as an afterthought 'Would you like supper Sir?'

He chuckled. Despite everything he had been through that day, he still had not lost his sense of humour. 'What would you like to feed me? Dry, mouldy bread? Fresh mouse droppings, perhaps?'

'I do have some soup,' she replied indignantly.

'*RATatouille soup,* by any chance?' he laughed, and then laughed even harder at the look of confusion on Eleanor's face. Clearly she had not understood the meaning of his joke, or this foreign word, having never set foot out of England, let alone Yorkshire. 'I've eaten,' he said suppressing his amusement further and feeling guilty for teasing her.

Eleanor left the room without another word. He sighed, staring into the blazing flames of the fire, his smile fading away now his thoughts drifted back to Victoria once more. What did she mean by *something happened?* What could have possibly happened that would cause her to turn her back on him and marry Robert?

Finally, after downing almost a bottle of brandy, he staggered to bed. He spent half the night knocked out, and then the latter part restless, tossing and turning, one bad dream after another, and finally he awoke to the sunrise and the call of the cockerel. The daylight filtered through the crack of the curtains. He looked down to notice he was fully clothed. His woolly head and sandpaper tongue, reminded him of all the brandy he had consumed. He wanted to get up, but instead rolled over and fell back to sleep, deciding the world could wait a little longer for his presence.

Eleanor had been up since dawn. She had collected the eggs from the chicken coop and was now preparing bread for James's breakfast. An appetizing aroma filled the air and the room was once more spic and span after her cleaning spree late the night before. She wiped her brow after taking the bread out of the oven, feeling tired after very little sleep. Still, she was one of the lucky ones, and would always be thankful to James for employing her. A soft smile crept across her face, thinking of George and how close they had come to being caught in Captain Hawkes's bed the night before. She planned to sneak out and see him later. They had a secret meeting place not far from the mill. On a sunny day, the River Esk, running past the mill, would sparkle like little tiny crystals and she loved to see it. They held hands, kissed, and laughed at the ducks with their frolicking ways. She sighed wistfully. Life was bliss with George and she was looking forward to spending the rest of her life with him.

After a hearty breakfast, James took to the back yard and chopped firewood for that night, taking out his anger with every violent strike of the axe into the logs. What was he supposed to do about Victoria, sit back and let her marry Robert? He needed to speak with her properly, and in private. But how? With her interfering mother, over-protective father, and nosy sister constantly around her, not to mention Robert too, it seemed almost impossible. His timing had to be perfect. He would find a way to speak with her, he just needed time to plan it.

'Robert, this is a delightful surprise.' Rose smiled, walking into the drawing room. The sun poured in through the tall windows, framed with deep red velvet curtains. It seemed to bounce off the expensive sofas, casting light on the many framed pictures sitting on an antique sideboard.

'I thought, with it being such a lovely day, Victoria could walk out with me,' Robert smiled. He felt it important to show willing.

'Oh dear, I'm afraid you may have had a wasted journey, Victoria appears to be a little under the weather.' Rose, always immaculately dressed, smoothed the back of her dress before sitting down. 'I am sorry to hear that.' Robert sat down opposite her, after her gesture towards the armchair.

'Robert, as we are soon to be related, may I speak frankly with you?' She asked with caution.

'Of course, I wouldn't have it any other way.' He sat forward in earnest, looking a little worried.

'Are you sure this marriage is what you both want? Victoria doesn't appear to be overly excited in the way one would expect a bride to be. I noticed yesterday evening a lack of...' she hesitated, finding the right words. 'Lack of affection on both parts?'

Robert appeared relieved, he thought for a moment she may have known about their secret. God forbid her finding out this soon. 'I can assure you, Rose, that this marriage is what both Victoria and I want. We are a perfect match in many ways. I am a private man, and I don't always feel comfortable making my affections known in public,' Robert replied, sitting back in his chair.

'Of course. I can see I'm being a little over-protective.' She seemed pleased with his explanation.

'It's a mother's prerogative,' Robert said reassuringly, and this time with a smile. She smiled back at him. She understood fully how Victoria had fallen for his charm. He was more intellectual than James, he had inherited his father's head for business and it was no wonder Joseph Hawkes had left the mill to him. He would make a good husband and a decent father one day too. 'Stay and have a cup of tea,' she insisted.

He glanced at his watch. The mill could wait, however, bonding with his future mother-in-law could not. 'Of course, I would be delighted to.'

Upstairs, Violet passed her sister's room and then stopped at the awful sound of wrenching coming from within. She tapped on the door. Victoria did not reply, and so she walked in anyway, catching her by complete surprise, wiping her mouth with a handkerchief and holding onto a bed-pan full of sick.

'You poor darling, have you eaten something that does not agree with you?' Violet had not been blessed with Victoria's beauty. Her features seemed rather narrow and pinched in comparison, and she wore her dark hair neatly braided to one side, rather than have it styled properly as Victoria and most young ladies of her age did. Violet was not concerned about fashion, she preferred to bury her head in a good book; her concerns were more with one's mind, than one's appearances.

Victoria promptly burst into tears. Violet rushed towards her and took her sister into her arms to comfort her. 'There, there,' she stroked her hair. 'I'm sure it's nothing serious. Whatever it is will pass. Would you like me to call for the doctor?'

Victoria pulled away from her and looked up at Violet with a forlorn and tear-stained face.

'No. I do not wish to see a doctor. I know what is wrong.' The burden of her secret was taking its toll. She had to tell someone and she could trust Violet.

'What is it Vicky?' Violet asked affectionately, pulling on her arm to sit down with her on the end of the bed. 'What's making you so unwell?'

'Oh Violet I've done something I am far from proud of, and now I fear I am to pay the price. A very high price,' she added, sorrowfully.

James had returned old Tom's mare and had spent the morning in Whitby catching up on errands. Now back in Ruswarp, he stood on top of the hill looking down at the view below. He could see for miles; lush green hills peppered with sheep grazing, trees now in blossom and the mill standing tall from every angle. He spotted a heron swoop down, flying just above the river. Having spent so long at sea, he appreciated the countryside more than ever. Being out in the open helped him to think. He was contemplating when to go and see Victoria. Should he go today, or should he let the dust settle and see her in a day or two? There was not a soul to be seen and the only noise that could be heard was bird-song, until the peace was disturbed by a rustle in a bush, and a sudden bright, silver, flash of a light taking him quite by surprise. 'Good heavens!' he jumped, startled. Domenico Cifaldi appeared as if from nowhere with his camera in hand as always. 'So sorry Captain 'Awkes, I didn't mean to intrude.' His Italian accent was still apparent, despite having lived in England since he was a small boy. His parents had stowed away on a boat for England, wishing to make their fortune, and ending up in Whitby, where they sold Italian ice cream to the tourists and locals. They did not make a fortune, but they made a living, especially from the tourists in the summer. Domenico, on the other hand, was making a fortune from his photography. 'I like to capture people naturally, and with a superb-a landscape backdrops. Forgive me, I could not-a resist when I saw your pensive expression.'

James smiled. 'You are forgiven.' He was intrigued by this little man with dark hair and neatly trimmed moustache. 'May I?' he pointed to the camera and Domenico came closer to him.

Violet looked deeply concerned and shocked. 'You are with child out of wedlock?'

Victoria nodded and wiped her tears. 'It was the night of the Galloways ball. I had a little too much wine,' she began to explain. 'Robert, in so many ways, reminds me of James, and I was missing James so much.'

'Really?' Violet could not see the similarity at all between the two brothers, neither in looks, nor personality.

'Being close to Robert brought comfort,' she continued.

Violet was hanging on her every word.

'We sneaked away from the ball and came back here.'

'Was anyone here?'

'No. Everyone was still at the ball. We drank another wine, and like a brazen hussy I gave myself to him.' She burst into tears again, sobbing into Violet's arms. Violet held her tightly, not knowing what to say.

'My first time should have been with James on our honeymoon,' she sobbed in her arms.

'Does he know? I mean Robert, about the baby?' Violet was falling over her own words.

'Yes. I stupidly told him. Why else do you think he would marry me?'

'For love of course,' Violet replied, but with uncertainty.

Victoria looked at her and gave a humourless chuckle. 'He does not love me.'

'Oh don't say that!' Violet grabbed hold of her hand. 'We will find a way through this terrible mess, please do not despair.'

'How? I must marry Robert now that I am carrying his child.'

'But you don't love him, do you?' Violet enquired, suspecting not.

'No,' answered Victoria, flatly confirming Violet's suspicions.

'Do you still love James?'

Victoria sighed. 'I've never stopped loving James.'

James, holding the camera, took his first photograph. This is amazing he enthused, getting excited about the technology and how it worked. 'I would love one of these. It is like a machine that freezes time. It's most extraordinary!'

'Kodak have since made even better models of late. This is a *three A,* and it is now two years old, but I'm happy with it. I'm not-a ready to buy another yet.' Domenico informed him, matter of fact. 'I know a supplier who could get one of these for you for the right-a price,' he said, as an afterthought.

James beamed. 'Name your price Mr Cifaldi, I would love one!' Far more interesting than investing in a motorcar, James thought. He was quite sure Robert did not own a camera.

'See me in my studio in Whitby later this week, Captain 'Awkes and I shall be only too 'appy to oblige.'

'Can you teach me the development process of photography too?' James sounded like an enthusiastic schoolboy, all thoughts of Victoria now brushed temporarily to one side, although most definitely not forgotten.

'Si, Signore! It would be an honour. I'll even treat you to Mama's ice cream. She have-a new recipe.' He kissed the tips of his own fingers, in typically Italian fashion and laughed. James laughed too. 'It's a deal Mr Cifaldi. I shall visit you later this week.'

Chapter Three

The loud clatter of machinery hammering, grinding and sifting was almost deafening. Each machine had an important role in the task of making flour, as did the workers operating them. Below the building a huge wheel churned and spat out water received from the River Esk.

It was nightfall now and most of the workers had gone home, leaving only Charlie Crouch, George Tanner and, Bill Sanders, James's missing servant who had gained employment at the mill, just as Eleanor had suspected. They were the only three left to finish work and close up.

Young Charlie made his way down to the granary with the last of the sacks, leaving Bill and George alone. 'You need t' be careful with Eleanor, she's cheap - give herself t' any man what give her the eye.' Pearls of sweat formed on his forehead beneath his shining bald head, his cheeks scarlet from years of drinking gin.

George grabbed Bill by the scruff of his collar, their noses almost touching. 'You disrespect Eleanor one more time and I swear I'll...'

'You'll what?' Bill snarled. Their eyes locked in anger. 'She pleasured me that young lass on many a cold night when Captain 'Awkes wor' at sea.'

George swung a hard and fast punch at Bill's face, causing him to fall backwards, and knock his head on an iron bar which led to a malfunction of the machine behind him. And as Bill toppled towards the erratic machine, he smashed his head again on the side of its large steel cog. He fell to the floor, blood dripping from a gash on the top of his head.

George stood over him. 'Bill?' No response came from Bill; his limp heavy figure lay helplessly on the cold stone floor. George stopped the machine. He knelt down and, placing his shaking fingers on Bill's neck, he searched for a pulse but found nothing. He checked both his wrists, again nothing. The blows to the head had killed him outright.

Charlie, not bothering to enter the room, whistled a cheerful tune and then shouted out as he made his way downstairs. 'Granary closed, see you int'mornin'.' The slamming of the large heavy door downstairs echoed throughout the building. George stood shaking from head to toe, his eyes wide with fear. Oh God, what had he done? He placed his fingers over each of Bill's eyes and closed them, not being able to bear looking at his wild, intense, stare.

Above rising fields, stood a cluster of six run-down cottages, where James went on the hunt for cheap labour. His father had owned the cottages and the land for many years and the Hawkes family had always maintained a good relationship with their tenants.

Lights were burning in all the cottages and he hesitated at first about bothering them now it was almost nightfall, but having spent many hours working on his land that afternoon, he decided he couldn't wait any longer, he needed help. In the last house in the row of six, lived the Horners. Mrs Horner's husband had died only recently from a long illness and Mrs Horner now lived with her four sons and one daughter. The boys, aged between fourteen and twenty, were in and out of employment, like most on that estate, scratching around to make a living wherever they could.

'Captain 'Awkes.' Mrs Horner's expression was one of surprise and worry. 'We've paid our rent - I know it was a couple of days late but...'

'Mrs Horner, I can assure you I am not here to determine if you have paid your rent. Forgive me for intruding at this late hour, but I wondered if I may have a word?'

'Of course, come in.' She held open the door for him to enter. She had always been fond of James and, in her opinion, he was the nicest of the Hawkes family. She didn't much care for Robert Hawkes, too full of himself, especially now he had inherited the mill from the late Mr Hawkes, and as for Miss Lillian, she was full of too many airs and graces.

Inside, the main living area smelt of stew, which was slowly simmering on the stove. Washing hung to the right, drying from the heat and what little furniture there was looked like it had seen better days.

Becky watched with interest as James walked in and removed his hat. She was the youngest of the Horner children at thirteen years old. Neat and trim with pretty hazel eyes.

'Have you forgotten your manners, you remember Captain 'Awkes don't you, Becky?' Mrs Horner stood with her arms folded across her large bosom, her cheeks flushed from cooking.

Becky smiled at James. 'Captain 'Awkes,' she curtsied, then crossed the room, while removing her apron.

'She's a fine lass… growing up quickly. You must be proud Mrs Horner.'

'Aye, I am that. Concerned though,' she gestured for James to sit down at the table. She too sat down. Becky had now left the room.

'Concerned?' James echoed her.

'She's a fine young lass. Many a boy in the village has eyes for her, but she's still a child.'

'I see.' James got the picture. 'I'm sure her brothers will keep a look out, and I too now that I'm back on leave,' he offered.

'That's most kind of you Sir.' It's Charlie Crouch, he works at mill. I caught our Becky down at riverside with him last week. I know his intentions, the dirty little...'

James said nothing but listened with interest. She stopped in mid-flow, realising she should perhaps not use inappropriate language in front of him.

'Any'ow, if you see her with 'im on your travels I'd be most thankful to you if you'd send her home, if it's not too much trouble t' you Captain 'Awkes.'

'It would be my pleasure to help,' he said sympathetically. 'And if the lad continues to trouble you, send word to me and I'll speak to him.'

'Really? I'm sure he would see sense if you were to speak with 'im.'

There was a moment of silence. She looked at him with a troubled expression, remembering he had come to see her about something and fearing he had come to bring her bad news. Now that the late Mr Hawkes had passed away, perhaps they had plans for the land? Perhaps they were all to be evicted and she would be cast out on the street with her family, with nowhere to go.

'I'm seeking help at *Heron House*,' James broke her train of troubled thoughts. 'It seems Bill Sanders has left my service and the fields are in desperate need of clearing.'

She looked relieved; at least her home was safe. 'I'm not one t' spread gossip, but I think Bill is working at mill.'

'You're not the first to tell me such news, Mrs Horner,' James admitted, remembering Eleanor's words on his arrival the night before.

Just then, the door flung open and Alfie darkened the doorway. Tall, strong, sixteen years old with deep brown eyes, he had grown considerably since James had last seen him.

He looked bemused, not recognising Captain Hawkes straight away.

'You remember Captain 'Awkes, don't you Alfie?'

'Good to see you again Alfie.' James remembered him as a small lad playing out on the field at the top of where the cottages stood.

'Aye, I do now. Ayup! Captain 'Awkes.' He shook hands with him.

'Captain is looking for 'elp, might you be able t' lend 'and, Alfie?'

'Aye, I dare say I could.' Alfie looked pleased at the prospect of working for James.

It was still not properly dark yet, when George arrived at *Heron House* and knocked hard and frantically on the back door. Eleanor, preparing supper for James, rushed to open it with a beaming smile. 'Can't keep away can you!' Her smile soon faded by the look on George's face.

'I need your 'elp? Is Captain 'ome?'

'No.' Eleanor frowned. 'What is it?'

'No time to explain now. Fetch an old blanket and meet me down at riverbank - at back of mill as soon as you can.' George was speaking so fast she could hardly keep up with him.

'But what if Captain 'Awkes comes back?'

'Then you'll think of somethin'. This is important El, there's no time t' lose.' With that he was gone.

Eleanor took everything off the stove and then made her way out to the stables. There were a couple of old blankets in there she remembered seeing. She grabbed one, went back to the house, and moments later she ran down the hill, away from *Heron House*. As she passed the little bridge she prayed James would not be on his way back. She had no idea what she would say to him if she were caught now. More importantly, she had no idea why George needed to meet her with an old blanket at such an hour. Then it dawned on her, this was it, the moment she had been waiting for. He was so romantic; he wanted to propose to her under the stars at night. He had been so nervous when he had knocked at the door, what else could it possibly be? Her heart fluttered with excitement as she rushed down towards the mill.

There were no lights burning at the mill, it was silent all around, other than the hoot of an early owl and the quack of a passing duck, flying over the river and then landing on the water.

She arrived at the riverbank panting, the blanket still draped over her arm. An attention seeking whistle came from behind in a bush and, as she came closer, she could see a rowing boat tied against a tree and George standing next to it.

'You're a dark 'orse - George Tanner – wantin' to take me out on boat this time o' night.' She beamed with excitement.

'Shut-up and come 'ere!' His tone was harsh and took her by surprise. Not waiting to be told twice, she ran towards him. He pulled her down to sit next to him. She loved it when he was being masterful, it excited her no end. She sat huddled up next to him, waiting for him to kiss her.

'El, there's something I have to tell you,' his hands were shaking so much as he reached out to her, his eyes were wild and gleaming.' 'It's aright, calm down. I do feel same way you know. I love you too.'

'What?' He looked confused. And as Eleanor's gaze wandered to the right of them she saw a hand poking out of a bush. She screamed. 'Over there!' She pointed to Bill's lame hand.

'Shush!' He put his hand over her mouth, her frightened eyes stared back at him.'

'If I release me 'and, promise not to scream?'

She nodded her head in agreement and he took his hand away from her mouth.

'There's been a terrible accident.' His voice was a hoarse whisper. 'I got into a fight with Bill Sanders. He fell, you see.' He paused trying to find his words. Eleanor stared back at him aghast.

'He's dead,' he said, without warning.

'Dead?' she threw her hand to her mouth, for a moment she thought she was going to be sick.

She stared back at him in disbelief. 'What was the argument about?' Not that it really mattered, but it must have been something important if Bill had ended up dead. She searched George's face for an answer. He contemplated telling her, but it wasn't worth it. He knew Eleanor was a decent girl and Bill's vicious tongue had regrettably cost him his life.

'Nowt! Look, I need to get rid of 'is body. If they find out it's me I'm finished.'

'It was an accident; you didn't kill him on purpose.' Eleanor jumped to George's defence. George was no killer; she was sure of that.

'They won't see it that way.'

'Were there any witnesses?'

'No, but Charlie Crouch may 'ave 'eard us arguing. All it takes is for 'im to open 'is trap and that's it, I'm done.'

Eleanor was shaking from head to toe, tears now rolling down her cheeks.

'Listen to me,' he held both her hands tightly. 'I need you to 'elp me wrap body in t' blanket and get it on t' boat. I will take it out t' sea and dispose of it.'

'And then you'll be back?' she asked, choking on a small sob that had caught the back of her throat.

He looked deep into her eyes. 'I love you, I always will, but I can't come back.'

'No!' she let out another heart-felt cry. 'You can't leave - you can't leave me.'

'El, I will 'ang for this. Would you rather see me dead?'

She shook her head, tears streaming. He leaned forward and kissed her on the lips. Their eyes met once more. 'Promise me you will not breathe a word of this to a living soul? If anyone asks where I am, you don't know, same as you don't know where Bill is.'

She nodded again. 'I promise.'

They wrapped Bill's lifeless body into the blanket. Eleanor stopped twice, retching in the bushes. Finally, they loaded him into the boat. George hugged her tightly and their lips met for the last time.

'I'll never forget you George Tanner, not for the rest of my days!'

He untied the boat, he too now crying openly.

Take care of yourself Eleanor Jones, were the last words he spoke as he rowed away down the river, leaving Ruswarp for good. He headed towards Whitby, his mission to then row out to sea to dispose of Bill Sanders' body, and with any luck he would find a boat he could stow away on, hide, and keep his head down for a while, before making a new life for himself in pastures new.

Chapter Four

Alfie arrived at six o'clock in the morning at *Heron House*, eager to start work. He removed his hat and smiled at Eleanor, who ignored his polite greeting. James watched from where he was standing, noticing Eleanor's dark circles and swollen red eyes. He sent Alfie to collect some tools from inside the barn and walked over to where Eleanor stood. 'You don't look well. Are you sickening for something?' He felt her brow and she shied away from him, shaking her head.

'No Sir, just a little tired, I'll be fine.' She picked up the basket of eggs she had collected from the chickens and made her way back inside.

James, with his shirt sleeves pushed up, not afraid of hard labour, joined Alfie clearing and cutting back the fields that had grown uncontrollably in his absence. The sun shone brightly and felt warm on his skin. He soon forged on in front of Alfie, driven by his own private necessity. The sweeping movements of the scythe in his right hand through the overgrowth, while his body pivoted to the same rhythm, helped him to lay those uncomfortable ghosts of discontent to rest, at least for now anyway. The grass toppled, bending over and sinking to the earth and, together with the grass, fell weeds, daisies, dandelions and buttercups. He took deep breaths and stopped to wipe his brow occasionally. A crow flew overhead, letting out a cry as its wings flapped, beating the air. He shielded his eyes from the sun, while watching the bird fly away and his gaze fell upon a female figure on horseback, approaching fast along the small dusty lane towards *Heron House*. For a moment he thought it to be Victoria and his heart gave a small lurch. He had made his plan of how he could speak with her alone, and had decided to take action soon, but had she arrived now, he feared himself somewhat unprepared. He'd been glad of a couple of days to think and calm his raw emotions.

Lillian stepped down from her horse. 'If my brother cannot spare the time to pay me a visit then I must spare the time to visit him.' She gave her horse a grateful rub on the nose and then turned to face James in anticipation.

James shook his head. 'It's not for the lack of want. As you can see, I have my hands rather full.' He pointed to the fields around them and his face softened with a small smile, before planting a dutiful kiss on her cheek. He took her horse and they walked towards *Heron House*, she quickened her pace in time with his. James tethered her horse and they walked across the courtyard. She looked back over her shoulder at Alfie, still hard at work in the fields. 'What's happened to Bill?' she enquired.

Eleanor was baking bread as they walked inside. She looked up, brushed her hands free of flour on her apron, and curtsied. 'Miss 'Awkes,' she greeted her as expected.

Lillian smiled politely and turned to face James, still awaiting his answer.

'Bill had a better offer, at the mill it seems,' James said at last. Lillian sat down, making herself at home.

James called over to Eleanor to make some tea for them both.

'Bill Sanders has gone to work at the mill?' Lillian repeated with confusion.

The very mention of Bill's name jangled Eleanor's nerves. She reached for the tea cups and dropped one, and it smashed all over the floor. James and Lillian instinctively looked up. Eleanor excused herself, flustered and embarrassed. Seconds later they dragged their attention back to the conversation in hand again.

'Has Robert been poaching staff?' Lillian asked.

'Poaching staff, the woman I love, the list is endless.' James's forlorn expression matched his tone. It was almost as if he was admitting defeat.

Lillian, not quite sure what to say, looked away, deep in thought.

'I had no option on Victoria - she is free to marry who she wishes - but…' The pain was very much etched over his face as he spoke.

'It was most strange, the way it all happened,' Lillian interrupted. 'Last autumn at one of the Beckwiths' dinner parties I noticed they hardly exchanged words - then in March they became friendly at the Galloways' ball - and then all of a sudden they announced their engagement - well you know yourself, you were there. I don't understand any of it I'm afraid, James.'

'How the prices have gone up since I've been away,' said James, looking out of the window. He found talking about Victoria too painful.

'James, I'm certain that neither of them wished to be unfair to you.' Well at least Victoria she was certain of, but with Robert she had her doubts.

Eleanor served them tea. James kept his tortured eyes firmly on the teapot, still uncomfortable with the topic of conversation. Lillian, oblivious to his discomfort, continued regardless.

'And then there was the rumour of you perhaps not coming back for quite some time. You – you taking another voyage departing Italy for Africa, they all said.'

Eleanor left the room. The ticking of the clock on the wall seemed extremely loud all of a sudden. James cleared his throat, trying to keep calm. 'Rumours started by Robert I dare say,' he replied sharply.

'We had no reason to question him.'

He slammed his fist down on the table, taking Lillian by surprise. 'Did you not?' he glared at Lillian.

She reached out and pressed his arm. 'I wish I could take away your pain James. Help you in some way. How about you come to the house more often now Robert has moved out into his new home?'

That would be the new home he would be sharing with Victoria once they were married, James realised, without airing his thoughts out loud.

'We have an excellent cook, she makes delicious pheasant pie,' Lillian continued. 'Better than Eleanor's,' she grinned, after checking Eleanor was not within earshot.

'Thank you, but I must find my own way out of this mess, and I'm happy with Eleanor's cooking,' he added, still sounding annoyed.

'I just want to help.' Lillian took a sip of tea. 'I feel ashamed of Robert. I feel I could have done more. I've let you down and I am so sorry.'

James sighed. 'You are not to blame for any of this. When are they to be married?' he asked, not really wanting to know, but needing to all the same.

'May the twentieth at St Mary's church in Whitby.'

'But that's only a couple of weeks away, why so soon?'

'I've no idea. Robert told me only yesterday.'

She decided to change the subject and chatted on about idle gossip, unaware that James was not really listening; his thoughts were still very much on Victoria and Robert's impending wedding.

'When will you be going back to sea?' she asked, catching James's attention once more.

'I'm not sure. I've taken a longer leave this time. I need to get this place in shape.' He rubbed his brow. 'Lillian, I'm not sure I want to go back to sea.'

'Nonsense!' Lillian reached out and touched his hand. 'You are upset, and quite rightly so, but don't throw away everything you have worked so hard for. Not over them, they are not worth it.'

James did not have the energy to explain. It wasn't just this business of Victoria that had affected his wavering mind, but an inner, nagging, feeling of wishing to change direction completely. He needed something more, but quite what he had yet to discover. All he knew was that being at sea no longer excited him.

He took Lillian's horse and walked back with her to the end of the lane.

'If I promise not to get in your way,' she said, with her wide eyes surveying his, 'may I come and visit you more often? I never get to see you with you being away all the time.'

He smiled at her. She was like a little girl that had never really grown up. Despite her being older than he, she was more like a younger sister and in desperate need of attention. He could see she craved love. It was such a shame she had still not married. *She would make a wonderful wife, and mother too*, he thought.

'You may visit whenever you like.' He kissed her cheek and helped her up onto her horse.

'Bye James.' She waved, and moments later she was gone, trotting down the lane into the distance.

James left Domenico Cifaldi's studio just after four O'clock, the day after Lillian's visit, having spent two and a half mind-blowing hours learning the art of photography. He could understand Mr Cifaldi's passion and he was quickly falling in love with the art himself. To have the ability and the power to freeze a moment in time seemed incredible, almost unthinkable. And as Mr Cifaldi had promised, Mama Cifaldi let him taste her new flavoured ice cream which was simply out of this world.

James, holding his very own camera like a prized possession, boarded first class on the train at Whitby station.

A thin, clerkly looking man with a narrow face sat next to his rather large wife who was holding a tiny baby. Its creased and pink features looked annoyed as the train chugged along the line. Moving his gaze away from the child, something caught James's eye as he glanced at the vacant seat in front of him. A tatty, black, pocket-size book. He picked it up. The train gave a loud whistle. Not bothering to look at it now, he tucked the book into his inside pocket. Whoever it belonged to, the owner was obviously long gone and, being curious, he would have a good look at it later when he was home.

Arriving at *Crawford House*, he was greeted by the Crawfords' butler and shown into the drawing-room as every guest was accustomed to, but it seemed strange to be meeting Victoria quite so formally.

Rose looked up from the colourful tapestry on her knee; her glasses perched on the bridge of her nose. 'Captain Hawkes! How splendid of you to drop by.' She had reverted yet again to calling him by his proper title instead of his forename, even though they were not amongst company.

James walked into the centre of the room, still holding his camera. 'Do forgive me for my intrusion, Mrs Crawford. I wonder if I might have a word with Victoria.'

Rose eyed him with suspicion and then her focus shifted on to the camera he was holding.

'I - I have recently purchased a camera.' He held it out for her to see.

She peered down her glasses at it. 'So I see.'

'And I – I would like to know if Victoria would approve of me taking some photographs at the…' He found it hard to say the word, but then soon found the courage to continue, 'at the wedding,' he said at last. She made him feel so nervous and he had no idea why. Even when he had spent much time with Victoria in the past, he still felt uncomfortable in her mother's presence. It felt like she was always looking down at him - perhaps even feeling sorry for him - the child that Joseph Hawkes liked the least - the son who inherited very little - the one that lived in his brother's shadow; he could imagine her saying that when mixing with her cronies at dinner parties. He would not be surprised if it was she who had put the idea into Victoria's head in the first place to marry Robert. It made sense now, watching her scrutinise his every move.

'How charming, but I am sure Mr Cifaldi will have it all in hand.'

'It's most kind of you to offer, James', said Victoria now standing in the doorway, overhearing the conversation. 'Isn't it Mama?'

Rose forced a beguiling smile.

'Mama, I wonder if you might leave us to discuss this further? In private.'

Rose looked at them both disapprovingly. 'I hardly think it appropriate, or necessary.'

'Thank you Mama,' Victoria stared harshly.

Rose reluctantly left the room.

'I'm sorry, I didn't mean to cause…' James placed the camera down on the floor next to him.

Victoria cut in on James's apology. 'Please, on the contrary, I should be the one apologising.'

He ached to touch her, hold her in his arms once more, but all he could think about was the fact that she was with Robert now. They were engaged to be married. How had he let her slip through his fingers like this?

'I'm pleased you will be attending the wedding,' she said. Her words cut through him like a knife.

'I have a confession,' he replied. 'The camera was a ploy to speak with you alone.' He had no intention of even being at the wedding, if it should go ahead, let alone take photos of her with Robert. The afternoon sunlight shining through the window caught the glimmer of the large sapphire ring on her hand. He tried his best to ignore it. 'Victoria, I need to know this marriage to Robert is truly what you want.' He moved closer to her and held his breath, waiting for her to answer.

A cloud of sadness wavered in her expression. 'Yes - Yes of course it is,' she replied, her voice nothing more than a just an audible whisper.

He moved closer to her, not buying her answer one bit.

'Look me in the eyes and tell me you don't love me and I shall never bother you again.'

She looked away from him, holding back her tears the best she could. Of course she loved him. She wanted nothing more than to say her engagement with Robert was none other than a sham, but what good would it have done either of them? With Robert's baby inside of her there was no way back now.

He waited with baited breath. She looked up at him at last. 'James, I love Robert with all my heart,' she lied, hating herself for it. She could see how much her words were hurting him, but it was for his own good too. To make it more believable she must add fuel to the fire. 'You must leave us to get on with our lives. We have a wedding to arrange,' she glanced at her ring then back at James. 'We are both looking forward to it so very much. I can hardly wait.' She had somehow managed to shield her dejection well this time.

He swallowed hard and turned away, embarrassed to let her see his tears. 'Of course,' he said. 'Then I wish you every happiness.' He picked up his camera and left the room in haste. There was nothing more to say, she had made her decision whether he liked it or not.

Victoria let out a pitiful sob once the door was firmly closed. She stood at the window and watched him walk away, not just from *Crawford House*, but from her life too.

Arriving back at *Heron House*, he placed the camera safely in his bedroom, then dashed through the house and back outside.

'Sir,' Eleanor called out, but he had already left.

'Damn!' She pounded her fist on the table. She had to warn him that the police had been round that afternoon wanting to speak with him about Bill Sanders.' She felt sick inside with worry for George, but she had kept her promise to him and not told the police anything.

James rode for a ng while out in the open fields, stopping eventually and looking down from up high on Whitby. Victoria's rejection and the pain he felt was unbearable, she had more than broken his heart; she had ripped it out and shredded it into tiny pieces. What's more, he hated Robert more than ever. He would never forgive him for stealing the woman he loved, not ever. Fire rose within him as he made his way down into Whitby. He needed to find a public house, to drown his sorrows to oblivion.

In the summer house Robert found Victoria. 'How are you feeling?' The miles of countryside spread way beyond the grounds of *Crawford House* and the sun shone a golden glow over the fields. She sipped her tea and turned to face him. 'Nauseous,' she replied coolly.

He chuckled. 'Gosh, is that how you feel about me? You certainly know how to flatter a gentleman.'

She looked at him with contempt. In the early evening sunshine her dark hair carried a hint of auburn, she looked radiant and even Robert could not fail to notice.

'Your mother said you were unwell yesterday.' He looked concerned.

'I had morning sickness, which seems to continue most of the day.'

'You poor darling, it must be awful. You know that you need to be careful. If your mother,' he paused, 'your father even, were to find out before we are married.'

'I'm quite aware,' she retorted.

He held her hand tightly. 'I know I'm not your first choice of a husband, and I know if circumstances were different you would not be marrying me.

She looked at him, a little surprised by his bluntness.

'I'm no fool, Victoria,' he said. 'But I promise I will do my very best to be a good husband to you and a good father to our child,' he smiled wryly.

Victoria rubbed his hand with affection, her anger now softening. He was not a bad man. 'I know you will. It was a moment of madness that has led to us being thrown together for the rest of our lives. We must make the best of it, or I fear we will both go insane.'

'Indeed. And we shall make the best of it. We will be happy, you will see, in time.' He kissed her tenderly on the lips and when she closed her eyes, for a moment, a tiny moment, she imagined herself kissing James.

The strong smell of ale hit James as he made his way inside *The Old Horseshoe* public house. Its low beamed ceilings and dim lights were the perfect setting for the locals who liked their drink. He ordered a brandy and sat at the end of the bar, away from the others who were quite rowdy, enjoying their banter. They didn't seem to bother about him being there, they were far too busy with each other.

'As you are soon to be my wife, I think it only appropriate you should come to the mill with me soon,' said Robert.

Victoria did not appear enthused by the idea. 'I know not the first thing about milling.'

'And you need not, my dear. It would look good if you showed some interest. There's been some problems,' he admitted, deciding that, as they were soon to be man and wife, he could share parts of his life with her.

'What sort of problems?' she asked, more out of interest than concern.

'Two workers have gone missing.'

'Missing?'

'Yes - lots of speculation, you know what gossiping tongues are like. One of the workers is James's former servant, Bill Sanders. He has no family, so there is no one to ask of his whereabouts.'

'And the other man?' Victoria put her tea cup down, becoming more interested.

'George Tanner. He lives with his old mother. She knows nothing of his whereabouts either. She said he frequently doesn't come home, has a lady friend apparently, not that she has ever met her, it's all very recent and they are keeping it quiet.'

'Good heavens! But how can two grown men simply disappear?' Victoria pulled her shawl up closer around her shoulders, now the sun had set and the temperature had dropped.

'Look at you, you're shivering, let's get you inside.' Robert took her hand as they walked back across the gardens and inside the house.

Rose walked towards them, happy to see the young couple, apparently spending some quality time together. 'Robert, are you staying for supper?' she asked, hopefully.

'I'm afraid not. I must get back to the mill.'

'There are problems at the mill, Mama. Two workers have gone missing,' Victoria informed her.

'Gracious! How frightfully troublesome for you Robert.' She appeared genuinely concerned.

'Yes, very troublesome,' he replied. 'I would have loved to stay for supper, if that was not the case.'

'Run out of brandy on your boat, Captain?' A female voice from behind the bar passed him his second glass of brandy. He had not noticed her on his arrival, but now that he was slightly calmer he recognised her. It was the girl from the market. 'Carry on like this and you won't be up for runnin' after waifs who go round stealin' apples.' Her whole face seemed to light up when she smiled.

A ghost of a smile appeared on his face. 'I don't believe we have been formally acquainted.'

'I don't believe we 'ave. Sophie Dickens,' she gave a small curtsy. Her blonde hair hung partly up and the rest a tangled mane of curls, in need of a good brush, but her dress was clean and her eyes bright and twinkling.

He took another swig of brandy and looked at her squarely. 'Captain James Hawkes, pleased to make your acquaintance.' He seemed pensive. 'Forgive me. I could easily have misplaced you for I thought you attended a stall in the market square?'

'I do. I'm just 'elping me uncle out. 'E owns this place. He's sick and I'm his only relative now t'others 'ave moved on. I do me best when I can.'

'It's no place for a lady,' James wiped his mouth with the back of his hand, glancing at the rowdy bunch of men around them.

She giggled. 'I've never been called a lady before.' He caught her infectious smile again, grasping her meaning. He hated the way that society was split into classes. She probably wasn't educated, wouldn't know how to read, or conduct herself at a formal social event, but that didn't make her less of a lady, and as the hours passed she only confirmed his thoughts. Her personality shone like a bright star on a dark night as they chatted. She helped him more than she knew, keeping his mind off Victoria. And he did not drown his sorrows as planned, although he did become a little tipsy. They talked about a number of subjects and he was surprised at the depth of her knowledge for someone of limited education, although she did admit she was teaching herself to read. He talked about places he had visited and she seemed captivated by the stories of his days at sea, and he also told her about his recent purchase, his camera.

'Perhaps you could be a model for me,' he suggested, in all seriousness.

'Captain! What, like painters 'ave models? I 'ope you're not expecting me to take me clothes off,' she blushed.

He laughed at her innocence. 'I would not expect you to remove any of your garments, please, I can assure you.'

'May I ask you a question?' she said, her smile turning into a frown.

'I said more ale!' A drunkard up the other end of the bar yelled out, interrupting her. 'If you can drag yourself away from your fancy man, that is,' he slurred, propping himself up against the bar.

James leaned forward. 'I bid you to hold your tongue, Sir. That's no way to speak to a lady.'

'She aint no lady,' he jeered.

James rose to his feet and the man suddenly appeared worried. James was far taller than he, much bigger built too, and given the amount of ale he had consumed, he did not fancy his chances with the captain. 'She's just a girl in my eyes, that's what I meant. She's just a girl.'

Much to his relief, James sat back down on his stool.

Sophie smiled, impressed that he had stood up for her and had come to her rescue once again. She poured more ale into the man's tankard and plonked it down in front of him, held out her hand for payment, into which he thrust a coin, and she threw her head up high and returned to James.

Remembering what she had been about to say to James, before they were interrupted, she said 'When you walked in, you looked sad - really sad, 'appen you were even angry. There's only two things what bothers a man and that's business and women.'

James did not reply, he just held her intense stare.

'Well?' she pressed.

He seemed taken aback by her directness. 'It doesn't matter which,' he replied.

'Ah, so it is one or t'other, I knew it. Now let me see. As you are a captain and on leave, I doubt you 'ave business problems, which leaves t'other – a woman. It's woman trouble int-it?'

'You're too sharp for your own good, and on that note,' he finished his drink. 'I must head home.' He stood up, said goodnight and left the pub which was now almost empty, all but a few punters who were too drunk to even notice him leave, including the man he'd had an altercation with.

Sophie folded her arms across her small bosom, disappointed he had gone. She had enjoyed her evening with him. He made a change from the many low-life drunks she normally had to serve. Captain Hawkes was interesting, not to mention very handsome, and she hoped she would have the good fortune to see him again.

Chapter Five

James awoke to a soft tapping on his bedroom door. 'Sir, two policemen are downstairs. They wish to speak with you.' Eleanor's muffled voice through the door urged him to get up out of bed.

He took a moment to pull on some clothes and then opened the door. 'What do they want?'

'To speak to you about Bill - 'e's – well – e's gone missing.' Eleanor's stomach churned with nervousness.

'He's hardly missing. I thought he was at the mill.' He pushed past her, annoyed at being disturbed.

'Sir,' she called out to him as he reached the top of the staircase. He turned to face her.

'E's not at mill - 'e really 'as gone missing,' she lied, knowing full well he was dead. 'George too,' she added, he would find out from the police anyway.

'George?' A look of realisation swept across his face. 'Oh you mean George, your gentleman friend,' he replied, with a look of intrigue. So that would explain the forlorn expression she had worn the past few days.

She nodded.

'Well I'm sure they'll turn up - they couldn't have gone far.' He made them sound like two pet dogs gone astray. He patted her arm and went downstairs, leaving Eleanor alone with her thoughts. He had no idea of the seriousness, and neither had anyone else for that matter. Eleanor had not breathed a word to anyone and did not intend to, but it was far from easy carrying such a burden; she feared someone would soon guess that she was hiding a dark secret. Fortunately, no one except James knew of her relationship with George. It had developed only quite recently and they had wanted to keep things private, but she did wonder if Bill had told someone while working at the mill. Little did she know that her relationship with George was the reason for Bill's departure from *Heron House*.

Bill had carried a torch for her the whole time they had worked together and, contrary to what he had told George, they had never been intimate. To see her in the arms of another man had forced him to move on. She was never going to fall for him, he was twice her age and had nothing to offer her. It so happened that Robert Hawkes had a vacancy at the mill and, despite what others thought, Robert had not poached Bill, although it would not have been beneath him to do so. It was a bonus that Bill was James's devoted servant, there was no denying that and Robert had been delighted to employ him. Another triumph for Robert Hawkes.

'Captain Hawkes.' The taller of the two policemen stepped forward, while the other listened.

'Gentlemen, what can I do for you?'

'We believe Bill Sanders was formerly in your employ, is that correct?'

'Yes,' James confirmed.

'When did he leave your service exactly?"

'Exactly? I couldn't tell you. I've been away for the past six months. When I returned my maid informed me that he had left.'

'I see.'

'Were you aware of his employment at your brother's mill?'

'Yes, I was. What seems to be the problem?' James asked, eager to get to the bottom of all this and then get some breakfast.

'Bill Sanders and another miller, George Tanner, have not turned up for work for the past three days. We are treating their disappearance as suspicious.'

'Well they are grown men, I'm sure they'll turn up,' replied James, not really grasping what all the fuss was about. His stomach gave an impatient rumble. He continued regardless. 'Have you tried all the public houses in Whitby? Bill likes his gin.'

'Yes. Nobody has seen them since Monday.'

'Forgive me for asking,' said James, 'but isn't this all a little premature? They've only been gone three days, not three months.'

One of the policemen moved closer to James and looked him directly in the eyes. 'Blood has been found outside of mill, leading down t' river. We have every reason to treat this inquiry seriously.'

Eleanor listened behind closed doors, her heart pounded and perspiration formed upon her forehead. Try as she might, it was not easy to hear what they were saying, their voices were far too muffled. She did, however, hear the words *blood found*.

'Perhaps the blood is from a drunken brawl? It's close enough to the public house,' James suggested.

'Perhaps, or perhaps something more sinister?' The officer replied, raising an eyebrow. 'We would like to have a proper word with your maid please,' he said.

'Of course.'

Eleanor stepped back from the door and James opened it. The policemen had already seen her; there was no time for her to hide now. She walked into the room with James at her side.

'Captain Hawkes, if you would kindly leave us alone for the moment.'

James nodded. 'I'll be in the yard if you need me.'

Eleanor wiped her clammy palms on her apron. 'Ow can I be of 'elp?' she said, holding her head high and pushing her shoulders back, trying to put on a brave face.

Within five minutes the policemen were back outside, they waved to James across the yard and walked away from *Heron House*, they had finished their questioning - for now.

Eleanor felt sick and weary. If she could sink into a bed as one did when exhausted, she would have willingly done so, needing to sleep and to forget everything. She shivered; the old French clock on the mantelpiece, with its painted and gilt figures, ticked loudly.

James found her sitting huddled on a chair. He picked up a blanket, used as a throw on one of the sofas, and placed it around her shoulders to stop her from shaking. He sat down next to her, still ignoring his hunger. This was more important. 'Eleanor?' She turned to face him, her eyes full of tears.

'Do you know what happened to Bill and George?' he asked, cautiously. He had his suspicions that she knew more than she was letting on.

There was chaos outside the mill. Workers gathered in their numbers and locals came to see what was going on, now that the police had closed it down. Robert stood amongst them all, trying to calm the situation, and he was relieved that he had not brought Victoria with him, as previously planned that day. Victoria had been feeling off colour again, so he had suggested she come with him another day.

Henry, a robust man, wearing shabby clothes and covered in flour, shouted out over the crowd. 'We can't afford to be laid off with nowt comin' in. We got families t' feed - food t' put ont'table.'

'And you'll be paid for today, I'll see to that,' Robert replied.

'And what about day after?' another bellowed. They all joined in with firing their questions, but Robert was already making his way across the crowd towards the police.

'How long is the mill going to be closed? These people need to get back to work.'

'Mr 'Awkes, is it a murder investigation?' Jim Johnstone, the longest serving worker, having spent forty years at the mill, called out. He'd heard about the blood found outside on the floor, as had everyone else. Henry joined in again. 'There'll be another bloody murder if mill int open soon - I tell ye.'

'I always knew he'd be trouble that Bill - had shifty eyes,' said Jim. 'And as for George Tanner - well don't get me started - he were a right one that George Tanner...'

A few photographers had turned up too, but not Domenico Cifaldi. He knew better than to upset Robert Hawkes, with the promise of commissioned work now that the wedding date had been set.

'We'll do our best to move things on quickly Mr Hawkes, that's all I can say for now.' Robert stared back in desperation at the policeman leading the investigation.

'No Sir,' Eleanor's voice trembled. The fire crackled and spat. A mangy looking ginger cat sat himself down next to the fire. James had allowed the stray animal to stay, since it helped to catch the field mice that had made a habit of coming indoors, with Eleanor leaving the house in such a state during his absence. He glanced at the cat and then back at Eleanor. She stared at him wildly. How could she tell him the truth? She had promised George to keep silent, but aside from that, she would be putting herself in trouble too, seeing as she helped George to put Bill's body in the boat and assisted his getaway.

'Then what is it? What's upsetting you so much?' James asked, pouring her a cup of sweet tea and handing it to her. Something was not right and he needed to get to the bottom of it.

'I…I loved him,' she sobbed, trying to find her words. 'I thought we'd be wed - spend rest of our lives together.' She really didn't know how to fight the awful heartache that had possessed her now that he was gone.

James nodded, satisfied the girl was nothing more than heartbroken and had no connection with George or Bill's disappearance. She obviously didn't know where they were or she wouldn't be in such a state, he decided, besides he needed his breakfast; he found it hard to think straight when hungry.

'Violet, where's Victoria? If she doesn't hurry, we shall be late for luncheon at the Beckwiths.' Rose prodded the last pin into her hair, then placed her navy-blue hat, encrusted with tiny, white lace daisies, on her head.

'She's not feeling well Mama.' Violet stood in the doorway, in a sunny yellow dress, with a blue and yellow hat to match.

'Still?' Rose frowned, then dashed past her, calling out to Victoria as she made her way upstairs. She found Victoria laying on the bed, staring into space with a vacant expression on her face.

'Violet says you are still ill. Darling, is this true?'

Victoria dragged her attention back to her mother. 'A little queasy, but I shall be fine.'

'I'll call Doctor Tailford, this sickness has been going on for too long.'

Victoria sat bolt upright with a look of horror. 'No!'

Rose, alarmed at her reaction, moved closer. 'Why ever not?'

'I'm feeling better than yesterday. I'm on the mend –I - I just need to give it another day.'

'But you are not well enough to go for luncheon at the Beckwiths.'

'I know and I'm sorry Mama, please make my excuses.'

'Such a shame, everyone is so looking forward to speaking with you about the wedding.' Rose walked to the door and then turned to face her again. 'I shall not be late, get plenty of rest.'

Victoria nodded. Once Rose was back downstairs and out of sight, Violet nipped back up quickly to see her sister.

'Vicky, you really should tell her,' she whispered loudly, on entering the bedroom.

'Are you completely insane? Of course not!' She gave a short groan of annoyance. If only everyone would just leave her be, she felt tired and emotionally drained.

'If you share this with her you can see the doctor, get something for the sickness. She is going to find out sooner or later.'

'Don't be so ridiculous Vi. Do you have any idea of how this could destroy our reputation? She'd be pushing me down that aisle to marry Robert tomorrow.'

'Well it's going to happen anyway,' Violet pointed out, for which Victoria did not appreciate being reminded.

'I know, and two weeks from now is soon enough thank you.'

Rose stood at the bottom of the stairs and called up to Violet. John Crawford waited patiently behind his wife, dressed in a newly tailored suit.

'Are you ready Violet? We're leaving now.' Rose called out.

'I'm going to have to go now,' she said to Victoria. 'Mama and Papa are waiting. Are you sure you are going to be alright?'

'Yes, go.' She shooed her away with her hands, as if she was a stray animal. 'I could do with the peace and quiet.' Victoria flopped back on the bed and gave another groan, once the bedroom door was closed again.

'This will not look good, Victoria not coming,' John moaned, as they walked towards the carriage waiting for them in the courtyard.

'These things can't be helped,' said Rose, accepting his hand to help her up into the carriage.

'Robert isn't going either, some crisis, apparently to do with the mill,' John added. 'If I can make time, I damn sure he could have.'

'Yes I heard about it. Don't be so hard on him darling.'

Violet sat next to Rose, opposite John, and said nothing. A moment later they were on their way.

Sophie tapped on the door of *Heron House*. Her hair, this time, was neatly brushed, and she wore a pale pink dress that had seen better days but was, nevertheless, quite pretty. She became aware of her heart beating faster as she waited for the door to open, and a moment later Eleanor appeared. She looked Sophie up and down, wondering what business she had at *Heron House*. 'Can I 'elp you?' she asked.

'I'm looking for Captain 'Awkes,' Sophie seemed unimpressed by Eleanor. She wondered if she was ill or tired, looking at the dark circles encompassing her eyes.

'E's not 'ere, but should be back very soon,' she added. She felt obliged to be polite in case James was acquainted in some way with the woman standing before her, although she doubted it very much. 'Do you want to wait?' she asked, as an afterthought.

Sophie looked back over her shoulder at the fields behind, where Alfie was hard at work in the distance. She contemplated walking home and then coming back later, but decided to wait now she was here. 'I'll wait, if it's all the same,' she replied.

Eleanor showed her into the parlour.

She sat down close to the fire; its embers were only a few crumbling, orange, specks. The cat got up, scratched itself, stretched and walked away.

'Captain 'Awkes isn't looking for another maid, if that's what you're seeking.' Eleanor said.

'I'm not seeking employment,' Sophie replied scornfully, rubbing her arms against the noticeable chill in the room. She had enough work balancing the stall and running her uncle's pub to even consider finding more work.

'Oh. So are you and Captain 'Awkes acquainted?' Eleanor asked, not really caring. Nothing much mattered to her any more, since losing George. The days were endless without his popping over to see her, or her going down to the river to meet him. What Captain Hawkes did in his private life was of no concern to her, but she made small talk, all the same.

Sophie nodded. 'Yes, we are acquainted.'

'Sophie! What a surprise.' James entered the room, his camera in hand after taking a few photographs of the landscape. He had walked for over an hour. He found taking photographs to be a very useful way of taking his mind off Victoria. The thought of going to the wedding filled him with dread. To sit back and watch the woman he loved marry another man, and not just any other man, but his own brother, was unthinkable. He had purposely kept his distance from Robert. In fact, he had not seen him since the day he had arrived at *Crawford House*.

'A nice one I hope,' she smiled.

'Of course. What brings you to *Heron House*?' I trust Eleanor has made you welcome.' The two women looked awkward. Eleanor left the room, having to attend to her duties.

'Forgive me for asking, but is your maid unwell?'

'She's having some personal problems at the moment,' James replied, then rapidly changed the subject. 'Anyway, it's lovely to see you again...' He looked genuinely pleased to see her.

'I agreed to be your model, if you remember? I see you may have started without me.' She pointed to his camera sitting on the floor next to them.

'Oh yes, you did indeed,' he grinned. Their eyes met in an equal fondness. Her smile lit up her entire face and he couldn't help but notice how pretty she looked in the pink dress she was wearing. He could see she had made an effort for the photography session, or perhaps the effort was for his benefit, he wondered.

The clouds were forming, thick and grey, and heading towards them. Sophie posed on the little bridge, dangling a stick into the water.

'Forget I'm taking your photograph. Think about anything, anything you like.' James fiddled to focus the camera on her.

A sudden ripple in the water caught her attention. 'There's a fish!' she shrieked, bending down to prod it with her stick and then toppling forward. The upper half of her body hung precariously over the stone wall, dangling into the river. 'I'm stuck!' she squealed, wriggling to get free from a low branch detaining her dress over the water. James pressed the button, not wanting to miss this opportunity to catch such an image on camera. As soon as it flashed he ran to help. 'Wait, keep still.' He leaned over her. She could feel the skin of his cheek on hers, his breath like a soft whisper in her hair as he untangled the part of her dress that was caught on the bramble. When he had finished he pulled her to her feet. 'Thank you, she grinned,' having enjoyed every moment of their close encounter.

Just then a clap of thunder sounded behind them on the hills, followed by a bolt of lightning and another huge rumble. They looked up instinctively, and then, the heavens opened. He pulled off his coat to make a cover for them both and to protect his camera too. But as he lifted his coat, the little black book he had found on the train the other day fell out of his pocket and onto the path before them.

'You dropped something.' Sophie shouted out against the noise of the heavy downpour, picking it up and running with him to the nearest tree for shelter. They were no more sheltered under the tree than where they had been standing. The rain was so heavy it simply poured through the leaves onto them. Only a few yards away stood an old run-down barn. 'If we can make it there, we can keep dry,' James suggested, pointing over at the barn.

'What are we waitin' for?' She ran next to him under his coat, acting as a makeshift cover, until they reached the barn.

The door creaked in protest when James pushed it open and they entered, dripping wet. He placed the camera down and wiped it dry with his shirt sleeve.

Apart from a few bales of straw, a rusty tin bucket, as well as a rust speckled shovel and fork hanging on the wall, there was little else. A field mouse scurried away to the other side of the barn.

'At least it's dry, and I think the camera has survived.' James sat down on the straw. Still gripping the little black book in her hand, Sophie perched herself next to him.

'Here. Is it important?' she handed the book to him.

'I found it on the train. I have no idea what is inside it,' he confessed.

'In that case…' She grabbed it back from him and opened it. 'I'm learnin' to read you know. Me uncle 'as books - dead educated is Uncle Nick.'

'An educated publican,' said James, half in jest, but with respect for the man too.

He was impressed by her hunger for knowledge. 'Tell me, what does it say?' he couldn't resist finding out himself now that she had raised his curiosity again. He had completely forgotten about the book.

Sophie tried to read the first few words but was not able to make head nor tail of what the scrawly handwriting was about. All the letters seemed to roll into one. 'Can't understand owt?' she thrust the book back at him in frustration.

'Don't look so glum, the hand-writing is dreadful.' Although it was not easy even for him to understand the unruly writing, he began to read it to her. *Ace always bet them. Kings almost always bet them, and Jacks risky at best. Numbers never bet them.* 'Gambling tips,' Sophie interrupted. James paused and then read on. *'If each player has at least four cards of a given suit...*

'Makes sense,' said James, coming to the end of the page.

'To you maybe, and what does that say?' she pointed to a mass of words written at the bottom of the page.

'Facial expressions and how to read your opponent with ease...'

The rain had stopped outside and the sun was now breaking through, although low, now it was late afternoon. He snapped the little book closed. 'Good to know; the author certainly knows what he's talking about'

'Are you a gambler?' Sophie eyed him with suspicion.

'At sea I played a fair hand.' He looked pensive, almost wistful.

'I should be headin' back. Uncle will be wondering where I am.'

'It can't be easy looking after him and the public house. And what about the market stall?' he enquired, opening the barn door for her.

'Jenny, she lives in Blackburn's yard, she's lookin' after it for me for a share of profits.'

'If your uncle needs help, I'm not averse to lending a helping hand.'

Sophie looked at him with surprise. 'I think it not fit work for a gentleman.'

'A gentleman of my calibre is fit for most types of work, trust me,' he grinned.

When he smiled, she noticed the sadness still there in his eyes.

'Did she hurt you?' she asked.

'Who?' They walked past the little bridge and onto the path. *Heron House* could be seen to the left in the distance, and above it a glorious rainbow, so bright with many colours.

'The girl that broke your heart.' She picked a daisy from the grass beneath them, tearing away at its wet petals as they walked on.

'Yes,' he replied, not bothering to ask how she had guessed. 'She is to be married to my brother very soon.'

Sophie gave a humourless chuckle. 'Talk about a kick int' ribs.'

'What about you?' he asked, changing the focus of the conversation to her.

'Well there was someone once, Paul. Paul Woods, 'e were fond of me and me of 'im. But 'e liked 'is ale, did Paul, and 'e were 'andy with 'is fists after a few ales.'

'Did he hurt you?'

'Not badly, 'e got arrested. 'E spent time in jail. Since then I've kept me 'ead down, worked 'ard, 'e's not bothered me since. 'Appen 'e's moved on with 'is life, cleaned up. Looking after me uncle takes up much of me time. 'E won't have many days left now, Uncle Nick.'

They reached the end of the path, the mill stood in the distance, silent and non-functioning.

'I'm sorry to hear that. What will happen to the pub, I mean when your uncle passes?'

'It'll be mine. Not sure it will be a blessin' though.'

'You could sell it, you'd have money then,' James pointed out.

''E'd turn in 'is grave if I sold it. That pub is 'is pride and joy.' She sighed.

'Would you like me to escort you back to Whitby? I can go back home and fetch my horse.'

'It's only a walk through them fields and I'll be 'ome in no time. Make sure to show me your photographs.' She pointed to his camera. 'Did it get wet?'

'I think I managed to keep it dry.' He smiled. Spending time with Sophie felt good. She lifted his spirits somehow. She had her share of problems and he felt in awe of the way she handled them and life in general. 'Visit whenever you like, as often as you like,' he shouted out with obvious fondness.

''Appy gambling,' she called out to him, walking away from him through the fields.

'Only gamble when I'm at sea,' he answered, but his words fell on deaf ears, for she was already too far into the fields.

Chapter Six

Jim rolled his tobacco, while sitting on the step outside of the mill with young Charlie. The mill was back to business as usual. The police seemed to have drawn a blank in their investigations. They had widened their search for Bill and George, but still no sightings had been reported.

'Still think you should of said somet' - t'police,' Jim said, taking a puff of his roll-up.

'There's nowt t'say. I didn't hear what they were arguing about, just heard 'em arguing.'

'I reckon Bill killed George. They say there's a rowing boat gone missing, he probably dumped him out at sea and made a run for it. Never liked him, had shifty eyes, did Bill.'

Charlie smirked. 'So you've said a hundred times or more. What's important is we're back at work. And what's more important is I'm meeting that lass Becky later. Getting closer to 'avin' a bit of…' He gave a small suggestive whistle, but Jim was clearly not grasping the point, so he felt the need to spell it out. 'Her dropping her knickers for me.'

Jim stood up. 'Not Mrs 'Orner's lass, surely not. You want t' leave well alone lad. You'll get 'assle from them 'Orner lads and you won't want that. Why, she's no more than a child.'

'Give over! She's ready for it, good and proper, and as for them 'Orner lads, I can 'andle meself.' Charlie walked back inside. Jim shook his head from side to side and followed behind.

'I'm pleased with your work Alfie, you've done a fine job,' James praised, looking at the land, back in good order once more. 'How do you fancy staying on permanently?'

Alfie's face lit up at the prospect. 'Permanently? Oh yes please Sir. I was 'oping you were going to ask me. Ma will be pleased with extra money coming in, it's been a struggle since Pa...' he hung his head low, unable to finish his sentence.

'I dare say it has,' James patted him on the shoulder. 'The stables need mucking out by the way.'

'Right you are Sir.' Alfie made his way to the stables without another word, feeling pleased with himself.

'Captain 'Awkes!' Eleanor called out across the courtyard. 'Miss Crawford is 'ere to see you.'

James stopped in his tracks. 'Miss Crawford?' he asked. 'Miss Victoria?' he checked just in case it was Violet, although he had no idea why Violet should visit him, no more that he did Victoria, since she had made her feelings very clear the last time they had met.

'Yes Sir, Miss Victoria,' Eleanor confirmed, well aware of how his relationship with Miss Crawford had broken down since his return. Victoria used to visit regularly, but this had been the first time since James had been back from sea that she had come to see him. It was common knowledge now, amongst the locals, of Victoria and Robert's engagement. Gossiping tongues had much to say about Victoria switching from one brother to the other.

'Tell her I'll be there right away,' he called back. He pushed back his shoulders, took a deep breath and headed towards the house.

He found Victoria in the parlour. Too nervous to sit, she stood in the centre of the room waiting for him.

She had taken off her navy-blue, fur-edged cape. The bottom of her skirt was black with dirt and splashed with rain from her walk over. She had been crying, her eyes were still damp.

'Victoria, what an unexpected surprise.' His words were welcoming, but his tone rather cool.

She gave a small cough to clear her throat, then spoke in a precise manner. 'The purpose of my visit was to ask for your forgiveness.' Her expression, one of sadness, made James ache all the more, longing to hold her and comfort her.

'Although, now that I am here, I fear I am most unworthy of your forgiveness.' She dabbed her tears away with a white linen handkerchief.

'My dear Victoria, why should you seek my forgiveness? You fell in love while I was at sea and now you are engaged to be married. If I am to feel betrayed it is through no fault of yours, but only my own. Had I proposed to you earlier you may not have agreed to marry Robert.'

'No!' She left out a small heart-felt sob. 'You do not understand.'

'Then try me,' James replied. 'Come, sit down.' They sat down side by side on the sofa together.

'I don't know where to begin.'

'Is it Robert? Has he talked you into this marriage?' James knew only too well how manipulative Robert could be. 'If you are having second thoughts…'

'I am carrying his child,' she said, catching him off guard. For a moment James did not speak, astonished, he needed to absorb her words.

'Did he…' he finally spoke. 'Did he force himself upon you?'

Victoria shook her head. 'No. I'm just as much to blame. I missed you so very much…' Her eyes were full of tears again. She reached out and touched his hand. 'I drank wine,' she continued, 'it was the night of the Galloways ball.'

'I'll marry you,' he interrupted her, not wanting, or caring, to hear what more she had to say. 'I'll bring the child up as my own flesh and blood. Victoria, you know how much I love you.' He went down on one knee before her. 'Victoria…'

'No! Please James, don't!' He stopped and looked up at her, with tears now in his own eyes.

'Robert knows about the baby - he will not give up his child.' James sat back down next to her. 'I'll speak to him, reason with him.'

'And say what? If you speak with him, he shall know of my betrayal... that I confided in you about the baby. He will also be aware we have met and spoken alone.'

'He will not want to marry a woman who is in love with another man, surely? Least of all if the woman he is to marry is in love with his own brother?'

'I came here only to explain and to ask for your forgiveness. I should have waited for you. My weakness has cost me dearly.'

'We can find a way through this together.' He held her hand tightly. 'No woman should marry a man she does not love, or bear his child through no fault of her own.'

She pulled her hand away from his. 'But it is my fault, this is all my fault!' she cried.

'No it's not, Victoria. You were lonely, vulnerable, and Robert took advantage of you. No gentleman would take advantage of a lady who was missing her true love.'

Victoria stood up, grabbed her cape and slipped it on. 'Robert is not a bad man. He did not take advantage of me, I gave myself willingly. I came to ask for your forgiveness but I can see it was a mistake and very foolish of me.'

'Victoria, please!'

'I know you owe me nothing, but if you really do love me, please don't tell Robert of our conversation. It's best to let me go.'

'Best for who? Not you, nor I!' he said with despair. 'I love you too much to let you ruin your life.'

'Then there could be terrible consequences for us all.' She dashed out of the door.

'Victoria wait!' he called after her. Her pace was fast as she walked quickly on. A moment later he had caught up with her out in the courtyard. He reached out for her arm and pulled her to a halt. 'I'm going to sort this.' He sounded resolute.

'Leave me alone!' she shook herself free from his grip and walked on.

It was not good for her to be so upset in her condition, so he decided it best not to follow her and he would deal with the situation in his own way. The mere fact that she had come to him asking for his forgiveness and needing to confide in him, proved that she loved him and she wanted to be with him, she just didn't know how to go about it. So now he must fight for her and get her back.

At the back of the mill was Robert's office. He sat at his desk and had a stack of paperwork to get through, having had to put much of his work on hold when the mill had been closed, under police investigation.

'Afternoon Captain,' Lizzy called out to James as he approached the entrance to the mill. She stood in the doorway, with traces of flour through her already peppery coloured hair. 'Afternoon!' He walked past the toothless, middle-aged woman, and around to the back of the mill. The familiar smell of grinding corn suddenly hit him, reminding him of the days he had spent at the mill when he was young, helping his father. His father had paid him a pittance of course, taking full advantage of his cheap labour, whereas Robert, even though being younger than James, was allowed to operate some important pieces of machinery, learning the ropes and being paid the going rate, sometimes more. Even back then, Joseph knew that he intended to leave the mill to his youngest son Robert.

Robert looked up with surprise at James as he opened the office door, without as much as a polite tap on it.

'My dear brother,' he took off his reading glasses and placed them on the desk. 'And to what do I owe this pleasure? Have you come to formally accept your wedding invitation?' he teased.

'There'll be no wedding.' James stood before him, looking down at him with eyes of steel.

Robert laughed. 'You do amuse me, James.'

'I know about the baby,' James continued. Robert looked momentarily surprised. 'Well, sometimes things happen not quite as planned. Victoria and I have a spark, an unyielding chemistry. It seems we could not put our passion for each other on hold until our wedding night.' He grinned, enjoying every moment of James's torture.

'Let's not play games here Robert. You took advantage of a vulnerable woman, but not just any vulnerable woman – Victoria, the woman I love. Why did you do that?' Before Robert had the chance to reply, James continued. 'I'll tell you why.' He leant closer to him. 'Because you wanted to take from me, as you have done all your life. Your scheming, manipulating ways…'

Robert threw up his hands in protest. 'Hold on, that's grossly unfair. I have not taken from you, not ever. Victoria's desire for me is such that…' James grabbed Robert's throat, unable to control his anger any longer.

'You used her to get at me. She doesn't love you, no more than you do her.' Their eyes fixed in an angry glare. Robert could hardly breathe. He struggled to get away from James's grip but James held on to him tightly, he wasn't finished with him yet.

'No one knows about the baby, other than you and I - I want you to end it with Victoria. Call off the wedding.'

'No!' Robert croaked.

'I will marry Victoria and bring up your child as my own,' James said, his voice now raised. Noticing Robert's blue lips, he released his grip from around his throat. Robert coughed, clutching hold of his throat and trying to get his breath back. And when he did he looked back at James in anger. 'She is carrying my child and I will not have you take it away from me.'

'If you go through with this marriage, I will take from you, just as you have taken from me,' he threatened.

Robert gave a humourless laugh. 'You're pathetic, do you know that? Coming in here, throwing your weight around like some ruffian because you can't have your way.' He stood up and walked around to the front of the desk where James stood. Their noses almost touched. 'I have everything you want…. the mill,' he threw his arms out showing off the mill. 'Victoria, and now I'm about to become a father too. The woman you love is carrying my child,' he gloated, pushing James to the edge. James threw Robert a hard punch, knocking him backwards. 'You're a low-life, dirty skunk that does not deserve a decent woman such as Victoria. I mean it, you marry her and you will regret the day you were born.'

'No! It is you that regrets the day that I was born!' Robert shouted after him. James slammed the door behind himself, leaving Robert with a bloody nose and fumbling around in his pockets to find a handkerchief.

James, in anger, marched along the river bed. Up ahead the sound of a scream brought him to a standstill. He listened intently, and on the second scream he ran in the same direction. He found Charlie Crouch on top of young Becky Horner; she was struggling and screaming to get away from him. He pulled the boy away by the scruff of his collar and punched him on the nose, the second punch on the nose he had delivered that day. Charlie cowered on the floor. Becky stood up quickly, straightening her dress, her cheeks flushed and bits of grass lodged in her hair.

'Did he hurt you?' James asked, beckoning her towards him. She shook her head nervously.

'Come on let's get you home.' He turned to face Charlie once more. 'You'd better have eyes in the back of your head, lad.' Charlie knew instantly what he meant. It was not a direct threat from James, but a warning about the Horner brothers.

Mrs Horner rushed out to meet them the moment she spotted James and Becky heading towards the cottage. 'What 'appened? Did you find 'er with that Charlie Crouch?'

'Your instincts were correct,' said James.

She slapped her daughter hard across the face. 'It weren't my fault Ma,' she cried, rubbing the side of her cheek from the sting. ''E said 'e wanted to talk to me, just talk 'e said,' Becky stood with tears streaming down her face.

'I told you not to go near that lad, not ever! Get indoors!'

Becky, with her head down, made her way inside. Mrs Horner looked up at James. 'Do you think 'e…?'

James shook his head. 'No, but if I'd been a moment later, it might have been a different story.'

'I can't thank you enough Captain. Will you come inside? I 'ave a bottle of brandy unopened, it were a gift, been savin' it.'

'No. Keep the brandy for a time worthier. I must get back.' He walked away feeling tired, dejected, and all he could think about was speaking with Victoria again and trying to reason with her. Mrs Horner frowned. The captain didn't seem his normal self, something was up, she could tell.

Fortunately, the Crawfords, apart from Victoria, were out when James arrived at *Crawford House*. The butler informed him that Miss Crawford did not wish to be disturbed.

'Tell Miss Crawford that I refuse to leave until she sees me.' He pushed past him and made his way into the drawing room, where he stood next to the fireplace, waiting patiently. He had no idea what reason he would give for his visit if the Crawfords arrived back before speaking with Victoria, but all he cared about right now was seeing her again.

Victoria entered the drawing room, her eyes still puffy from crying. 'You must not come here any more,' she said, without even greeting him.

'Victoria this is ludicrous, I cannot,' he paused to calm himself down, 'I will not allow you to marry Robert.'

'Well it is not up to you. It is my decision,' she replied indignantly, sitting down on the sofa. James remained standing.

'You came to see me today because you love me.'

'I came to see you because I thought you deserved an explanation,' she corrected him.

'But you still love me, don't you?' He sat down next to her and reached for her hand, she pulled away from him abruptly.

'My feelings for you are irrelevant. I love Robert and I am carrying his child.'

James smirked incredulously. 'You don't love Robert.'

Of course she didn't love Robert, but somehow she had managed to convince herself one day she would. Her mind was made up about the marriage and James was not going to stop her.

'I do, and I'll thank you to leave us well alone.' She stood up with tears in her eyes.

'Is that really your wish?' He looked distraught, still sitting on the sofa.

'Yes James, it is. I can't be with you. What we had...' she swallowed the lump at the back of her throat and brushed away her tears. 'What we had was special but a moment in time. My future is with Robert and not with you. If you really love me, you will not make this more difficult than it already is.'

'If I really love you, I will fight for you,' he said, tears brimming in his own eyes.

'You are fighting a losing battle. Give it up James before you hurt me further.'

He could see the pain etched all over her face and hated to see her this way. 'Am I really hurting you?' he asked sincerely.

'Yes you are. Your presence, you being close to me brings me much heartache and pain. It's not good for the baby either. I want you to leave and to keep your distance for my sake and for my unborn child, please James.'

He looked deep into her eyes. 'Please,' she begged again. It was killing him to walk away, but he knew in his heart he had to. Robert was not going to give up his child and he could not let

Victoria go through this torture. If she was to make a go of it with Robert, he had to stand back.

He nodded. 'If you need me,' he said. 'You know where to find me. I will respect your wishes, but I will never stop loving you.'

She let out a heart-felt sob of relief and left the room.

James took a deep breath and wiped his tears before leaving the room too. Putting on a brave face and forcing his emotions to bed was something he had become accustomed to over the years, Joseph Hawkes had seen to that, but this time it would be harder, and he had no idea how he would cope in life without Victoria, not to mention seeing her with Robert.

'Why did you go and see him? Why tell him about the baby?' Robert paced the drawing room floor. Victoria sat perched on the edge of the sofa.

'I wanted to explain...'

'Explain that you don't love me, that the only reason you are marrying me is because of my child?'

She didn't answer. He had hit the nail on the head.

'We said we would make the best of it, you and I.'

Victoria stood up and walked towards him. 'Don't play the victim Robert. You know that the baby is the only reason for our marriage.'

He ran his fingers through his hair and looked at her with despair. 'He offered to marry you, bring up my child. Do you have any idea of the humiliation I felt?'

'He had no right to say that to you.'

'Well he did, Victoria, he did.' He flopped down on the sofa. Victoria sat down next to him. 'I promise I will not see him again. For the sake of our child, our marriage must be a happy one.'

Their eyes met and he held her stare for a long time. She seemed sincere and he needed to trust her if this was to work.

When James arrived home, Alfie was just finishing in the stables. 'Miss Eleanor was looking for you,' he informed him, closing the stable door. A guttural snort came from within.

Eleanor walked across the courtyard to meet James. 'Message Sir,' she waved a piece of paper. When she caught up with him she handed it over. 'It seems you will be leavin' again then.' She watched him as he read it, accustomed to handing him messages when he was due back at sea. He read it, then looked at her. 'Just a week this time,' he said. If he was honest he would be happy to get away from everything, even if it was just for a week.

'Oh, by the way, Miss Lillian is waiting for you in the parlour.'

He rolled his eyes and sighed. That's all he needed, a visit from his sister after having the day from hell.

Lillian greeted him with open arms and a beaming smile, then frowned at his glum face. 'James you look weary.'

'I am,' he replied, making a beeline for the drinks cabinet and pouring himself a brandy, then turning to face her, 'Can I offer you refreshment?'

'No thank you. I came to speak with you about a delicate matter.'

'I see.' He sat down opposite her on a comfortable armchair.

'Jack Beckwith,' she began. 'Are you acquainted?' she asked.

'Yes.' James could not bring himself to dislike the seaman, despite his past reputation for drinking heavily, he was an intelligent man, rather charming and witty at times too. They had shared a couple of short voyages together but that was some time ago now.

'We met a couple of times prior to the Beckwith's luncheon last week,' she continued. 'Anyway, he asked me to dine with him yesterday and we had the most agreeable time.' She paused for breath and her expression turned from delight to concern. 'There are rumours you see.'

James was well aware of them.

'About his wife's untimely death. They say in a drunken outrage he pushed her down the stairs.'

'He was found not guilty,' James said. 'How long has he been sober?' he then asked.

'Three years and it's been three years since her death.'

'Have you spoken to him about it?'

'Yes. He approached me on the subject, said he wanted me to know everything.'

'And…' James encouraged, wanting to be sure that a relationship with Jack would be safe for Lillian.

'His drinking got out of control, so much so that he was dismissed from the navy.'

'Yes I know about that, but he was reinstated,' James said, matter of factly.

'They had argued that night,' said Lillian. 'He and his wife, about his drinking, but he swears he did not push her. In fact, he was not even in the house at the time she fell to her death.'

'I heard he had a reliable alibi which was why he was acquitted.'

'He's dreadfully ashamed about his drinking and the court case and so forth. The navy did take him back when his name was cleared. He is a good man,' Lillian said.

'I don't doubt that. So what is your concern? Are you afraid he might have a relapse?'

'No. I believe that he will not touch another drop of alcohol again. Reputation is what I'm concerned about. Some people still believe it to be true…about him killing his wife I mean.'

'I've never been one for gossips,' James said, taking another swig of brandy. 'Go with what your heart tells you. The Beckwiths have managed to forgive him, and still have a favourable reputation.'

Lillian gave a small smile of gratitude. 'I can never talk to Robert like I do you. Talking of Robert, will you be here for the wedding?' she asked with hope, but at the same time worried for him. She knew how terrible it would be for him to witness Victoria marry Robert.

'No. I am going away tomorrow.' The word *wedding* ripped at his heart and he was happy to have a plausible reason for not attending.

'Tomorrow? Pity.' She looked disappointed.

'You'll have to get used to that if you and Jack Beckwith are to be…well you know,' he managed a small smile.

'Yes, it's not easy, his going away, although he is talking about leaving the navy soon.'

'As I,' James said, catching her unaware.

'Really? But why, James? Being at sea is your life.' Not having much family, she had grown fond of her younger brother, although she did not see him as often as she would have liked. Secretly, she felt quite thrilled that he should give up his life at sea, but didn't want to appear selfish and felt obliged to at least try and persuade him to stay in the navy.

'Was my life,' he corrected her. 'I'm getting close to the end of my term. I think it's time for a change of direction.'

'Oh please don't tell me you are going to move abroad?' She would hate for him to move away. James gave a throaty laugh. 'Whatever gave you that idea? No my dear, I am an Englishman and a Yorkshireman through and through and will not leave these green pastures of Yorkshire!'

As the millers left the building, Jim and many of the others dropped into the White Swan Inn for a drink before heading home, many of them having a long journey to get to neighbouring villages, some of them many miles away. It was the only public house in Ruswarp and far nearer than walking into Whitby. It wasn't until a couple of hours had passed did Jim leave and make his way back past the river bed, and it was there he heard whimpering in the overgrowth.

'By-eck, lad! what 'appened ta' thee?' He bent down on his haunches to take a better look at Charlie Crouch covered in blood from head to toe, his face hardly recognisable. Charlie tried to speak but his lips were too swollen to move.

'Don't speak. 'Orner lads, right?'

Charlie nodded.

'Well I hate to say, *told you so*. Come, let's get you cleaned up.' He pulled him gently to his feet.

Chapter Seven

The night before Victoria and Robert's wedding the wind picked up with violence. Victoria stirred in bed, her eyes fluttered as she dreamt on. The church was packed with familiar faces smiling back at her, large as life. She walked up the aisle towards Robert, but when he turned around it wasn't Robert, but James, and he was holding a baby wrapped in a white crocheted shawl. The baby let out an almighty wail and, as she turned back to face the congregation, she noticed that every guest held a baby in their arms too. Each baby was crying at the same time. It soon became a cacophony of deafening noise. She awoke to the sound of crying still ringing in her ears. Her nightdress clung to her body with perspiration. She sat up in bed, took a deep breath and exhaled while listening to the wind rattling at the windows and whistling up the bedroom chimney.

In Whitby, Sophie sat holding her uncle's hand. The doctor had just been and the news was not good. He had told her to prepare for the worst. Nick Dickens's heart was not likely to last the next twenty four hours.

The room, dimly lit, hosted shadows on the thick stone walls. A solitary candle flickered on the table from the draft coming underneath the door, courtesy of the stormy wind whipping around the old building. Nick lived above the pub, and Sophie had moved in a few months ago to help look after him and also tend to the pub, it made it much easier, her being there. The pub was now closed. She had thrown out the last punter earlier than usual, eager to get back to Nick. She had been alarmed at how shallow his breathing had become and had sent for the doctor straight away.

She pulled up the extra blanket laid at the foot of the bed and tucked him in, before sitting down next to him once more with a sigh and laying her head next to his arm, like a loyal dog, watching her master slipping away before her very eyes. He had been like a father to her all these years. She could not imagine a life without him.

Crawford House was chaotic the following morning, as one would expect on such a big day. Downstairs, Meg, the cook, was in a flap over a mix up with the ingredients for her special soufflé recipe. There was an army of kitchen maids to assist Meg. Everything from consommé to horseradish sauce had to be made from scratch, no cutting corners on a day as big as today.

Nathaniel, the gardener, had accepted an elaborate bouquet of flowers sent to Victoria from overseas, a distant aunt; too frail to attend the wedding, and wandered into the kitchen with them. 'Not sure where these are supposed t'go?' He held them up for all to see.

'Well not in 'ere!' yelled Meg, shooing him out of the kitchen.

Upstairs, Violet flapped around the room trying to find a dainty silver broach she had dropped, while her maid waited patiently with brush and comb in hand to do her hair. Violet glared at her and the maid then got down on hands and knees and joined in the search.

Rose and John, surprisingly, were remarkably calm, drinking tea in the parlour. John was already tailored and looking every bit the proud father of the bride. Rose, on the other hand, had decided she would slip her dress on at the last minute to keep it free from creases, and wore an old favourite navy-blue dress that she felt most comfortable in.

She decided to go and check on the bride to be. Victoria had refused breakfast that morning and looked very pale again, which concerned Rose, no end.

Victoria's bedroom door was left open. Mary, the maid, fiddled with the wedding dress hanging up on the outside of the wardrobe.

Rose walked into the room. 'Mary, where's Victoria?'

'In the garden, My Lady.' She pointed to the window. Rose looked out and saw Victoria perched on a wooden bench, surrounded by flowers. She sighed. 'That girl will be the death of me. Thank goodness she is to be married today. She will soon be Robert's responsibility!'

Victoria closed her eyes for a moment. The wind, now much calmer than the night before, still whipped her hair across her face, but the sting didn't bother her. She had heard through the grapevine that James had returned to sea. It made it easier for her, knowing he would not attend the wedding, but it didn't make it any easier when it came to missing him and longing for him. She wondered if she would ever learn to live without him or even grow to love Robert. She placed her hand over her tummy. Her small protrusion, fortunately, did not show yet through clothes, although Victoria noticed it very well when naked. She felt no emotion for the baby, no joy as an expectant mother should feel, if anything she held a grudge against the tiny person growing inside of her, tying her to his or her father, rather than the man she really loved.

'Darling!' Rose called out from across the garden.

Victoria looked up, startled. Her time of being alone was over. From this moment on she would not be able to be herself, but the Miss Victoria Crawford they all expected her to be and then soon to be, Mrs Robert Hawkes.

The wind had picked up stronger yet again, much to the vexation of the wedding party. Much of the blue sky had now been covered by large, grey clouds and there was a definite threat of rain on the horizon. Victoria's veil of old fine lace blew billows around her small frame. Violet, dressed in a pretty pink bridesmaid's dress, slipped her hand into Victoria's. Victoria gave an appreciative sideways glance. 'You're doing the right thing, you'll see,' Violet said, fully aware her sister had no choice. Marrying Robert was the only option for her now. They had spoken about it secretly many times in recent days.

A little girl, of eight years old, in the same matching dress as Violet, held up a modest bouquet of lilies and handed it to Victoria. She was Victoria's youngest cousin.

'No, sweetie,' Violet cut in. '*You* must hold it until the bride is inside the coach.' The bridesmaid nodded and did as she was told. Victoria looked at her, wondering if the child she was carrying would be a girl. Would she look like Robert, she wondered? 'Come on,' Violet led her towards the coach and she brushed her thoughts to one side, for now.

The coach left *Crawford House*, bumping over rough terrain, followed by the rest of the wedding party in more coaches drawn by fine horses with braided hair and ribbons. News of the wedding procession moved fast as the millers lined up, waving and cheering them off. Cottagers and farmers turned out to see them all pass and, arriving in Whitby, the fishermen and their wives, workmen from the pier, shop-keepers and market stall holders all waved and shouted out messages to wish them well.

Outside the church Lillian fussed about Robert, brushing his lapel from the dust the wind had blown on him. 'I'm fine, will you stop it now?' He looked annoyed.

Lillian looked smart in a pale lilac dress edged with white lace, and her hair styled fashionably high above her head in ringlets. Apart from her oversized nose of course, she looked remarkably attractive. 'Promise me something Robert,' she met his eyes with a worried look. 'Please do your best to be a good husband to Victoria.'

Robert gave a small, nervous chuckle. 'Why wouldn't I?'

'It's just…' she hesitated for a moment. 'About what you said before, love being a strong word.'

'Well it is,' he replied, in-between smiling and greeting the guests that were now filtering into the church.

'But if you don't really love her, why marry her? You don't need to do this to spite James.'

'Dear God. Do you really believe I would marry to spite my own brother?'

Lillian appeared embarrassed. 'No. No of course not, forgive me.'

'Come on.' He ushered her inside the church before she could say another word. She, like Victoria, and probably most of the congregation, felt relieved James would not be there to witness the wedding. To see the love of his life, marry his own brother would have been very cruel indeed, his going away was a blessing to them all, and not least of all to James, she suspected.

St Mary's church, next to the abbey, was filled with approximately sixty guests. Family and close friends were invited, and acquaintances were to attend the *after wedding* party. The altar, decorated with golden and white chrysanthemums, looked very fine, accompanied by five musicians who played hymns on fiddles and violins, and a small choir ranging from children to adults sang beautifully.

The congregation listened to Reverend Alfred-Charles drone on with the legal and spiritual bond. Victoria looked radiant, but inside felt numb. And when it was her turn to say her vows, there was a noticeable quiver to her voice and a slight hesitation, but with an encouraging nod from Alfred-Charles and a pleading look from Robert to *not stop now*, she continued with greater conviction. In no time at all they were out in the churchyard again where there gathered a small group of villagers and the photographer, Domenico Cifaldi. They stood at a respectful distance. And as if it had all been rehearsed, they gave a cheer in unison as the couple appeared holding hands. Domenico Cifaldi, in his element, took as many photographs as he could.

'We've done it,' Robert whispered in her ear, still holding her hand.

'Yes, for better or for worse,' she replied. There was no point fighting it any more. She had made her choice, married Robert and she was carrying his baby. From this moment on, should any thought enter her head of James Hawkes, she would banish it immediately.

Robert watched her as she posed for a photograph with her bridesmaids. She was the mother of his child, a fine looking woman, and aside from the bonus of having the satisfaction of keeping her and James apart, his intentions were entirely honourable, he decided. He meant every word of the vows he had just made and would endeavour to keep them.

At *Crawford House* a banquet had been prepared, putting all other feasts in the shade. From freshly puréed consommés, poultry, game and fish, an array of wonderful vegetables, cooked elaborately with sauces and garnishes made from the freshest and finest mouth-watering ingredients. Meg's special soufflé went down a treat. She and her kitchen team had all excelled themselves, without exception.

Rose spent half of the time up and down, fussing around to make sure all was running smoothly. John, rising to the occasion, delivered one of his heart-felt speeches about his daughter and welcoming his new son-in-law into the family. Everyone raised a glass and cheered and to the outside world, it looked to be a happy event, two people in love, now united in marriage.

Dr Coker had attended the wedding reception with his silly wife who giggled nervously. Victoria's cousin William, an eligible bachelor, sat opposite Lillian, this had been Rose's attempt at match-making, little did she know that Lillian only had eyes for Jack Beckwith. They were deep in conversation and almost inseparable the whole evening. Lord Beckwith, sporting a fine red velvet waistcoat, led a political debate amongst the gentlemen. And amongst those gentlemen sat Uncle Albert Hawkes, in his early seventies and still going strong. He did, however, lend some solemnity and restraint to the conversation that was bordering on heated when it came to politics. Aunt Edith, taking her customary place at the foot of the table, wore an old-fashioned velvet gown, and a wig made from old hair in her brush to cover her thinning patches. And when she smiled she revealed her bare gums. At seventy seven, though, she still possessed a sharp mind.

On the other side of the table, in between members of the Beckwiths, sat Domenico Cifaldi and his lady friend Helena, who barely spoke enough English to string a sentence together, also George Leguey, a name well-known in the mining and banking circles, and Mr Shufflebotham, a banker, who was a rather large gentleman with pale blue eyes that carefully surveyed everyone for their worth. His wife, just as over-sized, sat next to him feeling a little out of her depth, not really knowing most of the guests.

Rose had seated the Beckwith family, eight in total, in various places around the table. A powerful, and somewhat rowdy crowd, although highly entertaining, she thought best not to be seated altogether. Mrs Beckwith's laughter, if you could call it that, was more like a hyena's call and it seemed to overpower all the chatting and clanking of glasses and cutlery at times. Unlike her husband, Lord Frank Beckwith, who was more refined, Verity Beckwith showed little elegance, or the grace of a lady. Having said that, Rose, like many other females present, did find her rather amusing and the Beckwiths were certainly a family to be reckoned with, with all their success and wealth and for this reason her outlandish behaviour would be overlooked.

When the banquet was at last over, the table was cleared and pushed away for guests to sit in a circle and watch the entertainment.

Victoria had not been impressed with the choice of entertainment, not really liking monkeys; too many of their features were similar to the human race which she found to be a trifle uncomfortable. Robert, on the other hand, had agreed with his new father-in-law that it would be fun for all the guests to see. Two squirrel monkeys shipped in from South America performed a lively array of tricks, ranging from cycling on tiny tandems to juggling balls, one of which managed to hit Aunt Edith on the head and knock her wig slightly out of place. Undeterred by this mishap, the show went on. Their frolicking ways brought much laughter and happiness to all and sundry.

Outside of *Crawford House*, the wind had dropped completely, and in the darkness a horse whinnied, its hooves sounded along the cobbles. A dark silhouette stopped the horse and looked up at the brightly lit house. The sounds of merriment and music echoed around the courtyard. For a moment he sat and listened, then continued on his way.

Arriving back at *Heron House*, this time the lights were burning brightly. No sooner had he put the horse back in the stables, Eleanor stood outside of the barn waiting for him. 'You have a visitor Sir,' she said, as James approached her side. 'I told her you only got back from sea late this afternoon, and you were out riding, but she's in a terrible state. I gave her a brandy, but it's been awkward, don't know what to say.'

'Who is in a terrible state?' His fair eyebrows knitted together trying to understand Eleanor's babbling words.

'Miss Sophie,' Eleanor replied. 'Her uncle passed away last night.'

James quickened his step. 'Make up the guest room, she can stay the night here.'

'But…'

It was too late he was already way ahead of her. 'But would that be proper her staying under your roof,' she called out, now catching up with him.

'Would it not be proper to help a friend in need?' he replied sharply.

Sophie sat staring at the roaring fire. The ginger stray, sprawled out in front of it, gave a yawn and rolled over. James burst into the room, startling it and Sophie at the same time.

'I'm so sorry,' he held out his arms to her and embraced her tightly. She cried and sobbed for a long while before finally speaking. 'I knew it would 'appen….' she said - 'him passing - but it doesn't make it any easier.'

'He'll be in no pain now.' James passed her the half empty glass of brandy, still sitting on the small table in front of them. He looked into her eyes, never had he seen them so sad before. She was always such a happy and jovial person. She looked like she'd had the stuffing knocked out of her now.

'I don't know 'ow to make the arrangements, never, 'ad to before.'

'Leave it to me.' James squeezed her hand tightly and she gave him a small, somewhat pathetic smile.

With the entertainment over and the monkeys put safely away in their cages, the dancing began and the drinks continued to flow. The strings, accompanied by the soft sound of the hautboy and the flute, were playing a familiar Italian minuetto. Strains of the music reached every corner of the ballroom and even through to where the refreshments were being served in the rest room. For the first time Victoria felt relaxed and sure that she had made the right decision to forget James and concentrate on a future with Robert and their baby. Robert found her taking a quiet moment to reflect.

'Do cheer up,' he said, giving her a peck on the cheek.

'Did I appear glum?' She looked up at him with eyes that were now smiling.

'Yes. Are you?' He asked, hoping she would learn to love him just as she did James.

'Quite the contrary!' She returned his kiss on the cheek and linked arms with him.

'Ah, what a handsome pair you make.' Aunt Edith toddled along with a glass of champagne in her hand.

'Aunt Edith,' Victoria smiled. 'Are you having fun?' Aunt Edith was John Crawford's sister, Edith Agnes Anne Crawford, being her full name.

'Why of course,' she replied, with a gummy smile.

'Robert, what a shame your brother couldn't be here, is he ill?' she asked, seemingly in her naivety. Most of the guests had managed to avoid the delicate subject in front of her, but she knew more than she let on.

'He's at sea Madam Crawford,' he replied tactfully.

'Would the navy not permit him leave? Surely, for his own brother's wedding?' She scratched at her wig and then took a sip of her drink.

'It was all erm…' Robert cleared his throat. 'A little short notice for him.'

'Yes, I suppose it was all a bit sudden. Weddings normally take months to arrange, why did you rush it so?' She looked Victoria directly in the eye. Edith Crawford may be old but she was no fool. Victoria turned a pale shade of pink. 'Well we um..'

'We didn't want to wait once the decision had been made to get married,' Robert stepped in.

'Yes we were keen to start our married life together,' Victoria added unconvincingly.

Robert, feeling hot under the collar from the interrogation, made his excuses. 'Oh I really must have a word with Mr Cifaldi about the photographs, if you'll both excuse me?' With that he was gone in a flash, leaving Victoria alone with Aunt Edith.

'Your skin is radiant. In fact, I'd say you are positively blooming!' She revealed her gums once again.

'Thank you.' Victoria felt Aunt Edith's eyes, through the spectacles on her nose, staring into her with suspicion.

'Is the sickness getting any better?' she continued.

'Sickness?' Victoria squirmed.

Fortunately, Rose arrived in the nick of time. 'There you are darling. This is your big day. You must enjoy it and learn to mingle. Aunt Edith, would you like a refill?'

Edith dragged her beady eyes away from Victoria and on to the half empty glass in her bony hand. 'That would be most agreeable,' she said.

James poured himself a brandy. Eleanor entered the room. 'Sir, I've made up the guest room. Will Miss Sophie be joining you for supper?' She glanced over at Sophie, who seemed to be staring vacantly back at the fire. She had not heard a word that Eleanor had said, or noticed that she was even in the room. 'Yes, Miss Sophie will be joining me for supper if she so wishes. He looked at her expectantly, but still saw no reaction. With a wink and a nod of the head he said 'Yes Eleanor, set a place at the table.'

'Very well Sir.' Eleanor left the room, still unsure if James was doing the right thing. Sophie was not really a lady of status, and her staying the night at *Heron House* might be frowned upon by most. Still it was not her business, she was paid to serve and serve was what she did, and that was just about all she did these days. Since George had left, her life seemed empty. She never went down to the riverbank, the memories were far too painful and, other than the odd trip to Whitby either to buy at the market or visit a friend now and again, her life was dedicated to *Heron House*. She had not even noticed young Alfie's attempt to catch her attention, the lad was smitten with her, yet she had no idea.

Lillian sat in the corner of the room next to Jack Beckwith, they were now both a little out of breath from dancing. They had chatted and giggled like teenagers all evening. 'I love to dance,' said Lillian. 'But I get precious little opportunity,' she sighed then smiled brightly. 'Tonight has been such a pleasure.'

'The pleasure being all mine,' he held her gaze for a long time. She had pretty eyes, beautiful bare shoulders, but most of all her warm and sincere personality shone through, so much so that her oversized nose was totally disregarded. Their interest for each other had not gone unnoticed, as gossiping tongues chatted about the pair.

'Do you think she is aware of his past?' Faith Tweddle, a pale and painfully thin girl in her late teens asked Violet.

'Of course! Everyone knows, it is old news, isn't it?' Violet took a sip of champagne. She felt a little fuzzy now, finishing off her third glass. 'So if she knows,' Faith continued, 'would she not worry about a possible future with him?'

'He doesn't drink any more, and no one believes he did actually kill his wife.' Violet swayed slightly, then sat down to steady herself.

'Don't they?' Mrs Tweddle, Faith's mother, interrupted after overhearing their conversation.

'You mean people do still think that he?' Violet asked, now lost for words, looking over at the couple chatting and having fun.

Robert, finally having the opportunity to speak to his sister, approached Lillian, annoyed at her flagrant *carrying-on* in public and more than anything, her *carrying-on* being with Jack Beckwith.

'Mr Beckwith,' he greeted him coolly.

Jack stood up and Lillian followed suit. 'Mr Hawkes, may I offer my congratulations to you and your beautiful lady wife.' He gazed around the room in search of Victoria. She was on the far side talking to guests. Verity Beckwith, standing near Victoria, gave one of her raucous hoots, overpowering the music. Heads did not even turn for they were so used to her regular outbursts.

'Lillian, may I have a word in private please?' he asked, paying no attention to Jack. Lillian frowned. 'Surely whatever it is you want to say, you can say in front of Jack? We're amongst friends here.' She tapped Jack on his arm affectionately and smiled at him.

'I'd rather not if it's all the same?' Robert pulled her arm with force.

'Steady on old chap, no need for that.' Jack was quick to intervene.

'Jack it's fine.' Lillian didn't want any fuss. Jack, sensing this, stepped back.

Robert flashed a look of disgust and marched Lillian outside, away from prying ears and eyes.

'You are embarrassing me, let go of my arm,' Lillian whispered loudly.

They stood in the foyer next to the front door. He released her arm from his tight grip. The butler made himself scarce after receiving a daggered warning look from Robert not to interrupt them.

'You are the one who is an embarrassment. You were practically throwing yourself at him.'

'Don't be so ridiculous,' Lillian scoffed.

'Are you aware of his history?'

'Well of course I am.'

'That makes it even worse.' He pushed his fingers through his thatch of hair.

'He makes me happy. For the first time in my life I have met a man who I truly connect with. Do you really begrudge me that happiness?'

'You cannot see him. I forbid you.' Robert folded his arms defiantly, having not listened to a word she had just said.

'Forbid me?' she gave an incredulous chuckle. 'I am a grown woman and I shall do as I wish.'

'Not if it is tarnishing our family name.' His voice was now raised.

'The Beckwiths are good people,' she replied sharply. 'How can it be tarnishing our family name?'

'Where do I start? Besides the fact that Jack Beckwith was a drunk and stood trial for his wife's murder, there's Lord Beckwith who talks about politics non-stop and knows not the first thing about the subject, the stupid old fool. Then there's his ridiculous wife. No woman should behave in such a fashion, and as for the rest of them, a bunch of...'

'Stop it!' Lillian yelled, not being able to bear any more. 'You can not, and will not, run my life. You have destroyed James's and I will not allow you to destroy mine.' Robert appeared stunned by her outburst, a vast contrast to the normally quiet Lillian who did as she was told.

'The Beckwiths -' she continued - 'have invited me away tomorrow, for the weekend. Everyone is going, including your in-laws. I intend to spend a lot more time with Jack, so you'd better get used to the idea.' She turned on her heel and left Robert speechless, watching her retreating back disappear back into the party.

Sophie sat opposite James at dinner, having reluctantly agreed to eating, but when it came to it, she really couldn't face food. James watched her chase a potato around the plate with her fork.

'I've left the navy'- he blurted out, in an attempt to distract her from her grief. She looked at him, baffled.

'Can you do that - I mean just leave?'

'I have served my time and I would either have to start a new contract or leave, so I've decided to leave.' He took a sip of wine to wash down the bread he had just consumed.

'But what will you do?' She finally popped the potato into her mouth without thinking, too busy concentrating on the conversation. He noticed and smiled inwardly, his distraction worked.

'Firstly, help you, and then I shall see further.'

'Help me?' she looked blankly at him.

'The funeral, the pub.' He reached out and touched her hand. 'Sophie, I'm here for you. I'm your friend, please let me help.'

She nodded gratefully. She had no idea why she had turned to him in her darkest hour, but perhaps that was it, she did consider him as her friend now, why else would she be in *Heron House* dining with him and staying the night in his guest suite? James Hawkes was a kind and decent man.

Chapter Eight

The weather was dismal with low, grey, clouds and a light drizzle which seemed appropriate on this sad day, the day that Nick Dickens was to be laid to rest. A long harsh caw, followed by a series of short ones, echoed around the graveyard as a couple of crows flapped from tree to tree.

The service was held at St Mary's church, of course. Locals and fellow publicans came to pay their respects to a kind gentleman who had lived life to the full and made the most of what he'd had, his prized possessions being his pub and - the apple of his eye - his niece, Sophie. He had never married or had the good fortune to have a family of his own, and so when his only brother and sister-in-law had died of diphtheria, ten years previously, he took Sophie in and looked after her as his own. The only Dickens left now was Sophie; most of their relatives had either died or moved on to pastures new years ago.

Reverend Alfred-Charles led the sombre service, his long drone of a sermon continued as Nick's body lowered into the ground. Sophie threw a single white carnation onto the coffin. James stood next to her for support. As she stepped back from the grave, her legs seemed to give way and, before he could catch her, she landed on her knees, draping herself over the coffin, crying hysterically. James helped her to her feet and she sobbed for a moment in his arms, then composed herself once more, a little embarrassed that she was making a show of herself in front of so many people. But the reality of grief had taken a grip of her and no one thought any less of her for her conduct. She had never felt so alone in the world and the only person who she could draw any kind of comfort from was James.

The wake was held at the pub. Everyone had rallied round to make a fine spread of food and any expenses were generously covered by James Hawkes.

'I couldn't 'ave got through today without you,' Sophie rubbed his hand with affection. He looked deep into her eyes, she seemed so lost and he wished more than anything he could take away her anguish.

'Nonsense! You are stronger than you think.' He patted her hand and gave her a reassuring smile.

Mary, a middle aged woman wearing a black dress that fitted where it touched, showing every ounce of her body fat, spoke quietly to young Emily who worked on the market stall. They sat in the corner surveying James and Sophie carefully. 'He's stayed all day with 'er,' said Mary.

Emily, her eyes fixed firmly on them replied, 'appen there might be somet going on between 'em.'

'It's not right - likes of 'im don't marry likes of 'er.'

'She don't 'ave anyone else to turn to right now.' Emily turned to face Mary with a frown on her face. 'Who said owt about marriage?'

'What would he gain from marryin' 'er, I wonder?' Mary continued, not taking any notice of Emily, lost in her own little world of thoughts. 'She's not got money or owt, well not like them 'Awkes's 'ave.' Mary took a swig of brown ale.

'It's not as if she's got nowt to her name. She will 'ave inherited this place now.' Emily pointed out. They had not noticed Anna, who had pulled up a chair and plonked herself down next to them while they were chatting. 'You know about Captain 'Awkes and Miss Crawford don't you?' Anna brushed the crumbs from her sandwich that were now stuck in her long, tangled hair. 'Dreadful business, cast aside like that and her choosin' his brother. Never did like her, *Miss High and Mighty*. Mind you, Captain always 'as been black sheep of 'Awkes family. Joseph 'Awkes never cared for him much, he proved that when he left mill t'other Mr 'Awkes, probably why Miss Crawford married him instead.' She gave a little snort and took another bite of her sandwich.

'Given the choice,' said Emily, 'I'd 'ave chosen the captain any day. 'E's a fine figure of a man and still has a lot to offer a girl. I say if Sophie's got a chance with 'im,' Emily grinned, 'she should grab it with both 'ands, better still grab 'im with both 'ands!' The other two women let out a raucous laugh and everyone turned to face them. You could have heard a pin drop once they had realised they were being watched and fell quiet. Looks of disgust that they should laugh at a time like this were cast upon them. Although many on that side of the room had overheard the conversation, and after all, they were only saying what everyone was thinking, but there was a time and a place.

Victoria and Robert left for London the day after the wedding. They travelled by train, due to Victoria not wishing to spend any more time than necessary in an automobile; the strange, new contraption on wheels she felt to be most unsafe, especially with her being pregnant. Robert had left the mill in the hands of Jim for the two weeks he would be away. He had every confidence in Jim; the old boy had been inherited by Joseph Hawkes, and now Robert. If anyone knew how to run the place, Jim certainly did.

Robert and Lillian had not exchanged another word since their argument at the wedding and Robert only hoped that no damage would be done to the family name if she was to be seen again in public, fraternising with Jack Beckwith that weekend. On his return he would make it his business to make sure Jack Beckwith would be staying well away from his sister.

It had been a cold and unsettled spring, with stormy winds and much rain, but by the middle of the month, spring and mid-summer had amalgamated into one week. In seven days of constant sunshine the countryside grew and set into its richest green. The delayed spring blossoms seemed to have come out overnight. Eleanor had not noticed it until now, as she walked past the river-bed on her way to Whitby.

'Eleanor!' Alfie called out to her. She turned left and made her way down the lane, basket in hand and lost in thought. He jumped up onto Blackie. James had asked him to take the horse to the blacksmith for a new shoe fitting. He still walked well, but the shoe was becoming worn. He reached Eleanor's side. 'I'm going t' Whitby, if you want a ride?'

She shook her head. 'I'd sooner walk.' She held her head high and strode on.

'Do you dislike me that much that you won't even accept a ride with me?' He wore an injured expression.

She stopped, shaded her eyes against the sun, and looked up at him. 'I don't know why you think I dislike you.'

He laughed without humour. 'You avoid talking to me, you won't accept a ride, what am I supposed t' think?'

A ghost of a smile appeared on her face, feeling sorry for him. She had been a little impolite at times, though that was through no fault of his, but of her own. Her anxiety had taken over her life of late, she had been so preoccupied with her worries of George and her deceit to the police, that she had hardly noticed or given the time of day to Alfie.

'Go on then. Drop me at market.'

His face lit up and he gave her a helping hand. 'Wherever the lady wishes,' he said. She wriggled to get comfortable, grabbing hold of her basket in one hand and Alfie with the other. Now that the ice had broken between them they made small talk, and were accompanied by bird song all the way into Whitby.

James, wearing a broad grin, walked into the *The Old Horseshoe* pub, waving an envelope. Apart from two old men perched up one end of the bar, the pub was empty. Most of the regulars had thought it best to give it more time out of respect to the grieving; drinking and becoming merry was not quite the *done thing* when old Nick Dickens wasn't even cold in his grave.

Sophie stood behind the bar polishing glasses. She had wanted to keep the pub closed, but then decided that would not have been her uncle's wish. He opened up come rain or shine and no matter what.

'What's that?' she looked at the envelope James had placed on the bar, there was evidence in her eyes that she had been crying again.

'This,' he said, pulling the photographs out, 'Is art at its best!' There were half a dozen pictures of Sophie. She picked up the ones of her hanging precariously over the bridge reaching for a stick. 'Oh 'eavens! Look at me!' she put her hand over her mouth then let out a small shriek of muffled laughter.

'Aren't they amazing?' He sounded proud, flicking through them again. 'Not bad for a first attempt, wouldn't you say?'

'You can't show folk these,' she said with a look of seriousness. 'Well, not that one anyway?' She pointed to the photo of her stranded on the bridge with her skirts caught on a branch.

'Perhaps not that one,' he grimaced. 'But the others are fine, very fine. You look beautiful.' Silence fell between them. Their eyes met and he reached for her hand. 'I mean it, you are beautiful.'

'Give over,' she blushed, then let go of his hand. Her lips broke into a soft smile. 'You're a budding photographer - 'appen this is your calling - 'appen this is what you are meant to do now you've left navy.'

When she smiled he realised how much she reminded him of Victoria. He had noticed it while developing the photographs. They shared the same shaped face, tiny dimples, only noticeable when smiling, and both wore their hair in a similar fashion, piled on top of the head with the occasional stray curl framing the face. Although Sophie's hair was not as immaculate, in fact quite messy by comparison.

'Wouldn't go as far as to say that, I'm merely an amateur,' he replied. 'I don't think it's my calling, but I do enjoy it. It's a bit of fun.'

'I'd say these are professional, not that I'm an expert or owt.' She studied them closely and then looked up at him with excitement shining in her eyes. 'You could open a studio, like Mr Cifaldi.'

'Mr Cifaldi would not welcome the competition, not to mention the fact that there are other very talented photographers at present in Whitby. I am sure I could never compete with the likes of Francis Sutcliffe, for example.'

'Says who?'

He admired the confidence she possessed and the way she made him feel, like he could achieve anything if he so wished. His mother had been the only person who had shown so much faith in him, and now Sophie did too. It felt uplifting and very good.

A group of fishermen walked in, after deliberating outside for a few moments on whether they should or not. They came to the conclusion that if the pub was open they would be welcome, despite it being so soon after Nick Dickens' passing.

James handed Sophie the photographs to put back in the envelope and jumped up to serve them. 'Yes, gentlemen, what I can get you?'

'Ayup captain, you're on wrong side o' bar,' one of them joked.

'I'd argue I'm on the right side of bar,' he pointed to all the bottles behind him and they burst into laughter.

Sophie smiled. He had a way with people, a knack of bringing out the best in folk and she loved him being there in the pub with her.

Eleanor, with her basket now full from the produce she had purchased in Whitby market square, and also having bought fish for supper from Anna down at the quayside, was ready to make her way back home. She had no sooner got on the path to Ruswarp when she heard the fast canter of a horse heading her way through the fields. Alfie brought the horse to an abrupt halt. 'Tryin' out his new shoe – It's as good as new.' He patted the horse and it gave a deep snorted reply.

Eleanor looked down at Blackie's foot. 'Aye, 'appen it's because it is new.' She looked back at Alfie with a smile. She couldn't help but like him, despite her previous lack of interest in becoming friends with the lad and her not in the slightest bit interested in him romantically, he was nice enough, but he was not George. She missed George and there was not a day that went past when she did not wonder where he was, if he was safe, and if he spared a thought for her too sometimes.

'Pass me your basket first.' He held out his hand and she passed it to him. A moment later she was sitting next to him again, and they trotted off back towards *Heron House* with the sun still shining brightly and the birds still singing their songs.

Chapter Nine

It was the last day of the long weekend away at Bramblewick Manor, the Beckwiths home, located inland from Scarborough. Everyone had enjoyed themselves. An already close friendship had flourished further between the Crawfords and the Beckwiths, and also between Lillian Hawkes and Jack Beckwith. The busy itinerary had not left them much time for talking during the day, what with hunting, shooting, archery, polo, and croquet. But this afternoon the Beckwiths had laid on a garden party and the young couple found a quiet corner of the rolling lawns to eat their triangle cut ham and cucumber sandwiches, drink tea and chat in peace. They were amongst friends and family now and there were no gossiping tongues this time, or Lillian's angry brother to argue with. There were only encouraging smiles and waves, from those who approved of their blossoming friendship.

'It's so lovely to see them getting along. Poor Lillian, she hasn't been blessed with finding the right man so far,' Rose said to Verity.

'I was beginning to fear Jack had lost interest in women after his terrible ordeal.' She took a sip of tea, enjoying the warmth of the sunshine on her skin.

'Clearly not,' Rose said, as they watched Jack reach out and touch the side of Lillian's face, looking so very happy.

'In this light she looks pretty. I mean her nose – her nose doesn't seem so – well, large,' Rose said.

Verity let go of one of her famous hyena laughs. 'Hope to God she doesn't catch a bad cold, going to need a large handkerchief!'

'Stop it!' Violet said, laughing, sitting down next to her mother and Verity. A maid poured her a cup of tea and handed it to her.

'It must be the name. Her nose rather reminds one of a Hawk's beak,' chuckled Rose.

'All jokes aside,' said Verity. 'I think she is lovely, very suitable for our Jack. I just hope that, should they marry, my grandchildren will not inherit the Hawk beak!'

Violet and Rose laughed and then Verity said thoughtfully, 'Robert hasn't got the Hawk beak.'

'Um,' replied Rose, pensively, thinking of Victoria and wondering how she was getting on in London.

'Well he has a large nose but not quite as large,' said Violet. 'But James's nose is perfectly normal,' she added.

'That's because he takes after his mother and not his father,' replied Rose, now focusing back on the conversation. 'Lillian, unfortunately, has inherited Joseph Hawkes's nose.'

'Fancy that. Don't think I'd like to wear a dead man's nose,' Verity joked, then followed it with her outlandish laugh.

'Lillian' - Jack said, stretching out his legs on the grass. Lillian's attention focused on two sparrows fighting over the crumbs she had brushed off her lap from her sandwich.

'Yes' - she replied - looking at him.

'Being with you brings out the best in me. I haven't felt this way for a very long time - if ever.' He then added, 'you and I, it feels so natural.'

'Yes Jack, it does,' she replied, wondering where he was going with all of this.

'What I'm trying to say is – well what I mean is – um - well, that I've fallen in love with you.'

For a moment Lillian fell speechless. Jack suddenly feeling panicked by her surprised expression.

'Oh no – perhaps - perhaps I shouldn't have said all that. I'm sorry – so very sorry.'

'Don't be. I love you too,' she said at last.

'Do you?' he appeared stunned.

'I do,' she nodded, with a big beaming smile.

Not caring if anyone should be watching them, he leaned forward and kissed her tenderly on the lips. A moment later he sat back, looking pleased with himself and very relaxed. She took a sip of tea that had gone cold, not that it mattered, for all she could think about was how deliriously happy she felt. For the first time she had found a man she could love, a man who loved her as much as she loved him. Whatever his past history, she did not care. He was perfect for her, in every way.

'I'm going to leave the navy,' he announced.

'Yes, you mentioned it before. So you really are leaving then?' She could not fail to hide her joy at the news of him leaving. It would have been terrible to say goodbye to him and go for months on end without seeing him. She would have done so if it had come to it of course. Nothing would have got in the way of them being together, not the navy and not even Robert, she thought.

'I want to live in America,' he announced unexpectedly.

She nearly choked on her cold tea.

'It's the place to live - the place to get on - it's where dreams become reality.' He smiled broadly, remembering the statue of liberty in his mind's eye. It had always impressed him, as did New York itself, such a busy, vibrant city with bright lights; so prosperous and full of opportunity. 'I promised myself last time I left that next time I would be back for good. By the way, I have a job lined up in banking,' he said proudly. 'It's a fine job and the pay is handsome, and it will only get better as I work my way up the ladder.'

She placed the cup down, her eyes already welling up with tears at the thought of him leaving her. She did not understand why he should declare his love for her if he had plans to leave England. He couldn't leave her, not now, surely?

'And I want you to come with me,' he said, taking her off guard once more. 'I want you to be my wife.'

Her eyes were wide with astonishment. She cleared her throat nervously and, when she finally spoke, her voice gave an unwanted croak. 'Are you – are you asking me to marry you?'

He nodded. 'Stand up,' he said. 'Stand up,' he repeated, holding his hand out to her. She took his hand and rose to her feet. He looked around the garden and frowned. He needed this moment to be special, and memorable for the rest of their lives. It had to be right. 'Not here,' he said, glancing over at his mother who was watching them both with interest, alongside Rose. 'We need somewhere more private.'

He led her away from the gardens and towards a stunning stone water fountain surrounded by roses, in full bloom now that summer had arrived. She panted from their running and they both took a moment to catch their breath. He then got down on one knee.

'Miss Lillian Hawkes, will you do me the great honour of becoming my wife?'

With a mix of tears and laughter she agreed.

'Thank goodness, my knee is killing me from this blessed gravel. I should have stayed on the grass.' He brushed off the stones that had stuck to the knee of his trousers and Lillian giggled.

They were blissfully consumed with happiness and the prospect of a wonderful future together, a future that awaited them the other side of the Atlantic Ocean.

'I should head back. Will you be alright to run this place alone for the rest of the evening?' James wondered if he should leave Sophie in her state of grief, but there were only a few people in the pub, nothing she could not handle. The fishermen had now gone, wanting to get some *shut-eye* before heading out to sea in the early hours of the morning.

'If you must go,' she didn't sound pleased at the idea of him leaving her alone so soon. It felt strange, empty and desolate without Uncle Nick upstairs waiting for her. She knew she would have to get used to it, her being alone, but it was not something she welcomed by any means.

He picked up a clean cloth next to a stack of dirty glasses. 'I can stay a while longer, clean these for you,' he pointed to the glasses.

'I can do 'em. But I would enjoy your company, if you'd stay a while longer, that is,' she said with hope.

He started cleaning the glasses and she sighed with relief. If he wanted to clean the glasses she would let him, especially if it meant him staying longer.

The garden tea party had now turned into a dinner party at Bramblewick Manor. A feast had been laid on to entice everyone to stay up for one more night together, not that many of them had much of an appetite after the delicious spread that had been put on that afternoon.

Not being able to keep their news a secret, Jack had announced his engagement to Lillian at the start of the evening. The Beckwiths and Crawfords, in particular, were delighted for the young couple.

'Jack?' Verity interrupted his conversation with John Crawford about banking in the US. 'May I have a word?' she whisked him away, to outside of the drawing-room.

'What is it Mama?'

'Your fiancé needs a ring,' she said in a hushed tone.

'I am aware of that fact. I shall buy her a ring first thing in the morning when the shops are open,' he replied with a trace of amusement. 'Mama, I only asked her this afternoon.'

'Yes, well most gentlemen would buy the ring first before proposing,' she pointed out.

'It felt the right moment,' he said in his defence.

'I want you - well, rather Lillian - to have this.' She handed him a velvet covered ring box. He frowned and then popped the box open.

'It was your grandmother's and I know she would have wanted you to have it,' Verity added. He took the ring out of the box and held it up to see. It was an exquisite ruby, encrusted with tiny diamonds in the shape of a flower.

'Wow, I'm lost for words.' He gave a small whistle of appreciation.

'Go and ask her properly this time and put the ring on her finger. If it doesn't fit we can get it altered tomorrow,' Verity beamed.

'You're a genius, Mama.' He kissed her cheek and gave her a small hug to show his gratitude.

'A genius!' she shrieked, followed by her signature hoot. 'Go on with you, you'll make me blush.'

'I doubt that,' he laughed, leaving the room.

James stifled a yawn. It had been a long day. The last of the few punters had just left. He had stayed the whole evening, not wishing to leave her side. The two of them had chatted about a number of subjects, he had at one point made her laugh and on occasions she had almost forgotten her grief. He knew how much she was hurting, and if his being there helped, it was worth it to him to have stayed longer.

'You're exhausted. You don't want t' 'ave t' walk back t' Ruswarp now. Stay - stay in my room and I'll stay in Uncle's,' she suggested.

'Don't you think that might be a little upsetting for you – I mean - staying in your uncle's room?' He also wondered what people would think, but he didn't really care enough to let that get in the way of him staying. If truth be told, he would be more than happy to stay. If he went back to *Heron House* he would only eat supper alone, left out by Eleanor for him and then probably read a little in front of the fire before going to sleep. Sophie needed him and he enjoyed feeling needed.

'No, if anything I feel closer to 'im, in 'is room.' She poured herself a small glass of brandy and sat down on a stool, then took a large swig.

'You will need to sort his things at some point,' James said, stating the obvious.

'At some point - but not yet James,' she replied. 'I've got some bread and cheese upstairs and a bit of cold 'am and pie left over from wake, if you're 'ungry?'

'Sounds like a feast,' he grinned.

Taking Lillian by surprise yet again, Jack proposed for a second time that day. This time his knee was firmly on soft carpet. When he held out the ring she cried with happiness. 'Yes Jack - I will marry you!'

There was a burst of cheering, followed by a string of people congratulating them both and, when finally, that had all subsided, she suddenly felt an enormous wave of worry wash over her. She would have to break the news to Robert on his return from London. James would wish her well, she was sure of it, but she knew she would have to work very hard to get Robert's blessing, if ever he would give it to her.

'Whatever is the matter?' Jack asked, noticing her agonised expression. 'You haven't changed your mind have you?'

She shook her head. 'Not at all – of course not.' She sighed and brushed all thoughts of Robert to one side. She would deal with Robert later.

In her bed, he lay staring up at the wooden beams. It seemed strange to be sleeping in a woman's bedroom full of her belongings, instead of his room at *Heron House*. His eyes strayed to her dressing table, cluttered with numerous feminine objects to do with hair, make-up and even a bottle of perfume. Funny, he couldn't recall her wearing make-up, well if she did he had not noticed, neither did she bother with her hair most of the time. Yet it made her all the more interesting than most women he knew. Sophie possessed a natural beauty, both outwardly and inwardly. He wondered if he was falling for her. He did feel a sense of belonging when he was with her. He could be himself and did not need to think before he spoke. He liked how she made him feel useful, needed, and had so much faith in him. His thoughts then drifted to Victoria…

There was no air tonight and the room felt stuffy. He got up and opened the window.

She was married now, married to Robert, and they were on honeymoon in London. He got back into bed and noticed he had let in a moth that now darted erratically around the room. As much as it pained him to think about Victoria with his brother, and them having a baby together, he did hope Robert would make her happy. For all the bad Robert had done, if he could do one right thing and make her happy he would find it in his heart to forgive him, one day. The moth landed on the curtains and he watched it for a moment.

There was a soft tap at the door. He sat up and pulled the bed clothes higher to cover himself. 'Come in,' he called out.

Sophie walked in holding a candle. The door swung closed behind her. 'This frock,' she said, placing the candle down on the table close to the bed.

'What about it?' he answered, trying to ignore how pretty she looked even in the soft dim light of the candle.

'I find it 'ard to reach last 'ooks at back - they stick you see. I 'ardly ever wear it but I thought I would today and, well it won't budge and I can't get into bed with it on.'

'Come,' he patted the bed for her to sit down, suppressing a chuckle. She did amuse him.

She turned her back to him. His fingers moved clumsily over the problematical hooks. She could feel his warm breath on her neck, just as she had before when she had been stuck on the bridge and he helped her. She pushed back her head and arched her back as the dress became loose. His hands touched her cool, naked, skin. She pressed backwards, enjoying the closeness. She turned slightly and rested her head on his shoulder and, when he had finished with the remainder of the hooks, he pulled her close. Unable to resist each other a moment longer, their lips met.

A moment later she spoke. 'I 'ave a confession,' she said, her voice hoarse. He kissed her neck and his hands slipped inside of her dress, cupping her breasts. 'I lied,' she said, catching her breath enough to continue speaking. 'I can manage them 'ooks, but I could sense you wanted me as much as I want you.'

He said nothing, for nothing mattered. He had no reservations in his mind or his heart. He removed her dress completely and laid her softly down on the bed.

The candle flickered, casting shadows on the wall and ceiling above them, while teasing the moth that was busy flying around its naked flame.

Chapter Ten

She yawned and rubbed her eyes, waking up to the early morning sunlight filling the room. She looked up at the familiar rafters, then at her dressing table and its clutter. At first she had completely forgotten all about the night before, until her head turned towards his fair tousled hair on the pillow. She lay still watching him while her mind went over every little detail from last night. What had possessed her? - The grief? What must he think of her, coming on to him like that? She sighed.

They were not the actions of a lady, a lady would never behave in such a fashion, but the actions of someone who needed love, to find comfort during such testing times. He had been there for her when she needed support the most. If he told her this morning it had been a mistake, she would understand and would not disregard him for thinking so.

The birds were now awake and full of song. The sunlight filtered brightly through the parting of the curtains. It promised to be another hot day. She contemplated getting up, but couldn't drag herself away from James, just yet. If he felt that last night had been a mistake, at least she could enjoy being close to him a little longer, she thought.

She rolled over on her side and cuddled up to him. In his sleep he pulled her close, and she snoozed contentedly, resting on his bare skin.

A little while later a loud thud on the door downstairs woke them both. Sophie grabbed her dress and climbed into it before pulling back the curtains. And there, standing at the door, were two men dressed in tall hats and black cloaks. They looked official.

'Miss Dickens?' One of them called out to her, spotting her at the upstairs window. She opened the window wider.

'Yes,' she replied.

'Open up or we'll force entry!'

James, now dressed and standing behind her said, 'You'll do no such thing. What business do you have?'

'Business relating to a Mr Nicholas Dickens,' he answered impatiently.

James and Sophie exchanged a baffled look.

James unbolted the door and let them in. The two men walked into the pub, one started busily surveying the furniture and the other pulled out a document from his cloak. 'Mr Dickens owes,' he begun.

'The late Mr Dickens - I'm afraid he passed away,' James said.

'Yes, I am aware of that fact.' He coughed to clear his throat and glanced over at Sophie, now feeling slightly ashamed at their intrusion. 'Sorry for your loss Miss Dickens. Unfortunately, your uncle owes quite a considerable amount of money to the bank and has done for some time.'

''Ow much?' Sophie asked, hesitantly, her eyebrows meeting together in a deep frown.

'Two hundred and twenty two pounds and eight shillings to be precise.' His long moustache gave a small twitch as he awaited her reply.

'I want us to marry in America,' said Jack, his eyes shining with excitement. The others had gone home now, but Lillian had stayed on longer at the request of the Beckwiths, who wished to have the chance to get to know their future daughter-in-law better. Since Robert was away, and had moved out anyway, now that he was married, there was no need for her to rush home and she was delighted at the opportunity to stay longer at *Bramblewick House*. She would tell James of her engagement later that week on her return from Scarborough, she decided, and as for Robert, she would tell him when he and Victoria returned from honeymoon.

'But what about family? - Friends?' she asked from across the breakfast table.

'Do you really want a big wedding? - Lots of fuss?' He placed the morning newspaper down, having folded it neatly.

She didn't reply at first, but instead tried to envisage a wedding in America without those she loved. She would have liked James to be there, and Robert, but she suspected, knowing how stubborn

Robert could be, that he may not attend. Other than a few close friends, Aunt Edith, and distant cousins, the more she thought about it, the more she realised that she really didn't have that many people to invite.

He suddenly feared he may have been hasty expecting her to marry in New York. 'If it's a big day you want then we shall marry here before we leave,' he said, trying to please her. He wanted her to be happy. After all, she was giving up her home to be with him in America, the least he could do was let her choose where they would marry.

'Will your parents attend the wedding over there?' she asked, with a pensive expression.

'Try stopping them. Mother wouldn't miss it for the world, even if it meant travelling halfway across it to be there!'

'I'm not sure if James would want to come and, well, Robert – he's a law unto his self, and as for Aunt Edith - she's getting too old to travel now – and…'

'Then we shall marry here. It was a silly idea.'

'No – no it wasn't silly at all – I'm just not sure if it would be practical.'

'You're absolutely right, enough said - the wedding shall take place here in Yorkshire my dear.' He blew her a kiss from where he was sitting and she giggled. She felt so very happy and could hardly wait for them to start their new life together. She would miss James, of course, maybe even Robert, her home for sure and of course

Yorkshire and its green, rolling countryside. New York seemed such a vast contrast and so very far away, but if it meant being married to Jack, she would have lived on the moon if he had asked her to.

Sophie sat down on a stool at the bar, dumbstruck by the news of her uncle owing so much money. She'd had no idea, not even an inkling; he had certainly hidden it well from her.

'Miss Dickens has inherited these premises,' James said, still standing and with his arms folded tightly across his chest, 'If the debt is not in her name, then surely she is not liable.'

'Correct. Miss Dickens is not liable,' replied the taller of the two men. 'But she cannot inherit Mr Dickens's estate until all debts are settled.'

'And 'ow are you goin' t' get money owed t' you if me uncle is no longer 'ere to pay it?' Sophie asked, with a spark of anger in her tone.

'Assets - stock, furniture and so forth.' The other man with him held up a chair to examine it thoroughly in the light. He then placed it down and went behind the bar.

'You can't do that, 'ow am I supposed t' run this place with no furniture or alcohol?'

'Will the contents here be enough to cover the debt?' James stepped in. 'And if so will Miss Dickens still own the dwelling?' he asked.

'Technically she doesn't own anything yet, and she'll need a license too, but in answer to your question, it depends as to how much can be raised from assets as to whether this debt can be settled,' he answered pragmatically. 'We'll need to access the living quarters too, by the way,' he added.

Sophie jumped up. 'No! – James - stop 'em! They can't take from upstairs n'all.'

Eleanor prepared a stew, unsure if James would be back for supper that night. He had not come home the night before but she had an idea where he was, he was probably with that Miss Dickens. She hoped he knew what he was getting himself into. She may have inherited the pub and have some kind of status now, but there was no hiding she was not suitable for marriage, not for the likes of Captain Hawkes. No doubt he was still sore from Victoria's betrayal; what other reason would drive him to spending time with Sophie Dickens?

Alfie wandered in and pulled up a chair. She put down the large wooden spoon in her hand and looked at him, with questioning eyes. 'What do you want? This int for you, it's for Captain 'Awkes's supper.'

'Smells delicious.' He sniffed the air.

She relented with a smile. 'I might let you 'ave a small bowl if you promise to behave,' she teased.

He laughed. 'Me? Behave? I always behave.'

She shook her head and turned back to the stove.

'El?' he said. She stopped stirring and froze on the spot. George had been the only person who had ever called her that. Her mother had barely remembered her name, muddling her up with her three older sisters, and her father addressed her as *girl*, or *wretched child*, when he yelled at her while growing up. She had been his punch-bag since she could remember, especially after a few jars of ale. Her mother, too scared of him, always turned a blind eye. Eleanor vowed that the moment she was old enough to leave home, she would seek work and never see her parents again, not even her three sisters. Contact with them would mean contact with her father and, to rid herself of him completely, she had to cut all family ties forever. George had been the only person who had shown her love and when he called her *El*, it gave her a warm lovely feeling of being wanted.

'Don't call me that,' she snapped, not bothering to turn around.

'Sorry, didn't mean to upset you.' There was something mysterious about her, and he couldn't quite fathom it. 'Eleanor,' he begun, using her full name this time. 'Want t' come fishin' with me this evening, t' Whitby?'

This time she did turn around. 'Fishin'?' she said.

'Aye – fishin'.'

'Never been fishin' in me life - don't know owt about it.'

'I'll teach you.'

She stared back at him in thought.

'Tide'll be high enough at nine t' row down river t' Whitby. Please Eleanor - please say you'll come - it'll be fun.'

She wiped her hands on her apron. If James came back to eat that night she would have finished work by eight o'clock and she'd be free to go, so no harm in her saying yes, she wouldn't be missed.

'S'pose - but as long as you behave yourself and keep your 'ands t' yourself.'

'I'll take that as a yes then,' he beamed.

'If you want a bowl of this,' she pointed to the pot on the stove, 'You'd best come back in 'alf 'our.'

'Alf 'our?' he repeated, 'I'm starving.'

'Tough! It's not ready yet.' She turned her back on him so that he could not see her smile.

Patches of clean floor could be seen where chairs and table legs had once stood. Without furniture the pub looked much larger. Behind the bar there were no glasses, no alcohol, and all that remained on the empty shelves was Nick's old silver tankard, which they had spared due to it being dented, heavily stained and Sophie had also pleaded with them not to take it for sentimental reasons. Upstairs was just as sparse with only Sophie's room that had been left untouched. From furniture to ornaments, portraits and family heirlooms, it had all been taken to pay off Nick's debts.

'They've left me no option but to sell this place.' Sophie wiped her tears again and sniffed.

'Come.' James held out his arms to her and embraced her tightly. 'Come back to *Heron House* with me. Stay for a while and we will sort this mess out together, I promise.'

'Ow?' she looked at him with despair. 'There is no way out. What good is a public 'ouse with no alcohol and no furniture? I don't even 'ave a license - you 'eard what he said - I need a license. There'll be paperwork, lots of it...'

'If there is one thing I have learned in life,' he brushed a stray tear away from her eye, 'is that there is always a way out.' He ushered her towards the door. 'With a good meal inside of you and a decent night's sleep things will look differently in the morning.'

As he swung open the door they were faced with a string of regulars waiting to get inside. 'We're closed,' James informed them sternly.

Old David Strachan, with his scruffy beard, still containing the remains of an earlier meal, pushed forward to get a look at Sophie.

'We're all truly sorry lass for your loss, but we've given time to grieve and Nick wouldn't want this place closed up now would he?'

'If I 'ad a choice, I'd keep it open for you,' Sophie replied, still in tears.

'What d'you mean, if you had a choice?' David looked at her through his narrowed, deep brown eyes.

'Have they closed it down?' asked John Barrow, another regular who had known Nick for many years.

'I don't want to talk about it,' she brushed past them all.

'You heard the lady, now leave.' James shielded her from the gathering crowds.

'It were 'is gambling what cost him,' John Barrow shouted out. 'E couldn't stop - like a man possessed when 'e were on a winning streak.'

Sophie turned to face him. 'You're telling me my uncle gambled?' She knew he liked the odd game of cards, but to be in so much debt - it must have been a serious addiction.

'Aye – lass - fraid so!' John replied with regret.

Jim stood, drenched with water right up to his knees and soaked to the skin from the spray of the wheel under the mill as it jolted back and forth, instead of the normal rhythm it was supposed to turn to. He knew exactly what was wrong with it. It was the pit wheel. The axle was also damaged, where the wheel was mounted. It looked like the shaft had broken completely, which had held the pit wheel together. Cursing under his breath, he waded back out of the water and up the muddy riverbank to the mill again.

Charlie came out of the granary and spotted him. 'Ayup, someone's been swimming?' He had recovered nicely from his beating, not even a scar to show for it, but he had learnt his lesson and would not be bothering Becky Horner again, that he was certain of. No girl was worth getting a battering for.

Jim reached for the tobacco in his pocket and pulled out a thin tin. 'Dam shaft 'as gone on pit,' he said, wiping his tobacco tin dry, before rolling a cigarette.

'Oh,' Charlie said, none the wiser. 'What does that mean then?'

'It means it's got to be fixed - and quick, or the main wheel will break altogether.' He took an appreciative puff, then pushed past Charlie and made his way to Robert's office.

Once in Robert's office he found the address book with the technician's address.

'Will there be anything else, Sir?' asked Eleanor, after serving dinner to James and Sophie. They had sat down to eat later than usual and seemed to be taking an age to finish their meal. She had been quite disgruntled at the task of serving Sophie, a jumped up barmaid who didn't as yet officially own her uncle's pub, and who now had her sights set far higher than she should have. What was the Captain thinking of, spending so much time with her? It wasn't long ago she worked on the market stall selling fruit!

'We'll have two brandies in the parlour in a short while and that should be all for the night, Eleanor.' He watched her with interest as she cleared away dirty plates in haste. 'Are you going somewhere this evening?' It was the only reason that sprung to mind as to why she should be in such a hurry.

'Fishin',' she replied.

Sophie tried not to choke on her wine. James seemed amused too. 'Is this a new passion of yours?' he enquired, trying to keep a straight face.

'No Sir. Alfie asked me t' go fishin' with 'im and I said I would.'

'Well have a good time. Perhaps you'll catch tomorrow's supper,' he smiled.

''Appen I might,' she answered and then left the room.

Sophie and James let out their laughter as soon as the door closed. Their eyes then locked from across the table. 'It's nice to see you smile,' he said.

'Not much to smile about these days,' she sighed heavily.

'Sophie,' he said, sitting forward in earnest 'I have a proposition for you.'

'Sounds intriguing. - And before you ask no I will not be your model again, last time my underskirt was ripped to shreds.'

'Well if you will hang over streams too close to trees, what do you expect?' he laughed, remembering the photograph he had taken of her.

'As you are aware I have now left the navy and I'm looking for a new venture.'

Her eyes were still fixed on his, listening with interest.

'I've enjoyed helping you out, and I quite fancy myself as a publican.' He sat up straight and puffed out his chest.

'You want to buy my uncle's pub?' she asked, her eyes widened with surprise. If she really had to sell, she'd rather sell it to James than a stranger who might even knock it down and use it as goodness know what - a fishery or something. At least she could still visit and he might even let her work there and run the place for him.

'Not exactly,' he said. 'I would like to buy into it.'

'I don't understand,' she looked confused.

'I would like to be your business partner. Own half of the pub. But instead of giving you money to buy my half, I'll invest it in the furniture and alcohol, maybe get upstairs furnished too. What do you think?'

She stared back at him, lost for words. 'I..uh..I don't know what to say.' This was far better than she had imagined.

'The paperwork would be drawn up officially of course, license in both our names.'

'And we'd run it together? - You and me?' She asked.

'Well, not all of the time. I may have other business to attend to. You are more than capable of running the place should I not be there all the time.'

Her face lit up. It was the perfect solution. She still owned half of her uncle's pub and was able to run it. James's money would bail her out and stop her from having to sell, what a genius idea.

'Yes! I think it's a perfect solution!' she got up and went to him and kissed him firmly on the lips. Her kiss was so powerful it forced him back in his chair.

The pale blue of the daytime sky was now mingled with swirling, low, grey, clouds and splashes of peach, orange and red, displaying a thick line across the horizon. Alfie rowed, and Eleanor watched as they made their way down the river towards Whitby. They headed under an incredibly high stone viaduct, and not long after that, the river met the harbour. The waters were calm tonight as they steadily made their way out into the open sea. Eleanor looked pretty in a small beige hat, dressed in a warm matching cloak. Her cheeks were flushed from the sea air, while she dangled her hand overboard and touched the icy cold spray, giving her an excited thrill to be out and away from her normal routine at *Heron House*.

They skirted the pier and the *walking man*, then they passed an abundance of fishing boats. They were the herring fleet heading out for the night. Alfie raised a hand in greeting to a few of them. To him this was all very familiar, but to Eleanor it was quite the opposite. She couldn't help but think of George. This would have been the route he would have taken when he left with Bill Sanders' body on board the little rowing boat he had used to escape. She could still see it in her mind's eye, a blue boat with a bright yellow stripe down the side of it. She wondered how far he would have gone before tipping Bill's body overboard, and where George had gone from there.

'Are you warm enough?' Alfie asked. 'There's brandy under that blanket.' He pointed to an old grey blanket behind her. 'Take a swig, it'll warm your cockles,' he grinned.

She smiled back. 'I'm fine. My cockles are nicely warmed, thank you.'

There were a group of small boats up ahead and Alfie moved closer to take a better look. The boat in front of them had let down the seine. The fine, strong mesh with corks on the upper side lowered overboard.

With the large net now in the sea they had enclosed a couple of acres, at least, of water and they hoped it would be sufficient to capture many fish. Salmon, trout and in particular herring should be plentiful now in mid-summer. More boats and their crews gathered around to watch out of interest. The boat that had lowered its net rowed around again within the same area while the tuck net was secured at various points. Alfie and Eleanor watched closely, as did the other spectators.

The moon was just starting to put in an appearance, as were the stars. During the summer the stars came out much later in the northern skies. The days were long and the nights so very short. Seagulls flapped and shrieked overhead, just as excited about the expected catch.

They began to haul it upwards. As it became obvious that the net was heavy, there was silence and all eyes watched, wondering in anticipation, if the catch was as good as they all expected.

'Maybe it's a dolphin they've caught,' Eleanor said seriously, sitting huddled up close to Alfie for warmth. He smiled at her and then dragged his attention back to the scene. Murmurs spread from each boat, which rapidly turned into shouts and then they cheered as the water disappeared from the net and there came into view an abundance of fish, which included herring, mixed with salmon and trout, wriggling and flapping, all jumbled up together and trying to escape. The men strained to hold the catch, and the tuck net moved fast as fishermen dived in with baskets, tipping the fish into the bottom of the boat. One of the fishermen threw a few herrings over at Alfie and Eleanor and then to a couple of others in boats nearby, there was plenty for everyone and at times like this it was a celebration. Eleanor squealed at the sight of them slipping and sliding next to her feet on the bottom of the boat.

Jim had sent Charlie off to fetch the technician, but when Charlie returned alone, Jim was not impressed.

'What do you mean 'e won't come?'

'E's done 'is back in - well so 'e says,' said Charlie, catching his breath after racing back from Whitby on his bicycle.

'What d'you mean so *'e says?*'

'Well you know what folk are like - after scandal with police and mill shutting down before. You see - word is - a murderer is workin' at mill.'

Jim shook his head with despair. 'A murderer? Oh for Christ's sake, I can't be doing with this, lad. That wheel needs fixing, and soon.'

It was dark, but not too dark, when Alife and Eleanor headed back up the River Esk. There were lights still burning up ahead at the mill, casting a golden reflection from the windows shining over the river. Alfie helped Eleanor out of the boat, the fish were now of course dead. He threw them into a bucket which had been beneath the old blanket and he handed it to her. Now that they were no longer wriggling around she didn't seem to mind them so much.

'Did you enjoy yourself?' he asked, now having tied up the boat. He helped her out of it.

'It were different - Aye.' She looked so pretty, she looked exhilarated from the sea air. He moved towards her and touched the side of her face with affection. She stood very still and did not flinch or object and so he kissed her. She pulled away instantly and slapped him hard across the face. It was not the reaction he had expected.

'You'd do well to learn some manners Alfie 'Orner – I told you to keep your 'ands t' yourself.'

He stared back at her as if she was insane. 'I thought you liked me. - Thought we had a lovely evening together.'

'We did until you wanted t' get your filthy paws all over me.'

She stormed off, still with the bucket in her arms. He ran after her, trying to understand what had just happened. She had sat close to him and she had let him touch her arm, even her knee at one point. She had that look in her eye, a flirtatious one whenever she had laughed, the one girls' got when they liked you, he thought. They had chatted all the way back with ease, they got on so well. How could he have got it all so wrong?

'Eleanor! Don't be like that, wait up!'

Chapter Eleven

James had agreed to meet Sophie mid morning at Blackburn's yard in Whitby, to visit the cabinet makers. They had planned on making an order that same day for the furniture; time was of the essence and they needed furniture for both the pub and the flat upstairs. The plan, after seeing the cabinet makers, was then to attend to some formalities, such as a contract to be drawn up between them both, and they also needed to apply for a licence, all of which could be done locally through James's solicitor.

He walked over to the stables. Alfie was attending to the horses.

'Alfie, prepare Blackie for me please,' he said. 'I think I'll ride into Whitby rather than walk.' Alfie nodded, down-mouthed and still peeved at Eleanor's reaction to his kiss the night before. James was too preoccupied in his mind to even notice.

The sound of hooves clip-clopping towards him forced him to instinctively turn around. He shielded his eyes against the bright sunlight, then he saw the slight figure of a woman heading his way on horseback. It was Lillian, he realised, as she became closer. She rode side-saddle and looked very elegant in a peach dress that matched her cream hat, edged with a peach coloured floral design.

'What a beautiful morning, isn't it James?' She said as she stopped before him.

He helped her down from her horse, wondering how long she was planning on staying. He really needed to leave soon.

'Yes, delightful.' He kissed her cheek. 'What a lovely surprise, but I'm afraid I have to leave soon. I have some business to attend to in Whitby.'

'Oh pity. Well I shall not keep you long. I have some news I wish to share with you.'

She looked positively radiant and he could not ever remember seeing her look so well.

'Do you have time for just a quick cup of tea?' she asked, with hope.

His face softened with a smile. 'I will always make time for a cup of tea with my only sister.' She picked her moments to visit, but he didn't have the heart to send her away, especially as she appeared to be in such high spirits.

Eleanor served them tea in the parlour. The sunlight poured in through the large Georgian windows and the room felt warm, but slightly stuffy. He opened the window and then turned to face her. The resident ginger cat strolled in and took up position in the sun, which was now shining in on the big red and cream rug.

'Jack Beckwith asked me to marry him,' she announced, smiling from ear to ear. She held out her hand for him to examine her ring.

For a moment he fell speechless, and a look of worry washed over her. She knew Robert would not be at all happy with her news, but she had not imagined that James would object.

'Oh say you are happy for me, James. Please give me your blessing.' She looked at him with pleading eyes.

'Do you think he will keep away from alcohol?' he asked.

She nodded her head. 'Oh yes, I'm certain of it. I truly believe he will never touch another drop again.'

'Does he make you happy?' It was a bit of a pointless question; he could see that she was very happy.

'Extremely,' she beamed.

'Then yes, you have my blessing. Congratulations!' He walked over to her and hugged her. When he released her from his arms she looked up at him and said. 'That's not all of my news.'

'You are not with child?' he looked down at her stomach with a frown. After Victoria falling pregnant before marrying, it no longer seemed unthinkable.

She looked insulted. 'No - no of course not. Jack has asked me to marry him and start a new life with him in New York.'

He looked crestfallen. 'New York? Why? - Why New York?' He sat down on the sofa and she followed suit.

'He loves it there, and he has a job lined up in banking.'

'They have banks in Yorkshire too,' he replied sharply. 'You've never been to New York.' His eyebrows knitted together again. 'It's not like here Lillian - nothing like here.' He had been to New York twice during his travels, in his early days at sea. His memory of it was of buildings and people, lots of people - a busy and chaotic place, not one he could envisage Lillian living in after her quiet and sheltered life in Yorkshire.'

'I know, but it's what Jack wants, and if Jack is happy then so am I. It might not have countryside and sheep but it has a lot of fine shops,' she said, in attempt at convincing herself as well as him.

'Shops it has, yes,' he replied. 'So when do you leave?' Perhaps he would have time to talk her round, he thought.

'Not until after the wedding. We are planning on marrying next month. August twenty fifth.'

'Right,' he still seemed somewhat taken aback by her news.

'You will come and visit won't you James?' She took a sip of her tea, her eyes fixed very much on his.

'Well it's a long way to go, but yes of course I will, if your mind is set on going.'

'It is, and no one is going to stop me. I've waited a long time to find happiness James, and now I have I will not let it slip through my fingers.'

He understood perfectly well what she meant. He had let Victoria slip through his fingers. 'Promise me you will write, and if anything should ever go wrong you will come back home to England at once.' He still felt very protective of her.

'Nothing will go wrong. You are forgetting, I have Jack now to look after me.' James nodded, hoping Jack would be up to the job. Everyone should be entitled to a second chance, but should that second chance be with his sister? She would be too far away for him to be able to keep an eye on her, or Jack for that matter, he pondered.

They chatted a few minutes more before Lillian said she must leave and let him get on his way to his meeting. They promised to meet up the following week; she was excited to see the public house he was about to invest money in, and to meet Sophie. She had her concerns about him spending time with a publican's niece who had previously worked on the market. She had heard the gossiping tongues and so had the Beckwiths and the Crawfords, but she was in no position to question him. He had just given her his blessing to marry a man who had once been accused of killing his wife while in a drunken rage. Of course, Jack had been acquitted, but the stigma might always stick, especially amongst the locals. And now more than ever she realised how important it was for Jack to start afresh in another country with his new wife.

James helped her up on to her horse. No sooner had she left, Jim came rushing up the path, having just missed Lillian, who was now riding off in the opposite direction across the fields. 'Captain 'Awkes!' he called out, panting and stopping for breath.

'Jim!' James walked towards him so that he didn't have to run and struggle for breath any longer. He remembered Jim well from his days working for his father at the mill. Jim had always been kind to him. He seemed to realise that James had been the underdog, the one Joseph Hawkes left out and used as slave labour. 'What can I do for you?'

'There's a problem down at mill,' he said, now gaining his breath. 'Mr 'Awkes is away on 'oneymoon and I can't get 'old of Miss Lillian, she's not 'ome neither.'

'You've just missed her.' James said, glancing over at Lillian's retreating back in the distance. He turned to face Jim once more. 'What's the problem, Jim?'

'Damn technician won't come out t' fix wheel – said he's got a bad back – I don't believe a word of it. 'E wants nowt t' do with us.'

'Why ever not?' James frowned.

'Well according t' young Charlie, they all think a murderer is workin' at mill.'

'That's ridiculous.'

Jim shook his head. 'You're tellin' me.'

'So what are you going to do?'

'I managed to get 'old o' someone. E's come over from t'other side of Scarborough - Made it clear 'e wants paying now - soon as job is done, like. E's not prepared t' wait until Mr 'Awkes is back.'

'I see.' James now realised it was money Jim needed.

'I wondered if you could pay invoice. Mr 'Awkes will pay you back – you know 'e will.'

James didn't doubt that but why should he help Robert?

'I know you and Mr 'Awkes don't see eye t' eye - especially with 'im and Miss Crawford getting' wed n'all.' He felt uncomfortable bringing the subject up but needed to make his point. He shuffled his feet nervously on the dusty path. 'And - and I wouldn't blame you if you don't want t' help 'im - but you'd be 'elping me - and not just me - but t'others as well - folk need your 'elp Captain 'Awkes.'

'Alright!' James held up his hands in defeat. 'Wait here a moment.' He turned back towards the stables, leaving Jim looking relieved.

'Alfie, I want you to ride over to Blackburn's Yard and meet Miss Dickens for me. Tell her I've been held up and she is to go to the cabinet makers without me. I'll join her just as soon as I can.'

'Right you are, Sir.' Alfie saddled up the mare, leaving Blackie for James whenever he was ready to leave.

Workers hung around outside of the mill, chatting amongst themselves and with the locals who had wandered out of their cottages to take a look at all the fuss. Some of the millers hurled abuse at the technician, Samuel Abell, waiting down on the river bed. He had half fixed the problem, but was not willing to continue unless he was sure of payment.

They gave a cheer and applauded when Jim turned up with James. Anyone would have thought that James had been brought to fix the wheel himself. They were all aware there was not enough money to pay the technician and their only hope was either Lillian or James to pay the bill on behalf of Mr Hawkes and save the mill from temporary closure. After the recent closure by the police another catastrophe was most definitely not wanted.

'Don't just stand there,' shouted Jim. 'You'll 'ave your money - get fixing that wheel.' Samuel rushed back down to the wheel. Jim and James followed. It didn't take long for the problem to be solved.

'Good as new.' Samuel collected his tools and walked back to the two men waiting. He scribbled an invoice and handed it to Jim, who then passed it to James. James nodded and handed the money over.

'Bloody mercenary,' Jim mumbled. Samuel shrugged and walked off, showing no shame.

'Get back t' work – shows over,' Jim shouted over at the workers. They expressed their gratitude towards James and went back inside.

'You've done a good deed, Captain 'Awkes,' Jim thanked him, 'and I'll personally make sure Mr 'Awkes pays you every penny back.

'I dare say he will,' James replied, checking his watch and thinking of Sophie at the cabinet makers.

'Captain, do you play cards?' Jim presumed he probably would, didn't all sailors?

James smiled. 'Yes, I play.'

'Do you remember Albert Fisher?' asked Jim.

James shook his head, opening his mouth, about to make his excuses to leave, but Jim talked on and James could not get a word in edge-ways.

'You were only a lad when you worked 'ere. - Thick grey 'air 'e 'ad and wore a moustache - 'ad a stutter and a big pot belly.'

The description did ring a bell. He then remembered him as the man who used to sit out in the sunshine whenever it was a sunny day and he was on a break. He told stories of his days at sea, working as a fisherman before joining the mill. 'Aye, of course I remember him. – Albert Fisher.'

'E used to love a game of cards did Albert - gave many a local a run for their money.' Jim rubbed his chin in thought. 'E started this - well, sort of a cards night once a month - anyone who wanted to join in could – millers – villagers - anyone was welcome.'

'Oh, I see.' James had no idea where any of this was going and he was very conscious of the fact he really should be heading off to Whitby to meet Sophie.

'Since 'e died last year,' Jim went on, 'we still continue with it. It's a week on Tuesday - would you like t' come?'

'I presume Ro – Mr Hawkes - does know about this?' He asked cautiously.

'Aye – 'e plays when 'e can too; quite the gambler is Mr 'Awkes. 'E won't allow it int' mill - doesn't allow gamblin' or alcohol ont' premises so we play int' stables.'

'And will he be there?' James enquired, not sure when he was due to return and surprised to hear his brother was good at cards. He had never seen him play, or played against him, before.

Jim wrinkled his nose. 'Don't think he'll be back from London on time and probably won't want t' leave Mrs 'Awkes with them, just being back off 'oneymoon so soon.'

'Probably not,' James said, cringing at the sound of his own bitter tone. 'I'm not a big gambler Jim - probably not a good idea…'

Jim looked disappointed. 'Please Captain - we'd be most honoured and it would be a chance for folk to thank you personally for 'elping us out today.'

James sighed. Seeing as he put it like that he felt he couldn't really refuse. Robert was not likely to be there and so what harm could come of it? 'Of course - I will be delighted to attend,' he smiled graciously.

Chapter Twelve

The first class section of the train was decorated in deep burgundy and beige tones. The headrests, edged in lace, complemented the same dark red and cream curtains framing the windows. The mahogany tables were dotted with little lamps that also matched the panelling throughout the compartments; it was most definitely first class throughout. The countryside whizzed past as Victoria sipped her tea, staring absently out of the window. Robert sat opposite reading the morning newspaper. Their honeymoon, which had been rather like two companions travelling together and getting to know each other, had been both pleasant and interesting. They had visited all of the many sights in London. Robert had treated Victoria to afternoon tea at The Savoy on their arrival and he had surprised her with a beautiful gold bangle as a wedding present and, during that same week, she had bought him a new watch - a classical, Swiss design which he was positively thrilled with. They had grown fond of each other after spending so much time together. Her morning sickness had now passed and for the first time since becoming pregnant, Victoria felt more at ease about the baby. She did not resent the tiny life growing inside of her any more. The baby was not to blame for its existence, only she and Robert were to blame for creating it.

A clergyman and his wife sat on the other table eating breakfast. Neither of them spoke, both lost in their own thoughts as they too watched the countryside pass them by.

Robert, finishing his breakfast, while still reading, suddenly coughed, spluttered, and threw the newspaper down on the seat next to him. He took a gulp of tea, ignoring the stares from the clergyman and his wife, and even his own wife who looked at him alarmingly. 'Robert, are you alright?'

'No!' His voice was a raised croak and his face was scarlet, but not only from choking, from anger too. When he could finally speak he said, 'how dare they make a mockery of me – us - put our good family name in jeopardy!'

Victoria looked at him, confused. 'Who?'

He picked up the newspaper and thrust it at her.

At Bramblewick Manor Lillian and Jack were the first to be sitting at the breakfast table. Lillian glanced through the pages of the newspaper and then suddenly stopped at the announcements page. 'No! Who gave permission for this?' Lillian handed the page to Jack, aghast.

He placed his cup of tea down, read it and then grinned. 'It's good isn't it? Or are you ashamed to be marrying me?' he teased.

'Of course I'm not ashamed,' she replied sharply, 'it's just...'

'Ah - you've read it then,' said Verity, sitting down at the table and allowing the maid to pour her a cup of tea.

'You mean you...' Lillian couldn't quite find her words. Why had Verity not mentioned this before, not even asked her first?

'Yes, I thought it time everyone knew,' said Verity, nonchalantly.

'Everyone does know - well everyone that matters,' Jack said, looking over at Lillian, still trying to fathom why she appeared so flustered by the announcement.

'Formally I mean – everyone to formally know,' Verity corrected herself.

'But I have not told my brother yet,' Lillian said, with colour still rising through her cheeks.

'But you said you visited James only a few days ago.' Jack reached out for her hand and she pulled it away abruptly. He knew full well she was referring to Robert and not James. He had no time for Robert, neither did he care whether he approved of their marrying or not, and he wished Lillian would forget Robert and enjoy planning the wedding.

'Not James - Robert. I wanted to tell him in person - not for him to find out like this.' She pointed to the newspaper lying open on the table.

Jack sat back in his chair. 'Well I wouldn't expect him to do cartwheels.'

'Why ever not?' Verity patted the sides of her mouth with the starched white napkin. 'It will be wonderful for the Hawkes's and the Beckwiths to be united by marriage.' She smiled brightly. 'Had Joseph been alive, and your dear mother - she was such a lovely lady,' her voice trailed off in thought and then she quickly brought her attention back to the conversation again, 'had they been alive - they would be delighted at such a match - I'm sure of it.'

Lillian smiled ruefully. 'Sadly, Robert is not of the same opinion.'

Verity let out one of her uncaring hoots. 'Well that is his problem and certainly not yours, my dear.'

'Couldn't agree more,' Jack added. 'We'll tell him together if you so wish.'

Lillian was not sure if it would be wise for Jack to accompany her, but on the other hand she knew how bad tempered Robert could be and she would rather have Jack there to support her than to go alone, so she agreed.

'Well, according to Rose, Robert and Victoria are back this afternoon, so you won't have long to wait,' Verity said. 'Best get it out of the way today - tomorrow we need to make a start on choosing your wedding dress.' Verity lightly clapped her hands with glee. Lillian drank her tea, unable to share her excitement. A terrible feeling of dread was rising from the pit of her stomach at the very idea of facing Robert.

Victoria and Robert changed trains at York for the last leg of their journey back to Whitby. The new train was furnished in emerald green with a tiny cream motif on the curtains, neatly tied back at each window. Victoria chose a seat nearest the window. Robert sat down opposite her. The table between them, laid with fine china and sparkling cutlery, was set for afternoon tea. It wasn't quite The Savoy, thought Victoria, but it was comfortable. She was relieved to be sitting back down again after standing and waiting for the connecting train in York for nearly forty five minutes.

Robert was still seething about Lillian and Jack's announcement in the newspaper. 'Over my dead body will she marry that low-life, waste of...' His voice was much calmer than his initial outburst but his anger was certainly not abating.

'Robert!' Victoria snapped. She looked slightly embarrassed, noticing two men sitting on the other side of the carriage who seemed to find her most interesting. One of them flashed a flirtatious smile. She did not react. 'Lillian,' she said in a loud whisper, 'is a grown woman and free to marry whomsoever she likes.' Her back was aching, her ankles were starting to swell from either standing or sitting for too many hours and Robert's moaning about his sister was starting to grate on her nerves.

'I disagree,' he retorted. 'Not when she's marrying a murderer.'

'He was found innocent,' Victoria sighed, rubbing her back discreetly, ignoring the men who were still eyeing her up.

'Innocent?' he gave a small guffaw. 'Victoria, there is no smoke without fire. Just because he had a "so called" alibi and there were no witnesses, it does not make him innocent.'

'Well I beg to differ - innocent until proven guilty and he was not proven guilty. Do you really think the navy would have taken him back if he was?'

'The navy? - 'They took James for God's sake – the bloody navy will take anyone!' He shook his head. 'Talking of James - I bet he has given them his blessing,' he sighed. 'The man is a walking liability!'

'Who - James or Jack Beckwith?

'Both,' Robert retorted angrily.

Victoria looked back out of the window, knowing better than to argue with Robert, especially when it was about James.

'Are you happy?' James asked Sophie as they left Blackburn's Yard after spending a considerable amount of time choosing the type of furniture they wanted. Sophie had spent even longer, having arrived before him. Peter Crags had made her welcome, even made her tea and showered her with samples of his work. By the time James had arrived she had a fair idea of what she would like to order but it was a difficult choice between the light oak, or darker cherry wood. In the end they opted for the cherry wood and stools with plush red upholstery.

She nodded with a big beaming smile. She had big plans to turn *The Old Horseshoe* more upmarket, although James had warned her not to. *'Make it too lavish,'* he had said, *'and you'll scare off all the regulars.'*

'I've got an idea,' she quickened her pace to catch up with his. 'Another one,' he laughed. They were too busy chatting to notice some of the locals stopping and gawking at them. Word was already out about the captain buying into *The Old Horseshoe* pub and spending a lot of time with Nick Dickens's niece, Sophie. There were mixed opinions. There were those who thought Captain Hawkes was more like one of them and would make a great publican, and why shouldn't he be fond of the former publican's niece? But there were those who thought it not proper that James should be interested in a girl below his status, let alone run a public house. But whatever their opinions, James and Sophie really didn't seem to care as they chatted animatedly, walking along the street.

'The wall next t' bar, I was thinkin' you could display your photographs - you know - for folk to buy 'em.'

'You're quite the entrepreneur, aren't you?' he grinned.

'What's an entreper... whatever?'

He noticed that when the sun shone on her hair it showed off tiny strands of auburn. He wanted to kiss her right there and then but of course didn't dare, not in public. It wouldn't be right in front of so many prying eyes. He laughed again. 'It's a French word I learnt when I was in France - it means business minded – someone who is good at setting up new businesses.'

'Appen I am,' she smiled proudly. 'But 'appen I'm not good at fancy words with me not bein' so well travelled as you, Captain.' She raised her eyebrows at him and he laughed at her. Their shadows in the sunlight along the cobbled stones made them look an even more unlikely pair than they did in real life – he, tall and muscular, and she small and thin trotting next to him to keep up with his big strides.

It was late afternoon before they arrived back at *Heron House*. Sophie had agreed to stay with James until the furniture arrived at the pub. They rode back through the fields, Sophie holding tightly onto his chest, enjoying feeling close to him. The sun shone brightly and there was a mild southerly wind blowing for a change.

Chatting playfully and feeling relaxed, they both wandered into *Heron House*. Unaware of Eleanor, who appeared from behind them, they were startled when she spoke out. 'Sir,' she said, forcing both James and Sophie to turn around and face her. 'Miss Crawford – I mean Mrs 'Awkes - is 'ere t' see you.' James frowned and Sophie's heart gave a small skip. What did Victoria want with James? She was a married woman now, she had no claim any more on James.

'She's int' parlour,' Eleanor added.

Victoria, having seen James and Sophie arrive, could not wait a moment longer. She burst into the room where they all were. She stopped in her tracks and gave Sophie a look of disapproval.

'Victoria - what a pleasant surprise.' He could feel the colour rushing to his cheeks, feeling somewhat uncomfortable with Sophie and Victoria being in the same room at the same time. Somehow he had hoped that since his feelings had flourished towards Sophie that he would be immune to Victoria's charm and beauty, but unfortunately this was clearly not so. She looked positively radiant, although troubled, it seemed.

'Victoria, may I introduce you to Miss Sophie Dickens?'

Sophie gave a small, courteous bow and Victoria forced a polite smile. 'I don't wish to intrude,' said Victoria. 'But I – I am afraid I am here on a delicate subject which requires only your attention, James.'

He looked at Sophie apologetically. 'Could you please excuse us Sophie?'

'I'll – I'll go - I could do with stretchin' me legs after ride over from Whitby.' Sophie reluctantly left them alone, wondering what this delicate matter could possibly be.

Victoria gave another look of disapproval as Sophie left the room and then turned her attention to the matter in hand. 'I fear for Lillian,' she began with urgency. 'It's Robert - he saw the announcement about their engagement in the gazette this morning.'

'Oh,' James said. 'And I'm guessing he's not too pleased?'

'To say the least,' she replied with worry. 'Lillian came to visit us with Jack this afternoon to tell him of her news – an argument broke out between he and Jack and then Lillian too - and well it became all rather heated.'

'I see,' said James. This news did not come as any surprise to him. He knew full well Robert was as stubborn as a mule.

'After they left,' Victoria continued, with tears falling, 'he started drinking - threatening to go over to *Somersby Hill* to find them both. – A while later I heard him leave the house.' Her eyes were wide with fear. 'James – I - I fear he will hurt Jack – maybe even Lillian - I beg of you to find him and bring him to his senses.'

Somersby Hill, a small late seventeenth century manor house, still belonging to both Robert and Lillian, had been only Lillian's home since Robert moved out to be with Victoria. Ivy crawled over the walls of thick stone, spreading onto a couple of the window frames. A sweeping driveway, lined with an array of flowers, made it look pretty and welcoming.

When James and Victoria reached the entrance of the house James had once lived in too, when his parents had been alive, they could hear raised voices coming from within. Victoria looked at him with worried eyes.

'I told you - you should have stayed at home,' he said, picking up on her fear.

'And I told you, I want to help,' she replied indignantly.

'Very well - Come on.' He pushed his shoulders back and led the way.

Once inside they found Jack standing next to the fireplace with Lillian at his side and Robert standing opposite them. Their arguing was in full flow.

'I have a right to be happy!' Lillian shouted out above them both. They stopped momentarily at her outburst. 'Go outside, this is no place for you here.' Robert snapped.

'Her place is at my side,' Jack retorted in anger.

Robert turned around to see James and Victoria standing in the room. 'Oh look, the cavalry has arrived.' He then glared at Victoria. 'What are you doing here? And what is *he* doing here?' he pointed over at James.

'Robert, you need to calm down,' Victoria said.

'Don't tell me what to do, woman!' his eyes were red from drinking and she could smell the whisky on his breath.

'Victoria, please go outside with Lillian,' James instructed. Both women exchanged a concerned look but then left. They had confidence that, now James had arrived, the situation would simmer down.

'I think we should all calm down,' James strode into the middle of the room, tall, broad, and assertive.

'Calm down!' Robert raged. 'This dirty skunk has been worming his way into our sister's affections - a wife murderer, no less...'

'How dare you refer to me as that?' Jack moved forward. Standing in front of Robert he looked more youthful, compared to Robert's sturdy, almost middle-aged, *old before his time*, appearance. 'Look at you, so self-righteous, the son of a miller - that is all you are and you lecture me on your good family name - our family is worth ten of yours, no disrespect, James,' he said, glancing over at James.

'None taken,' James said, shaking his head and just wanting the fuss to stop.

Robert swung a hard and fast punch at Jack, but Jack, reacting quickly, hit Robert hard, knocking him to the floor.

James stepped in, not unaccustomed to brawls having seen many during his time at sea. 'That's enough! Let's settle this as gentlemen.' He offered a helping hand to his brother lying on the floor with blood all over his face. Robert, humiliated enough, refused his help and stood up without any aid. He couldn't bear looking at either of them. James was just as much to blame for his anger, supporting this ludicrous engagement. With all his hatred welling up from their previous encounter at the mill too, he caught James unaware with a punch that surprised and winded him, sending him to the floor. Robert despised him for not stopping Lillian, and more to the point, he despised James for the fact that Victoria still loved him and probably always would.

James tried to stand up but Robert fought back with violent strikes one after the other, until Jack stepped in, not being able to watch James get beaten to a pulp - none of this was James's fault. But as he tackled Robert, it seemed an inner strength had possessed Robert and he continued to lash out fast and furiously, while James lay on the floor, unable to move.

Robert then turned on Jack, again with one fierce punch after another. All of Robert's anger was born out of the fact that

Victoria had only married him for the baby's sake, and Jack, now wishing to steal his sister, gave him good reason to lash out.

Jack could take no more of his beating and collapsed on the floor in a pool of blood next to James. James, with all his strength, struggled to his feet and managed to stand up, feeling woozy. Lillian then entered the room and screamed hysterically, followed by Victoria, crying, terrified, and clearly shaken up by the sight of so much blood.

Lillian knelt down next to Jack. There was too much blood and she couldn't see where it was coming from. 'Fetch a doctor,' she yelled at Victoria.

'No!' James stood with Robert firmly in his grasp. 'He'll be imprisoned for this.' Lord knows, *he deserves it*, thought James, but for Victoria's sake he would not see her bring her unborn child into the world without its father. Robert struggled free from James, too exhausted to battle any longer, and staggered out of the room, bumping into Victoria in his haste to get away. She then rushed after him.

Lillian knelt by Jack's side, tears streaming down her face and praying Robert had not killed him. She felt for his pulse frantically and finally found one. Jack groaned as if to confirm he was still alive and she let out a heartfelt sob of relief.

James walked over to Lillian. 'Let's get him onto the couch.' He groaned from his own pain as they heaved Jack up.

'I'm going to need a bowl of warm water, salt, towels, old cotton garments.' He had dealt with many fights at sea and knew exactly how to treat open wounds. He only hoped there was no serious internal damage to Jack, if so, Jack would need to see a doctor.

'And I'll see to your wounds afterwards,' said Lillian, very much aware of the pain James, himself, was in.

Chapter Thirteen

It had been seven days exactly since the fight. Jack's wounds, fortunately, had turned out to be only external and were now healing nicely. Jack was staying at *Somersby Hill* with Lillian, and James, who had also now recovered, visited daily to make sure of no infections. Word had been sent to the Beckwiths that Jack had fallen whilst out riding, but all was well and he was taking it easy in Ruswarp with Lillian.

Out of respect for Lillian, Jack had agreed not to tell anyone of Robert's beating to ensure the Hawkes' name would not to be dragged through the mud, or that there be any legal implications for Robert, bringing embarrassment to Lillian. For Lillian, this showed Jack to be a far better man than her brother. She felt nothing but shame and humiliation at Robert's behaviour and doubted whether she would ever speak to him again.

'I've been thinking about the wedding,' she said, sitting in the garden summer house with Jack. The sun had disappeared under mounting grey clouds, but it was still warm and pleasant, although the air was muggy and threatened a thunderstorm. Jack looked at her through his puffy, bruised eyes. 'I'm surprised you still want to marry me.'

'Shouldn't I being saying that to you? I'm surprised that *you* want to marry me after the way Robert has behaved.'

'He thinks you are about to marry a wife murderer – we know he is wrong - but one could hardly blame him for wanting to protect his sister - although I don't agree with him turning on James like that – very uncalled for.' He groaned a little as he changed position to try to get more comfortable. His ribs were still very sore.

'You are a remarkable man.' She touched the side of his face gently, with affection. 'So noble - I love you very much.'

'Lillian,' he said quietly, 'you do believe that I didn't kill my late wife – don't you?'

'Of course I do.'

Looking in her eyes he could see she genuinely did believe him and he felt relieved, he did not want her to enter into their marriage with any doubts about his past.

'You - Mr Beckwith – are not capable of killing a fly,' she smiled softly.

'Actually, I have a confession - I have killed a fly – just the once,' he said in all seriousness. 'It was its own fault – it should not have buzzed around me while I was trying to read the morning newspaper – any self-respecting fly would have known better!'

Lillian giggled.

'One fell swipe of the newspaper,' he continued, 'And boom - dead.' He showed the action with his arm and then grimaced at the pain in his ribs.

'And you show no remorse?' Lillian laughed.

'Not the slightest bit - lock me up and throw away the key. Anyway, my dear – you - you were saying about the wedding,' he reminded her.

'Yes - I want us to marry in New York, Jack' she said, taking him by surprise.

'But we discussed this and you said…'

'I know, but I don't want Robert anywhere near the wedding.'

'Lillian, you can't be afraid of Robert. I'll make sure he stays away – both James and I will make sure of it.'

Lillian shook her head. 'I don't want you to have to deal with him any more.' She sighed heavily. 'I don't want to have to see him any more either. I have spoken to James and, although he won't make it to the wedding, due to business commitments, he has agreed to come and visit when we are settled. Aunt Edith, I'm sure, will forgive me for not marrying in Yorkshire.' She sounded resolute. He squeezed her hand and she laid her head gently on his shoulder. He stroked her hair and said, 'then a wedding in New York it shall be, my dear.'

Roselea House, located alone on a hill top, enjoyed views directly across Whitby and the abbey. It was an impressive Victorian house with much land and plenty of room to raise a family. Victoria gazed out of the upstairs window of her new home. She had not exchanged a single word with Robert since the fight, appalled that he could even be capable of so much violence. He had spent a few days at home until his face had healed, sending word to the mill that he wished to extend his honeymoon, which could not be further from the truth.

Violet had been around that morning and had persuaded Victoria to see the doctor. Rose and John still had no idea of their daughter's pregnancy or what Robert had done, having seen them only briefly on their return before Lillian and Jack had visited. They had decided to give the newlyweds time to themselves. Victoria agreed with Violet about seeing a doctor, she knew it was time to seek medical care.

Dr Coker seemed puzzled and sighed. 'I would say that you are four months pregnant.' He appeared baffled, he was rarely wrong.

'Promise me you will not say anything to anyone - especially not my parents.' Victoria said, anxiously.

'I would not dream of breaking patient confidentiality, Mrs Hawkes, but can I enquire as to why you did not ask for me to visit before?'

She sighed and sat up straight on the bed. 'It's complicated,' she said.

'I see - is Mr Hawkes not the father?' he asked warily.

'Oh yes he's the father - it's just – well - we weren't married at the time the baby was conceived.'

'Well I gathered that, seeing as you have just come back from honeymoon. Mrs Hawkes, if I may speak plainly - I don't think you have cause for concern having now married the father. Although -

questions maybe asked when the *babies* are born sooner rather than later.' He raised his eyebrows and patted her hand.

She suddenly picked up on the fact that he had said *babies*. You said babies – you mean baby of course?'

Dr Coker shook his head. 'No - you are expecting twins, Mrs Hawkes.'

She stared back at him in utter amazement. 'Are you – are you sure?' she asked, in a barely audible whisper.

'Positive,' he replied, tapping her hand again. 'Don't look so worried - you are in perfect health and at a good age for childbearing.'

James sent word to Jim at the mill that he would be unable to attend the card night at the mill. As much as he hated to disappoint them, tonight was all about the opening night of *The Old Horseshoe* under James and Sophie's management, and it would have been impossible to be in two places at the same time. Aside from the opening, he did not relish the idea of a possible chance meeting with Robert. He had not seen him since the fight and had put off collecting the money Robert owed him for paying the invoice for the technician to fix the wheel.

The furniture looked splendid, as did the new panelling, fixtures and the bar now stocked with a wider selection of ale, liquor, wine and cider. Small lamps were placed on each table, giving a warm and inviting appeal. The plush-red covered stools matched the larger comfortable chairs, placed strategically around the tables and the bar area. Largely, the locals were impressed. There were those who worried the price of their favourite tipple might have gone up, which it hadn't, thanks to James making sure the old brands remained the same price and there were those who thought it to be a bit upmarket and not what they had been used to under Nick Dickens's ownership. But they did not really expect anything less of Captain Hawkes - he was hardly going to run a scruffy, run-down backstreet boozer. Of course, tongues wagged, watching James and Sophie working together side by side, although James and Sophie tried hard to keep professional and not give reason for idle gossip.

'Your uncle would be proud of you, lass,' John Barrow said, eyeing the pub with admiration.

Old David Strachan grunted and sipped his ale, saying nothing, not sure what to make of it all. He was used to the old tatty furniture, the familiar darkness, as well as sticky tables and floors. He scratched his beard against a louse, crawling around in his matted maze of facial hair.

'Couldn't 'ave done it without Captain Awkes,' she replied. James was up the other end of the bar serving, unaware of them talking about him.

David Strachan grunted again and then spoke, 'needs t' make an honest woman of you.'

'Well that's none o' your business,' Sophie replied, looking annoyed at him.

'Aye, 'appen it isn't – take no notice of 'im,' said John. 'One step at a time lass - you've only just lost your uncle and got this place up an' runnin' again - don't listen t' what 'e says or t'others for that matter – you don't want t' be fussing about no wedding.'

Sophie smiled gratefully at John. She glanced over at James, wondering if he would ever ask her to marry him. It seemed unlikely he would choose her for his wife. Captain Hawkes could have the pick of any fine lady, and she suspected there were many who had their eye on him. What she and James shared was special, but she knew she was probably fooling herself if she thought she was anything more than a distraction from Victoria and all that had gone on with his brother of late. His buying into the pub was probably temporary, she thought, and once the turnover became substantially higher, thanks to her many great ideas to improve the business, she could always offer to buy him out when they were ready to part their ways and he had had enough of her. However, thinking of them parting filled her with sadness and she hoped it would not be any time soon. She didn't care what people said, or thought, they had no proof of what went on behind closed doors - that was hers and James's business and nobody else's.

Jim knocked on Robert's office door and then popped his head around it. 'Joan Tither 'as gone 'ome, Sir - not feelin' well - terrible fever 'as Joan.'

Robert glanced up at him over his reading glasses. 'Anyone else ill with this fever?'

'Not so far, no.'

'Good - last thing we want is them all off sick with this big order just in.'

'Aye Sir - oh 'ave you settled that invoice with Captain 'Awkes for repairin' wheel? It was most kind of 'im to 'elp like that.'

'You should never have asked him,' Robert replied angrily. Just to hear James's name sent prickles up his neck.

'Well there weren't anyone else I could ask for that kind of money - it was either Captain 'Awkes 'elping out or mill would 'ave come t' a standstill till your return.'

Robert groaned. 'Is there anything else?'

Jim hovered in the doorway. 'You will pay 'im, won't you? I did give 'im me word and I'm a man of me word.'

'You're a man of too many words — now get out!' he yelled, losing his patience. Robert showed no gratitude for James bailing him out while he was away on honeymoon or for James having spared him from being arrested last week. All he felt was anger and bitterness towards the brother who seemed to have such an easy life and take everything in his stride. James didn't know what it was like to run a business, the whole community relying on you for money. It was a far cry from sailing around on a boat from one port to the next. Neither did James know what it was like to take responsibility for one's actions and marry a woman who was carrying your child, even if you did not love her. He had heard about James and his floozy barmaid. It seemed to Robert that James had soon got over Victoria and was now having fun again, something Robert could not foresee ever having again, now that he had tied himself down to Victoria. James had it far too easy and so why should Robert rush to pay him. No, there would be no rush at all to settle the outstanding invoice - James could ask for it, beg for it even, before he would pay him.

Alfie had not once entered the kitchen since his and Eleanor's fishing trip. This had not gone unnoticed to Eleanor and she couldn't help but feel guilty for the way she lashed out at him. He had only tried to kiss her, and if she was honest, she actually felt flattered that he cared that much about her. She found Alfie in the fields, thinning out the turnips. He thrust his hoe rhythmically, cutting down young weeds at the same time. His strong arms were big and muscular and flexed with every move. Eleanor enjoyed watching him for a moment, shielding her eyes from the sunlight.

'Alfie?' she called out. At first he did not hear her, but on her second call he turned to face her and wiped his brow with the back of his hand.

'You don't come in to eat no more.'

He shrugged. 'Me Mam gives me bread – it's enough till I get 'ome for me supper.'

'Is it cause of what I said, t'other night?' She cocked her head to one side, studying him closely. 'If it is what I said – then- well I'm sorry.'

He started working again and spoke without looking at her. 'It's alright - you don't need t' apologise - I shan't bother you no more.'

'But I want you t' bother me – I want us t' be friends.' A smile appeared on her lips, not that he noticed. He took a moment to gather his thoughts, looking the other way. 'That's just it,' he said, turning to face her again. 'I don't want t' be friends – I want more - but it's obvious you don't feel same way.'

She looked down at her feet, feeling shy. An awkward moment passed between them as he awaited her reply.

'I – I best get back,' she said, disappointing him yet again.

He watched her retreating back for a minute or two and then, still clutching the hoe firmly in his hand, he continued thrashing the overgrowth but this time with far more aggression.

Robert, feeling tired and weary, poured himself a whisky and flopped down on the couch. He took a large swig, enjoying the sensation as it hit the back of his throat. He sighed out loud and kicked off his shoes. Victoria walked into the room and sat down in the armchair opposite him. She looked pale and withdrawn. 'We can't go on like this,' she said, referring to the silence they had been living in since the fight.

He took another swig and looked at her squarely. 'You're right - we can't.'

'What you did,' she continued.

'What I did was wrong - I took it too far - I know that now.' He spoke the words he knew she wanted to hear. He felt no remorse for what he had done to Jack and, as for James, well he deserved everything he got, but for a quiet life and to appease Victoria, he thought it best to pretend at least that he was sorry for his actions.

'You nearly killed Jack Beckwith.'

'Things got out of hand - I just got so angry.'

'And whatever your feelings towards James...' Now she had hit a nerve again by bringing James into the conversation.

'We know my feelings towards James and we both certainly know your feelings towards him,' he cut in, his tone as bitter as ever.

'That's what is eating you up isn't it? What James and I had is in the past, Robert - and it will remain there - I gave you my word - why don't you believe me?' She held his stare that seemed to go on far too long. He finished off the whisky in his glass, contemplating his answer.

'I want to - I need to - I just feel second best.'

She rushed over to him and took his hands into her own. 'You are not second best.' She looked him in the eyes. 'You are my husband now and soon to be a father.'

'What kind of father am I going to be?' he asked ruefully, pulling his hands away from hers. He ran his fingers through his hair, looking uptight again.

'A good one - if you will let rest your hatred for James,' she sighed. 'Robert?' she said, 'I have something to tell you – I – I have some news.'

He looked at her with a frown. 'What is it? - Have you seen the doctor? – Is there something wrong?

'Yes I've seen the doctor and no - nothing is wrong – not as such.'

'What do you mean as such?' he seemed genuinely worried, scared even, and inwardly she felt pleased that he cared so much. Underneath his resentment and all that bitterness, she believed there was a much better man, a kinder man, a decent man, waiting to have the chance to become a good husband and a good father. 'We are having twins,' she announced.

He stared back at her, lost for words. 'Twins?' he repeated.

'Yes,' she nodded.

'Oh my goodness - Come here!' he grabbed her into his arms and held her. She snuggled close to his chest feeling loved again. Whatever he had done, he was still her husband and still the father of her babies and, for their sake, if not for her own, she had to find it in her heart to forgive him and to move on.

The flat above the pub was decorated just as tastefully as downstairs. A large double bed replaced Nick Dickens old tatty one. The long sash window on one side of the room, and the small window in the alcove on the other side, were framed with expensive velvet blue curtains. An old French clock that Sophie had bought from an antique dealer stood on top of the carved pine mantelpiece, with its metallic bell that had been chiming for more than fifty years. A Queen Anne table stood under the window. There was also a cane rocking chair and a chest of drawers, with two stunning candlestick holders stood upon it. The wallpaper displayed crimson poppies on an ivory background. It was certainly a vast improvement on when Nick Dickens had lived there.

James lay in the new bed with Sophie in his arms. He had been too tired to go back to *Heron House* after such a busy night, but not too tired to make love with her again. Their love making was always passionate, needy and fulfilling. She laid thinking of that night in the pub and how it all went.

'Tongues were waggin' tonight.' She propped herself up on one elbow, her hair cascading over her bare breasts. She ran her fingers lightly over his chest.

'I know,' he replied, understanding exactly what she meant.

'Does it bother you?' she asked.

'Not really – Does it you?'

'No – course not.'

He wondered if it did, otherwise why had she mentioned it to him?

'They don't know what goes on behind closed doors - we are business partners,' she said.

'It's unusual for a man and a woman to be business partners - one can hardly blame them for their suspicions.' He kissed the tip of her nose. She smiled at him. 'Unusual is good.' She glided her hand downwards beneath the sheets.

'You are - a rather mischievous business partner – I can see I am going to have to keep an eye on you,' he laughed, enjoying the sensation of her teasing hand that was now sending excitement through his entire body.

James arrived back at *Heron House* the following day. He planned to spend a little time in his make-shift photography studio. He still had a number of photographs that needed developing and, now that he had the wall in the pub to display his art, it seemed like a good time to get on with his new found passion.

Stripped to the waist and busy washing, he suddenly remembered he had to check on Jack Beckwith later that day. He had not had time to go and see him the day before, but he was confident that his wounds, by now, should be healing nicely. No sooner had he put on a clean shirt, then he heard the familiar call of Eleanor.

'Sir! – Sir! - Miss 'Awkes is here t' see you, Sir.' He rolled his eyes. Lillian certainly picked her moments to visit. He buttoned his shirt and went downstairs.

'James,' Lillian kissed his cheek.

'How's Jack? – I was planning to visit this very afternoon. - Does he find himself well?'

'Jack's fine - all thanks to you,' she smiled gratefully.

They sat down and Lillian continued. 'I know you and I spoke recently about the possibility of Jack and I marrying in New York – well - I just wanted to tell you that I've decided,' she paused a moment and gave a small cough to clear her throat, 'we've decided,' she corrected herself, 'to get married in New York. - After everything that has happened of late - we feel it to be a wise decision.'

'I see,' he seemed a little lost for words. He had hoped she would change her mind. 'I am saddened that I cannot be there on your big day. – It would be impossible for me to leave the public house so soon after opening - not fair to Miss Dickens, I fear.'

'I understand,' Lillian said, not expecting for one moment that he would be able drop everything and go to America at such short notice.

'I can speak to Robert - if it helps – perhaps even to Victoria to reason with him – keep him away on the day.'

'It is not only because of Robert. Jack and I are about to start a new life together and – well - we feel it somewhat romantic to get married in America – the country we plan to spend the rest of our lives living in.'

A moment of silence passed before James spoke again. Her words were slowly sinking in. He couldn't imagine a life without Lillian. She was always there, always visiting him and now the prospect of waiting for letters from her to hear her news instead of her regular visits seemed rather daunting.

'When will you leave?' he asked, with eyes full of sadness.

'Next Friday - the tickets are booked. We shall be sailing from Newcastle - Jack's parents will also be travelling with us.'

He felt relieved to know that Lord Beckwith and Verity would be there by her side too, but he regretted deeply he could not see his only sister marry. America would be too long a voyage. It would mean at least two months, or maybe even three, away from Sophie and he felt she needed him at the moment - it was too soon to leave her.

'Verity would like to throw a farewell party the night before at *Bramblewick House*. - You will come, and bring Miss Dickens with you? - I should very much like to meet her properly.' She had no intention of judging the poor girl, especially without meeting her first.

He wondered how to answer her request. Would Sophie want to accompany him to a social event? She was rather shy about meeting strangers, especially of a different ilk. 'I'll certainly pass on the invitation to her,' he said tactfully.

'Good. - Are you serious about Miss Dickens?' Lillian asked, throwing caution to the wind. She would soon be on the other side of the world and did not have time to tread carefully. It would be nice to know her brother's intentions.

'We're business partners.' He could see in her eyes she was not buying his story. 'And very good friends,' he added.

Lillian sighed. 'Victoria has moved on, James, and so must you.' She reached out and held his hand.

'I presume an invitation has not been extended to Robert and Victoria?' He teased, tongue in cheek.

The look in Lillian's eyes said it all. Well at least he wouldn't have to deal with Sophie meeting Victoria again, or have to be on his guard that Robert wouldn't do or say something to upset the party.

Sophie stood behind the bar polishing glasses. The rain was pelting down outside, splashing and bubbling at the windows. 'Me? Go to a party with you? Oh I don't think it's such a good idea, James.'

James placed the last photograph on his display wall and turned to face her. 'Why not? It will be fun, and a chance for you to meet Lillian properly before she leaves for America.'

'Will Victoria and Robert be there?' She suspected not, but she couldn't bear the thought of being in the same room as Victoria again. It was so blatantly obvious she still had feelings for James, and he for her. She also did not want to fall victim to Robert's vicious tongue. If he did not approve of Jack Beckwith, what would he think of her? An ex market stall worker and the niece of a publican who had gambled all his fortune away, leaving her in debt and James to pick up the pieces. He would revel in the idea of James coming to rescue her from a life of poverty, then ending up back on the market once more. Not only that, at the party they would all display such fine manners and speak with airs and graces. She would be embarrassed that James might see, amongst all the others in the party, that she was not right for him and question his own interest in her.

'I don't think it is my place to go with you - I'm not their sort.'

'You were born from your mother - you eat – sleep – laugh – cry - we are all of the same sort.'

'You know what I mean – I'm not educated,' she pointed out, with a slight pout to her lips.

'You are learning to read and you are very business minded.'

'An entrepreneur.' This time she pronounced it correctly, impressing him. She had practiced saying it many times.

'An entrepreneur,' he laughed. 'If you should use that word you will certainly impress.'

He was not the least bit ashamed of Sophie. She was bright, and possessed a curious charm that all the tuition in the world could not teach. Knowing Verity and her hoot of a laugh and Jack Beckwith's past, Sophie should not fear being ashamed in the slightest.

'It would be a great honour if you would accompany me and I'll be most upset if you don't.'

She nodded in agreement but it was clear to see she was not comfortable with the idea. For a start, what would she wear to such an event? She would need to have something made and would there be enough time? Her mind became a frantic muddle. 'And what about this place?' she asked, suddenly remembering she had a pub to run. Who's goin' t run it that night?'

'We'll close it - it's only one night - I'm sure everyone will survive.' She looked at him with worried eyes, they might survive but would she?

Chapter Fourteen

'Sophie's eyes were wide with wonder as she and James entered Bramblewick Manor. She gazed up at the opulent paintings hanging on the walls, mainly portraits of the Beckwiths' ancestors. The high ceilings and thick heavy drapes framing the large windows were impressive.

'It's like a castle - I've never seen owt like it,' she said, in a hushed tone. James glanced at her and smiled. She looked like a child who had entered a shop full of sweets and wonderful things - she was completely struck with awe.

The first hour of the party was a little trying for Sophie as she sipped on her wine and tried not to speak unless spoken to. She stuck firmly by James's side, scared that if he should leave her sight she might have to make conversation with people whom she didn't know, and worse still, say the wrong thing simply because she didn't understand the topic of conversation. She could feel perspiration dripping down between her shoulder blades and she hoped it would not leave a stain on her new dress, the dress James had bought for her. To calm her nerves, he had taken her himself to the dressmakers, helped her choose the material, and paid for it. He had insisted on treating her, seeing as he had invited her.

Heads turned as she gracefully walked around the room with James at her side. Her tiny figure moved elegantly in the dusky, pink dress with its slender fitting bodice; revealing, though decent, amount of cleavage, and flowing long silk skirt to complement it. Her hair was piled high in a formation of soft curls.

Rose and John Crawford, and Violet too, were present, but not Victoria and Robert. The Crawfords had informed everyone that Robert and Victoria would not be coming this evening due to Victoria not feeling well. Little did the Crawfords know that Victoria had made this excuse, knowing full well that had she and Robert turned up at the party they would not have been welcomed by their hosts, Lillian and Jack. The Crawfords were still not aware of the fight that had taken place and neither were the other guests present for that matter, other than James and Sophie of course. Lillian and Jack, after much deliberating, had only sent the invitation to Victoria and Robert out of a sense of formal duty, certainly not out of sincerity. Robert, for a peaceful life, had for once done as he was told by Victoria and stayed away. It wasn't common knowledge yet that Victoria was pregnant, but there was much speculation that she was suffering from morning sickness, having conceived on honeymoon. But of course in reality, Victoria was now past the morning sickness stage.

Aunt Edith, never missing the chance of a party, arrived wearing a terribly old fashioned gown. She had been a close friend of the Hawkes family for many years and was fond of Lillian, as she was of James. They had called her Aunt Edith since they were children. She had never really warmed to Robert though, he was too much like his father and she had not cared much for Joseph Hawkes either.

'So, this is Miss Dickens -' She stretched out her bony hand and touched the side of Sophie's face. 'Pretty little thing aren't you?'

Sophie smiled politely, unsure what to think of this frail old woman inspecting her, as if she was about to be sent off to market.

'And is this your intended?' She turned to James, screwing her eyes up at him.

'Sophie is a very dear friend, Aunt Edith - and we are also business partners,' James replied.

'Business partners - and what business may that be?' she frowned.

'Sophie's late uncle owned a public house in Whitby,' he began to explain, 'leaving it to her in his will. I bought into the business and I'm helping her to manage it.

'A public house,' she repeated, wrinkling her nose. 'Dirty places - full of drunks - wouldn't catch me stepping foot in one of them.'

'Oh no, it's really, well, upmarket - since me and James took it over that is – not that there was owt wrong with it when uncle owned it,' said Sophie. 'You get a few drunks now n' again but there's never any trouble or owt – James makes sure of that.' She smiled at James with admiration.

Edith studied her with interest, trying to make out exactly what she had just said. There was a moment of awkward silence. James could sense Sophie's discomfort rising as the old woman poured over her with her beady eyes. He politely excused himself and Sophie too, and then promptly whisked her away to meet Lillian, leaving Aunt Edith mystified and rubbing her whiskery chin in thought.

'How good of you to come Miss Dickens,' Lillian gave a small courteous bow. Sophie hesitated, not knowing if she should bow too, but instead she froze on the spot. 'Please just call me Sophie,' she blushed, trying to ignore Lillian's nose.

'So, I hear my brother is helping you with your late uncle's public house – how delightful. James has always been most helpful.'

'Aye, he's been a great 'elp - couldn't 'ave done it without him.' She turned to face James but he had disappeared, slipped off suddenly, in an attempt at leaving the women to get to know each other better. Sophie felt a panic wash over her, now that she realised he had gone.

'James is very kind hearted,' Lillian said. 'After all this business with Victoria and then James leaving the navy - I – I fear he could be a little vulnerable.' She eyed Sophie with suspicion. Sophie tried hard to compose herself and not let her anxiety show. She could feel the colour rising in her cheeks, now realising what Lillian was meaning. 'I'm not taking advantage of 'im or owt - if that's what you're thinkin'. 'E were the one that wanted to 'elp me – and - and I never asked 'im for no money – not a single shillin'.'

'I'm sure you didn't.' Lillian replied, wondering what to make of the girl. She looked presentable, quite pretty in fact and she could see James's attraction, and she could also see the striking resemblance between Sophie and Victoria. But Sophie did not have the same air of sophistication that Victoria had. This was a girl from a poor background, who had probably worked hard all her life. She was out of her depth amongst all these people surrounding her this evening and Lillian suspected Sophie was well aware of it. In a way it made Lillian feel a little more sympathetic towards her.

'Look,' Sophie said frankly, 'I know from the outside it might look like – well that I'm usin' James - you know for 'is money and suchlike - but I'm not – I can assure you - I'm fond of 'im – very fond of 'im.'

'Fond?' Lillian asked. It was more than a business relationship, she felt sure of it now.

'Yes - well more than fond – I - I,' her face had now turned a deeper shade of pink. 'E means a lot to me, does James – a great deal in fact.'

Lillian smiled, getting the picture clearly. She linked arms with Sophie and spoke in a loud whisper. 'If you love him - then promise me that you will treat him well. He doesn't deserve to have his heart broken a second time – and I shall not be here to comfort him next time.'

Sophie, with her eyes open wide, nodded in agreement. 'I shall never do anythin' to 'urt James – I promise you that.'

'He's a good man and he will make a fine husband to a lucky lady one day,' Lillian said, wondering if that lucky lady would be Sophie.

'I dare say,' Sophie replied, wondering the same as Lillian.

Lillian smiled brightly. 'Then my dear – you have laid my worries to rest.'

Sophie grinned, looking relieved. 'I'm glad,' she said.

Now that she had passed the test, and after chatting a little more with Lillian, Sophie realised she quite liked her and felt strangely disappointed that she was going away.

Rose stood on the other side of the room next to Verity. 'So that's James's new love interest is it?' Rose watched Sophie with curiosity.

'I believe so - attractive girl - isn't she?' Replied Verity. 'She reminds me a little of your Victoria - a blonde Victoria,' Verity mused, thinking out loud, much to Rose's disapproval.

'I fail to see the likeness,' replied Rose haughtily. 'Victoria is far more beautiful and – and well – refined too.'

Verity sighed. 'I hope she treats James better than Victoria did - choosing Robert over James like that - the poor man - he did not deserve it.'

Rose looked at Verity unfavourably. 'What do you mean?' Robert is a far better match for Victoria, anyone can see that.'

'I beg to differ,' replied Verity. 'They don't strike me as being madly in love.'

'They don't outwardly show their affections for each other - I agree with you on that but I do believe that they shall be very happy together. Anyway - as for James – well - he is hardly heartbroken - look at him.' James was now back, chatting and laughing with Sophie.

'But Victoria and James were once inseparable,' Verity continued. 'Everyone presumed that they would marry - and I for one…'

'It was nothing more than a childhood romance,' Rose cut in. 'And look at his choice in women now - she hardly matches up to Victoria. She can't even speak properly and spends her nights working in a backstreet public house. It's nothing more than a step up from the common prostitute.'

'Rose! I think not,' replied Verity sharply.

Rose shook her head with discontent, her gaze still very much on Sophie. 'Thank goodness Victoria isn't here this evening to witness this.'

'Victoria shouldn't care any more,' Verity replied indignantly. Sometimes Rose could be too pretentious for Verity's liking. Verity always tried to keep an open mind and give people the benefit of the doubt, unlike Rose who was always quick to judge.

James and Sophie spent the night at *Bramblewick House*, in separate rooms. Verity had arranged their rooms to be as far apart as possible, avoiding the chance for others to gossip, least of all Rose.

Sophie had been relieved to get up to her room and relax at last. It had been a long evening, quite interesting, and she wasn't sure if she had enjoyed it or not. She had enjoyed wearing her fine dress though, acting as a lady, and some people were friendly and welcoming while others had been cautious, not really sure what to make of her. It was a strange insight to see how they all socialised with one another and how they spoke, so correct, so very posh. She giggled and drew the heavy curtains. It had been a far cry from a night at the pub. She then wandered over to the big bed and pulled back the fresh linen. Everything smelt so clean. Having managed to climb out of her dress, she snuggled under the bedding and the last thing she heard before drifting off to sleep was the soft pitter patter of rain on the window pane.

James got undressed and pulled back the sheets. His thoughts drifted to Sophie, wondering what she was thinking, lying there alone in a great big room. She had handled the evening well and most people, especially Lillian, seemed to be taken with her. He wished he could have sneaked into Sophie's room, but didn't dare for fear of being caught, neither was he sure of which room she was even in. His eyes became heavy the moment his head hit the pillow and, while listening to the rain outside, he fell into a deep sleep.

It was still raining the following morning. Suitcases and boxes were stacked high at the front door. Most of the guests had either left the night before or earlier that morning.

'You look radiant,' James said, standing with Lillian in the foyer. Sophie had gone back upstairs, having forgotten her shawl.

'Take good care of yourself, won't you?' He said.

She nodded, holding back the tears that were starting to form. She glanced to her right and saw the drawing room door left open. 'James,' she said, beckoning him to come with her through the open door. 'I want you to give this to Robert.' She handed him a sealed cream envelope. 'Ordinarily I wouldn't ask this of you - what with things being rather delicate between you both – between all of us - but it is important.'

James frowned, studying the envelope as if hoping to read it without opening it.

'It's my written permission, should Robert wish to sell *Somersby Hill.*'

'But you can't sell.' James looked horrified. '*Somersby Hill* has been our home since we were children. We all own a share of the property - all three of us.'

'And what use is it to any of us?' Lillian sighed. 'Robert lives at *Roselea* – you have *Heron House* - and I – well I shall not need it now.'

'But I don't want to sell *Somersby Hill*,' said James with desperation.

'I'm not forcing you to - or Robert for that matter - but should you wish to ever sell - you have my written consent.'

He sighed heavily. 'I think a decision about selling should not be entered into in haste. If you are not happy in New York - you will have a home here in Yorkshire to come back to.'

She smiled at him. He was always so very sensible.

Sophie poked her head around the corner of the door. 'Sorry James - it's just that our train leaves soon.'

James checked his watch. 'So it does.'

'Promise me you will visit soon - both of you,' Lillian said, holding a hand out to each of them. Sophie held her hand tightly.

'We will,' they both replied. James had no idea how they would manage it without closing the pub, unless they could find someone trustworthy enough to manage it while they were away, which would not be an easy task, but it was not a problem for today. They had time to find a solution.

'Please write - tell us about your weddin',' Sophie smiled. 'I love a good weddin' – I always cry.'

Lillian looked at James, but he was not picking up on the hint. There was a last emotional hug between brother and sister, and then James and Sophie left Lillian alone in the drawing room, while she dabbed her eyes and tried to compose herself before facing the others. She would miss James and her heart ached already at the thought of not seeing him for a long time.

James shook Jack's hand and made him promise to look after his sister and, with a final farewell to the Beckwiths, James and Sophie left *Bramblewick House.*

'It's such a shame she 'as to go,' Sophie looked up at him as they walked away from *Bramblewick house*. 'I really like Lillian.'

'I'll miss her,' James admitted. 'I wish I had given her more time instead of always being so damn busy. One never appreciates what one has until it's gone.' He looked pensive as they walked on.

'Let that be a lesson to us all - to appreciate what we 'ave before it's gone.' Sophie grabbed hold of his arm, thinking of Uncle Nick. She snuggled up close to him as they walked on.

'Ready?' Jack asked Lillian. The coach needed six horses to pull so much luggage. Verity and Lord Beckwith were already seated inside.

Jack held out his hand to Lillian and she accepted. 'Yes I'm ready,' she answered. She had never felt so sure of anything in her entire life. Jack was her future now and a new life awaited her, awaited them both.

The coach rocked gently from side to side. She wiped away a small tear as they passed familiar landmarks and through lush green countryside. She savoured every moment, embedding the views firmly in her mind so that when she was far away, she could remember them with fondness. New York may hold her destiny, but Yorkshire would always hold her heart.

Chapter Fifteen

It was late afternoon when James went to the mill to see Robert. He found him chatting outside to a well-dressed man, looking important. As he approached them both, Robert shook the man's hand and walked away in the direction of the entrance to the mill. The man got into a motor car and drove away.

'What do *you* want?' he asked, as James reached his side.

It was the type of greeting he had expected. 'Charming as ever.' James quickened his pace to keep up with him. Robert walked through the mill in haste, heading towards his office and not bothering to stop to find out the answer to his question.

Jim raised a greeting hand from the other side of the room at James, James raised one back. There was so much noise from the machinery that it was a relief to be inside the relatively quiet office.

'Lillian left yesterday,' said James

'Left?' Robert looked startled, sitting down behind his desk full of paperwork. 'You mean she has gone through with that ridiculous plan of hers? Gone with him to New York?'

'Yes, and why shouldn't she?'

'Where do I start?' He ran his fingers anxiously through his hair, 'how about the fact that she is running away with a murderer?

'She's a grown woman - she knows her own mind.'

'Of course she doesn't - a woman in her right mind would have no interest in Jack Beckwith - she's clearly deranged.'

'For once in your life, shut-up and listen.' James leaned forward, losing his patience with him.

'She is in love with the man - and - for what it's worth - I truly believe he loves her too - I also believe he wouldn't hurt her.'

'What you believe is neither here nor there,' flashed Robert.

'She has to be stopped. Do you know of her travel plans?'

'No,' he lied. 'And even if I did, I would not tell them to you. You've done enough damage - let the poor woman have some happiness for once. I know happiness is not something you condone as a rule - but people are entitled to it.' He pulled out the sealed envelope from his pocket. 'She wants you to have this.' He threw it in front of Robert.

Robert ripped it open, read it, and then threw it back down on the table without comment. 'Does that conclude our business?' Robert glared at him with annoyance.

'Not quite - there's the small matter of an invoice that needs to be paid?'

'You can wait for that,' Robert picked up his reading glasses ready to get back to work.

'No, I won't wait - I bailed you out. This place would have come to a standstill while you were in London if it wasn't for me.'

'Then they should have let it.'

'You ungrateful... - Jim was going out of his mind with worry.'

'Jim is an old fool who thinks only about playing cards and drinking whisky.'

'Rich coming from you, isn't it?'

'What is that supposed to mean?'

'Apparently you are quite the card player - happen we should play – you and I - and a few of the millers.'

'Don't be so ridiculous.'

'Worried I'll beat you?' James held Robert's concerned stare.

Robert licked his dry lips. 'Of course not.'

'Then prove it – play. Whist – nap – poker - I play them all.' He walked around the other side of the desk and perched on the edge. 'If I lose you can wipe that invoice clean – and if I win -you pay up.'

Robert stared at him and gave an incredulous chuckle. 'This family is messed up - you are as insane as Lillian is.'

'What's the matter Robert, scared you are going to lose?'

'Alright!' He held up his hands. 'If it shuts you up and gives you some amusement in your sad little life - stables tomorrow night.'

James walked to the door then turned to face him. 'I'll invite the workers - they'll enjoy it,' he grinned. 'Enjoy me wiping the floor with you.'

Robert tried not to look intimidated. 'As you wish – as you wish, dear brother.'

'James, I'm sorry but I don't agree with it.' Sophie flopped down on a stool. There were only two regulars in but it was early yet.

'I know how you feel about gambling – after your uncle - but I'm not really gambling - I'm teaching Robert a lesson. I want to humiliate the little…' he stopped what he was saying and helped himself to a brandy.

'It won't change anythin' – 'e'll still be a little… whatever it was you wanted to call 'im - if anythin' you are encouraging 'im - you know what that temper of 'is, is like.'

'Yes I do - and its time everyone else knew too. I've spoken to old Jim and he's assured me there'll be a good turn-out.' He downed the brandy in one.

'Well don't expect me to come and watch - I'll be workin' 'ere and even if I wasn't - I still wouldn't support you - I want nowt to do with it.'

Their eyes met challengingly. 'I'm not asking you to be there,' he replied abruptly, before going up the other end of the bar to serve two men who had just walked in. 'I'm merely telling you about it,' he said.

James sat in the parlour in his favourite chair having just finished a large slice of pie served to him by Eleanor. She had been pleased to see him back home, alone this time, without Sophie. The evening had remained quiet at the pub and so James had left Sophie to close up, wanting the chance to have an early night and to be in his own bed for a change.

The cat lay in front of the fire, hoping it would soon be lit. The evening was too warm for a fire, but the rain was back again and lashing firmly at the windows. James held in his hand the little black book of card tricks. He studied it carefully under a burning lamp. It all made perfect sense. The author had obviously written it from a wealth of experience. James was no stranger to many of the games himself and had won many while at sea, but it didn't hurt to learn new techniques and some of these were useful, very useful indeed.

Robert said nothing to Victoria of James's visit to the mill, over dinner that evening, neither did he mention about the scheduled cards night tomorrow. He decided the less he said about James, the better. Victoria had noticed he was uncharacteristically quiet and she wondered if he had found out about Lillian leaving. She decided to broach the subject gently - he had a right to know, all said and done, Lillian is his sister.

'Violet came by today,' she said, pushing a potato around her plate. She looked at him to see if he had heard her. 'She told me that Lillian left with the Beckwiths for New York, yesterday.' She half expected an explosion of outrage but instead he took a sip of wine, staying remarkably calm. The clock ticking in the background sounded louder than ever.

'Sometimes you have to let people make their own mistakes in life,' he said, coolly.

'Perhaps it will not be a mistake,' she said pointedly, hoping her own decision to marry Robert was not one.

He met her gaze from across the table. The look in his eye was a warning for her to not continue with the conversation.

'How's things at the mill?' she asked, pretending to be interested.

'Running like clockwork.' He forced a small smile. 'Victoria, you really must come to the mill and let me introduce you properly.'

'I'd like that,' she lied.

'As my wife,' he said sternly, 'you now have a responsibility to the millers - they look up to you - it would be nice for you to show them that they have your support.'

He had a way of making her feel guilty, making her question her own integrity, but he was absolutely right she thought. She needed to show her support and to be more involved, it was just that she had no interest in the mill and, furthermore, no knowledge of the industry either.

'I'll make the effort, I promise. I'll come by and make myself known.' She smiled her best beguiling smile.

'Good,' he said, placing his knife and fork together on the plate and sitting back in his chair. His right hand glided over his protruding stomach. Robert had gained weight recently. His stomach was bigger than Victoria's small bump; a bump that she was still managing to keep hidden for fear that people would guess

- 214 -

that her newly announced pregnancy was a stage further than it should have been.

Chapter Sixteen

Thunder rumbled through a blanket of grey and purple clouds, covering Whitby and Ruswarp, most unseasonable for August. It would not have mattered to anyone in the slightest what the weather would be like on this *all important* cards night, least of all James. He had brought brandy, wine and ale from the pub, slipping it out of the cellar before Sophie had time to notice. He had also brought some tankards for them to drink from.

Four round tables had been set up in the walkway of the stables, the floors brushed clean to show the concrete instead of hay. The horses stood tethered outside, having being turfed out of their home for the evening, and a mild aroma of horse manure unfortunately still lingered; not that anyone seemed bothered by it. There was a good turn-out. A good number of the work-force had come over from the mill too. Not all of them were playing, most were simply there for the entertainment. There had been a lot of speculation over the past couple of days about the two Hawkes brothers fighting their battles out over a game or two of cards. It was no secret that there was no love lost between them, especially now that Robert had stolen and married Victoria, James's sweetheart.

Robert had an air of austerity about him, aware that he had a reputation to live up to as their employer. If he was scared of losing, he certainly didn't show it as he walked in and took his place at the first table of three men, one of them being James. James showed no emotion. Likenesses may have been remarked upon between the two brothers; their features in particular, the same square jaw line, defined cheek bones, and both possessing a thick head of hair, but that was as far as the likeness stretched.

Robert took out the invoice and placed it on the table in full view. 'If I win,' he said, 'then James - you pay this invoice,' he looked at him with a stern expression from across the table.

'And if they win?' James pointed to Harry, a local shopkeeper, and Frank, a middle-aged businessman who had done well from his investments in mining.

'Then I shall still pay,' replied Robert. 'You must win the game for me to pay you.'

The two men both gave an encouraging nod of their heads.

'Very well,' James sighed.

'So, what are we playing?' Robert asked impatiently, picking up the cards.

Victoria glanced at the clock for the fourth time in the last five minutes. Robert must be working late. Shame, she had planned for them to go for an evening stroll and, despite the threat of rain looming, she had been looking forward to it all afternoon. She loved the long summer evenings. It did not get dark much before ten o'clock and became light again by four o'clock, a vast contrast to the short winter days and long nights that seemed to go on forever in Yorkshire. It made sense to enjoy the summer while it lasted, even if it threatened rain at times.

She looked out of the window to check the weather. Large dark clouds still lingered over the abbey and the harbour in the far distance, but to the east, over Ruswarp, it appeared a little lighter. If Robert did not show soon, she decided, she would walk to meet him. Perhaps he could then introduce her properly to the workers as he had suggested, that would make him happy.

Sophie checked the clock on the wall, it was still early. The pub, typically, as James was not there this evening, was busier than it had been in days. As well at the locals, a group of ten tourists had arrived all at the same time. They were making merry in the middle of the room, singing and dancing. The locals did not seem to bother, in fact they welcomed the entertainment, joining in with well known songs, apart from old David Strachan that is, who sat stroking his long matted beard, grumbling under his breath that these kinds of goings on never happened in Nick's day. Sophie tried hard to put out of her mind the image of James gambling with Robert at the mill. The whole idea was foolish, and she had an uneasy feeling in the pit of her stomach about it. She knew how violent Robert could be. The man was a monster. If James were to win this game, things could turn very ugly and she felt sick with worry contemplating the outcome. The last thing she wanted was for James to get hurt again.

In the stables, acting as a card room, all four tables were occupied by businessmen, fishermen, farmers and millers, an unlikely mix, but they all shared something in common – their love of gambling. The venue was of no importance, or who was playing for that matter, just as long as they could play and feel the competitive thrill of gambling, pushing the boundaries to the limit every time. The far two tables played "Napoleon," widely referred to as just "Nap," the second table closest to the entrance "Basset," and the first table at the entrance "Whist." At this table sat Robert, James, Harry, and Frank. Robert sat back in his chair with a smug look upon his face. 'Seems there's no need for me to pay this invoice then.' He ripped it up and threw it back down on the table, having won the first game. Harry and Frank sat back in their seats with disappointment, not because of James losing the right for his invoice to be paid, but for their own losses.

'Int fair!' Jim shouted out in protest, having watched the entire game. 'E shouldn't 'ave to pay – 'e 'elped us out in our hour of need, did Captain 'Awkes.' The other tables momentarily stopped playing and glanced over, while the rest of the millers joined in, disgruntled about the way Mr Hawkes had treated the captain.

James held up his hands for them to calm down. 'It's fair, gentlemen.' He then noticed a few women watching him. 'And

Ladies,' he added quickly. 'I agreed to this game and I lost it. Mr Hawkes won fair and square.' A small smile appeared on his lips. 'But that doesn't mean to say he will win the next - the fun is about to start.' The others jeered and laughed.

'What fun?' Robert took a swig of brandy, not amused by James's attempt at making a spectacle of him.

'What are the stakes gentlemen?' James enquired, without answering Robert's question. On the other tables the games had already resumed.

'A crown,' Frank suggested.

'It's more than my customary stake,' said Harry.

'Well 'appen you should find another table to play at then,' Frank said with annoyance in his voice.

'How about half a crown,' Harry offered, trying to keep the peace.

'Half a crown?' Frank almost laughed.

'Gentlemen, let's not begin with an argument. Half a crown will do fine,' James said, tactfully.

'I came here and I played you - and now I bid you gentlemen a good evening.' Robert stood up, grabbing his hat from the spare chair next to him. The spectators behind the table groaned and muttered amongst themselves.

'Are you going to show this lot that you are too much of a coward to play for money?' James provoked.

Their eyes locked in another challenging stare. Robert glanced at them all as they nodded and waved at him to sit down and play. Without saying another word, he pulled out his money and placed it on the table then sat back down. Everyone cheered. What choice did he have? But if he was to play, he was determined to wipe that smug smile off James's face once and for all.

Alfie placed the tools down he had been using to fix a fence in the barn, then wandered over to the stables to give the horses a last feed before heading home. They seemed unsettled tonight. He patted Blackie on the neck. He gave a snort, followed by a loud whinnying sound, scraping his back hooves behind him. 'What's up lad? - Shush! - Come now!' He patted him again and then went to fetch his food, and on his return, an almighty clap of thunder echoed around the courtyard and throughout the stables, forcing Blackie into a fright as he bucked his back legs, kicking Alfie to the floor with such force. He then made his escape through the open door, leaving Alfie on the floor and unconscious.

Robert waited patiently for his turn, with glazed, beady eyes. James pondered his next move. The question in James's mind now, was just how far to take things. If he was in for the kill, he'd need to sit tight and play the long game. The little black book had given him some handy tips, especially when it came to reading an opponent's expressions. Robert was not as sure as he had previously been.

A spate of muttering and whispering took place amongst the spectators, and was then replaced by sympathetic groans as Harry sat back with disappointment, while glaring angrily at Frank.

'Well don't look at me,' said Frank. 'You did not return my trump lead, had you done so you might have saved the game.'

The tension grew thick, now that it was just down to Robert and James, and not a sound could be heard, other than a rustle in the hay as a mouse quickly scurried away. James took out two pieces of paper and a pencil from his pocket. He scribbled on both bits of paper as the others watched with interest. 'I wish to make this game a little more interesting.'

Robert's forehead creased in a frown. *As if it wasn't already.*

'Let's raise the stakes? This piece of paper,' he held it up for all to see. 'This paper says *Heron House.* You have it here in writing, that should you win, you take my home, my land as well the money on this table.' The crowd gasped and muttering broke out again.

'You're insane - I'll beat you hands down and you'll be out on your ear - homeless.' Robert stared at him, amazed that he could be so stupid.

'That maybe so,' James replied. 'And this one,' he picked up the second piece of paper, 'says The Mill - should I win I take the mill and all the money on this table.' The crowd now broke out into an uproar, mixed messages shouted, many not happy about their futures being gambled with and others wishing that James would win and take over the mill.

Robert stood up. 'This is outrageous – how - how can you expect me to gamble the mill?'

'Take a moment to think about it. It's your chance to show them all how good you really are.' James met his angry gaze from across the table.

Robert left the table and went outside for some air. It was spitting with rain and the thunder was becoming noticeably louder. He looked up at the sky and saw a flash of lightning on the hills. His focus then moved to the mill. Only a solitary light shone from one of the windows upstairs, most of the workers were either in the stables or had gone home by now. He sighed heavily. What was James's game? He had so far lost every single hand, so why would he risk losing *Heron House*? The man was a fool, and he needed to be taught a lesson once and for all. If he should win this game, it would make James a laughing stock and he the hero. This night could make history - the night Robert Hawkes won every game and the captain lost everything, except it wasn't quite everything, he realised. If he was to do this properly, he had to clean James out completely. He took another deep breath and wandered back into the stables, resuming his place at the table. Silence fell. All eyes were on Robert, waiting for his decision. The other tables were still busy playing and had not really understood what was happening, neither did they care. Their own games were of far more interest, but not for the millers, this was their future they were gambling over.

'What will it be?' asked James. He studied him carefully, waiting, as everyone else did for his answer.

Robert turned to face the workers. 'I will not let you down – I - I promise you that.'

''Ow can you promise us that?' Mary shouted out as others joined in.

'Look at him!' Robert pointed to James. 'He's lost every game so far – he – he isn't even capable of winning.'

'Wouldn't be a bad thing if he did,' mumbled Jim, and those who heard agreed and nodded.

Harry and Frank said nothing, unsure what to think about it all. They respected both men, but this was between the brothers now, and their feud still seemed a long way from being settled.

'I'm only willing to finish this game with you,' said Robert, 'if you include your share of *Somersby Hill* and that public house of yours.'

An expression of concern swept over James's face. 'But I only own half of *The Old Horseshoe*.'

'Half will do - I'm not greedy,' he smirked, as the others laughed.

James chewed his bottom lip in thought. Could he risk it? Could he do that to Sophie? She would never forgive him if he lost his share of the pub, especially to Robert, which meant he could not afford to lose. Losing *Heron House*, he could live with, losing

Somersby Hill, he would not be happy about, not at all, but losing the pub would be far worse as that affected Sophie as well as himself. He had to pull this off and he knew he was more than capable if he set his mind to it.

'You don't need to accept, Captain 'Awkes,' Jim reminded him, with a tap on the shoulder.

'I know Jim – thank you - but I will – all the same.' There were more gasps.

'Great!' Robert rubbed his hands together with glee. Everything was going to plan. Soon he would be even wealthier, but more importantly, James would be left in the gutter and made a laughing stock, and that was worth ten of *Heron House* and *Somersby Hill* and that grotty little pub of his. 'Let's sign these papers, then.' Robert added *Somersby Hill* and the share of *The Old Horseshoe* to the paper.

Eleanor looked out of the window. She had heard another loud clap of thunder and, pulling back the curtains to reveal the pouring rain on the window, she spotted Blackie in the courtyard, not tethered and running back and forth in terror. She looked for Alfie, but he did not appear to be in sight, so she grabbed her cloak and ran outside. The rain lashed down and Eleanor struggled to calm Blackie. Finally, she led him back to the stables, suddenly stopping in her tracks. 'Alfie?' she pushed Blackie into his box and closed the door securely, then went back to Alfie. Still unconscious and with blood now trickling from the back of his head, there seemed to be no life in Alfie. She searched for his pulse and, relieved to find one in his wrist, she sighed heavily. 'Thank God.' Alive he was, but for how long without medical attention, she had no idea. She pulled a pile of hay from a spare horse-box, together with a blanket and propped up his head with the hay, holding the blanket against the wound to stop it from bleeding. It slowed a little. With the rest of the blanket, she draped it over his body to keep him warm, and then dashed outside. He needed help, urgently.

James could see the colour rising in Robert's cheeks. Robert moistened his lips, not giving into the want of having another drink right now. He must stay focused.

The fifth page of the little black book sprung to James's mind, remembering it well, he applied the instructions accordingly. He may have lost all the games so far this evening, but that had been intentional, he did not want Robert to be aware, or anyone else for that matter, of just how good a player he really was.

John Barrow walked into the pub much later than usual and pulled up a stool to sit down. Sophie looked relieved to see him. She served him and then leaned over the bar to talk in private. 'Can you do me a favour?' He nodded, waiting to find out what would be asked of him. 'I need you to watch this place for me. Something has come up and I must go.'

Always happy to help, John agreed. 'Aye lass - of course - you go.'

'I'll be back before closing. Just serve and keep everyone 'appy, especially that lot.' She pointed to the tourists who were now gathered around a table, laughing and still singing songs.

'You 'ave my word.'

'You're a life saver.' She managed a small smile and then dashed out of the door. The feeling of worry had not subsided all evening and she needed to get to the mill before it could be too late.

Robert felt tiny droplets of sweat dripping down the sides of his temples. *Damn him! Damn the bloody cards too!* He could have done with a much better hand than the one he had. The crowd watched on, holding their breath, as did Frank and Harry, still sitting at the table. Never had they watched a game so intense and with so much at stake.

Eleanor stood at the top of the hill for a second, panting and gaining her breath. She could see one light burning at the top of the mill. Should she go to the mill for help, or carry on a little longer down the path to the estate where the Horners lived? Lightning flashed, illuminating the whole sky as if someone had just turned on a big, bright, fluorescent light. She had never seen anything like it, but she had no time to watch or be scared, Alfie needed help. An almighty rumble of thunder sounded from right behind her as she ran on.

All eyes were on James now. No one knew what would happen next, it was too difficult to call. Robert swallowed hard. He could not lose - under no circumstances could he lose. A rush of panic came over him, and for a moment he thought he might pass out. His heart fluttered but he sat still, frozen to his chair, waiting for James, his eyes fixed on the cards he was about to reveal.

James smiled inwardly. Now it was time to put Robert in his place once and for all. He had messed with him too often and for too long. This was sweet revenge for all to see, pay-back time for all the hurt he had caused him over the years. This was for driving Lillian away before she had been ready to leave, for inheriting the mill and being their father's favourite, but more importantly for taking Victoria from him, and not even because he loved her. And finally, tonight, Robert would get his comeuppance. James laid down the highest trump.

For a moment a stunned silence fell upon them all while realisation sank in. Then in one almighty swoop, Robert picked up the table and threw it on its side. All the other tables stopped playing. Mayhem broke out as Robert reached for James by the throat, but Jim and the others stepped in and pulled Robert away. 'E beat you fair and square, take it like a man!' Jim yelled at him, while a group of men held him back. The others shouted their opinions, some agreeing with Jim and others not. But even the ones who were not happy about James winning the mill were filled with anger. What kind of man gambles his livelihood? Their loyalty to Robert had now suddenly diminished and it seemed they had no choice but to stand by James and make sure he kept the mill running, or they would all be out of work.

In a rage of anger Robert broke free from the men's clutches and raced out of the stables. James stood up to go after him, but Jim put out his arm stopping him. 'Leave 'im be! - Give 'im time to cool down,' Jim advised.

James, knowing Jim was completely right, turned to face them all. 'I want to reassure every single one of you,' he said, gaining their full attention, 'that your jobs are safe with me.'

'And there'll be no big changes?' Mary asked, speaking out for the others.

'No changes,' James confirmed. 'You won't notice the difference.'

'But you don't 'ave years of experience – like – like t'other Mr 'Awkes 'as,' said young Charlie Crouch. He did not agree with James winning the mill.

'That maybe so - but I have *some* experience - I worked there for many years when I was a lad.' Looking at their worried faces, he needed to reassure them; he owed them that at least. 'And with all of you at my side, and Jim as my right-hand man, we'll manage just fine.' He smiled with confidence and that smile of confidence won them over. A cheer of appreciation rippled through the stables, even the other tables had stopped their playing and were aware now of what was going on. 'To Captain 'Awkes!' They applauded. 'To a new future!' Jim shouted out, more than happy with the outcome.

'See you in't morning, Captain 'Awkes.' Charlie, put on his cap and was the first to leave. He didn't feel it right to celebrate, not at Mr Hawkes expense. Robert had always been good to him and he didn't know what James would be like to work for, he had already had one run-in with him when James had caught him with young Becky Horner.

James banged his fist on the table to gain their attention once more, picking up on what Charlie had just said. 'Seeing as I'm no longer a captain - I think you should all call me Mr Hawkes – what do you think?'

Henry from the mill, standing next to Jim shouted out, 'You'll be Captain of Mill - I say we continue to call you Captain 'Awkes.'

'Aye!' they all agreed at once.

'We run a tight ship at mill,' grinned Jim. 'It'll not be too dissimilar to your days at sea.'

'You'll always be Captain 'Awkes to us,' Mary said, with a toothless grin. 'Be difficult t' remember t' call you owt else.'

'Then Captain Hawkes I shall remain!' he laughed in amusement. They were a good crowd and he was very much looking forward to working with them all.

Without warning the stable doors suddenly flung open and Charlie ran in, red faced and with eyes as big as saucers, breaking up the party atmosphere. 'It's mill – it's on fire!'

James led the way as they all tumbled out of the stables, greeted by the flaring orange and red billowing flames through at least half of the building.

Charlie shouted out to James, 'Miss Dickens was seen goin' in - lookin' for you - she was.' The colour drained completely from James's face. 'Sophie - Oh my God, Sophie!' He pulled his jacket from his back, placed it over his head like a tent to protect himself and ran straight into the mill, while others shouted and begged for him not to go inside. Their attempts to stop him were in vain, for he was already inside the blazing building. The only thing on his mind was to save Sophie.

Broken masonry fell around him as he shielded himself as best he could from the extreme heat of the flames, sneering angrily before him as he tried to make his way through each room in search of her.

Charlie ran around the back of the building to find Robert. 'All done,' he said. 'I told 'im.'

Robert took an appreciative puff of a cigarette to calm his nerves and then looked at him. 'And did he believe you?'

'Aye - fell for it good n' proper. He's gone in lookin' for 'er - can I 'ave me money now?'

Robert slipped him a coin. 'Don't breathe a word, or your neck'll be on the line too.'

Charlie nodded then ran off back to the crowd, which was larger than before, now that many of the locals from the village and neighbouring farms had come to offer their help.

Wooden beams collapsed and floorboards gave way to the side of James and behind him too. He coughed violently and found it so very difficult to see, but there in the next room, he could make out an outline of a body on the floor, covered in debris. He ran over broken glass from the shattered windows and then jumped over burning wood, and when eventually he arrived at her side, he pulled away the debris to discover it was not Sophie after all. The woman, lying in front of him was Victoria. With tears, immediately springing to his already stinging eyes, he felt her neck to see if she was alive. She was, although unconscious. He picked her up and put her frail, limp body over his shoulder, trying desperately to find the safest exit. He needed to get her outside, and then a thought sprung to mind. Where was Sophie? Had Charlie mistaken Victoria for Sophie, or was Sophie still in the mill somewhere? A sudden explosion erupted from the granary downstairs and part of the building began to crumble.

The gathering crowds outside screamed at the terror unfolding before their eyes. Word had been sent to Whitby for help, but help would not arrive soon enough. James carried on through the crumbling building. His foot suddenly slipped and he fell, still clutching hold of Victoria. His coughing became extreme again, and through the smoke he could see the remnants of the grey night sky shining in from the outside. He stumbled again towards the front exit of the mill, then everything went completely black.

Several people, including Jim, ran towards the entrance as soon as James was in sight. James had passed out momentarily, but was now conscious and back on his feet again, spluttering and struggling for breath. They took Victoria from him and laid her down on the grassy riverbank.

Sophie pushed through the crowds, having just arrived. Waves of panic flooded her. James! She needed to know James was safe. There was so much noise and her head was spinning from all the chaos.

James, now next to Victoria, realised she was covered in blood, mainly from the abdomen downwards. He crawled closer to her and knelt over her, still coughing and crying openly.

Sophie had now reached the front of the crowd and stopped in her tracks. She could see him, he was alive. But who was that next to him? And then, realising it to be Victoria, she flung her hand to her mouth as she watched James distraught and sobbing. 'Don't...don't you leave me,' he croaked. 'Victoria!' Her eyes opened, rolled and closed again. Tears rolled down his face and then, wiping them away, it dawned on him that Sophie could still be inside the burning building. He didn't want to leave Victoria's side, not even for a second, but he couldn't leave Sophie either. He struggled to get to his feet. He had to go back and find her, but his body would not let him. He felt as if every inch of his being was made of lead. Every time he got up, he fell back down again.

Robert walked back up from the riverbank and could see the commotion. Jim shouted over to Robert. 'It's Mrs 'Awkes!' With a panicked look, he raced over to her. 'Get help!' he yelled at them all impatiently, pushing James away from her.

'It's on its way,' Mary called back.

Distraught at the thought he might lose her, he shouted at everyone to step back. His eyes fixed on the blood. There was so much blood, too much blood, and he knew then it had to be the babies. The thought of losing the twins filled him with more dread. He felt sick to the very core.

James attempted to speak, seeing Robert so devastated and full of despair. 'She's - she's not de –de.'

Robert could not make out what he was trying to say. James tried again to get back up, he needed to find Sophie, but his legs would not let him and instead he lay helplessly on the grass.

'He's saying she's not dead,' repeated Jim to Robert, now standing over James. 'He pulled 'er out of fire – 'e saved her,' Jim explained.

There was a glimmer of gratitude in Robert's eyes, but it didn't last long. 'Why? - Why was she even in there?' His tone was a mix of anger as well as sorrow.

'Looking for you I presume,' said Jim, and then he turned around and spotted Charlie. 'Charlie!' he called over. 'You said Miss Dickens was in mill - not Mrs 'Awkes.'

''Appen I got confused,' Charlie snapped. 'There's Miss Dickens.' He pointed to Sophie. She walked towards James and knelt down next to him. He grabbed her, so relieved to see her well and alive. 'I thought….' He coughed again. 'I thought you were…'

'Shush! Don't speak. I'm 'ere now,' she replied, cradling him in her arms.

Chapter Seventeen

The cottage was in its normal state of disorder, clothes hanging everywhere, plates on the table, still with the remains of that evening's supper on them.

'Ow bad is he?' Mrs Horner asked Eleanor, her eyes wide and tearful. She had sent Tommy to find Dr Coker the moment Eleanor had arrived.

'Not good.' Eleanor didn't want to lie, as Alfie's mother she had a right to know.

'Becky, stay 'ere lass and wait for your brothers.' Mrs Horner grabbed her cloak and flung it over her shoulders.

'Can't I come? He is me brother.' Becky stood up quickly, grabbing her shawl from the chair it was hanging over.

'No!' Mrs Horner replied sharply. 'And clear table - make yourself useful.'

Becky threw the shawl back down, pouting her lips in anger and frustration.

The lights were burning inside Dr Coker's cottage and Tommy Horner sighed with relief. The little cottage stood isolated, looking down over the rowing boats lined up on the river Esk. There was a strong smell of smoke filling the air. Looking down across the riverbank, Tommy saw the mill on fire, but he had no time to stop and investigate, his brother needed urgent help. He arrived at the cottage and banged both fists on the door. A moment later a disgruntled Mrs Coker opened the door. 'What's up with you lad? You'll break bleedin' door down 'ammering away like that.'

'Where's Dr Coker?' Tommy asked, without an apology.

'Just left – gone t' mill – there's a fire goin' on down there - can't you see it, lad?' She pointed at the smoke billowing from the building in the distance. Without another word Tommy sprinted away, having caught sight of Dr Coker walking down the lane in the distance.

'Dr Coker!' he called out, but the doctor did not stop; he was on a mission to help those at the mill.

'Dr Coker,' Tommy panted, now falling in step with him. 'We need you up at 'Eron 'ouse, it's me brother…'

'Sorry lad but I'm needed at mill.'

Tommy yanked his arm firmly and the doctor nearly dropped his medical bag, annoyed, he pulled away from Tommy and continued to walk on.

'There'll be 'elp coming from Whitby. Me - me brother Alfie - he's got no one – he might be dying!' Coker stopped and looked at him, hesitantly, trying to determine if the lad could be over dramatising the situation.

'Unconscious, Eleanor said – blood gashing from 'is 'ead like a waterfall.'

Coker scratched his small, trimmed beard. The lad was probably right, help would be on its way from Whitby and, as he looked down the lane, he could already see men on horseback arriving. He didn't like the sound of Alfie's condition, not one bit.

'*Heron House* you said?'

'Aye!'

'Come on then – there'll be no time to waste.'

When they arrived at *Heron House* Eleanor and Mrs Horner were already there, kneeling next to Alfie, still lying on the stable floor. Mrs Horner was covered in Alfie's blood, crying hysterically.

'Mrs Horner – please - move out of the way.' He pushed her back to make space for himself and to open his medical bag. The running blood from the gash on Alfie's head was minimal now, but Alfie was still unconscious. Coker could see how much blood he had lost from the dark, sticky pool next to him on the floor.

Victoria was lifted up into the hospital coach driven by four horses, with Robert at her side. She was still unconscious and covered in more blood. A moment later they were on their way.

A doctor from Grape Lane Hospital, in Whitby, had seen to James, cleaned up his wounds, and bandaged him where needed. He could stand on his feet again; the doctor had informed him the temporary loss of feeling in his legs was purely down to shock. Amazingly, he had come away with only surface wounds and no real internal damage, although his voice was hoarse, his lungs being still full of smoke. Sophie had promised the doctor she would take him home and she would be his full time nurse. James looked dejected, a broken man in many ways, as he left the hospital with Sophie. He wanted to wait, to see Victoria, but he knew full well that Robert was with her and the Crawfords would soon be at the hospital too. It was not his place to be at her bedside, she was not his wife, she was Robert's and the awful fact that he had no place in her life any more tore at his heart.

'You'll be fine – you'll see.' Sophie held out her arm to him and they walked towards the coach and horses waiting for them. James managed a small smile of gratitude. She was a good woman and he cared deeply for her, but she wasn't Victoria and she never would be.

Meanwhile, back at the mill, firemen had the blaze under control. The mill looked in a sorry state, nothing more than a burnt out, black, smouldering shell.

The rickety coach shook from side to side as it made its way up the old dirt track towards *Heron House*. 'Appen we should 'ave waited for Victoria and Robert,' Sophie said, thinking out loud. She looked him in the eyes, waiting for his reaction. Why didn't he love her, like he loved Victoria? He stared out of the window, unable to look her in the eyes. 'We would have only got in the way.'

'Do you think,' Sophie said hesitantly. 'Do you think Victoria will survive this?' The moment she had asked she regretted it, feeling guilty for implying Victoria might die, although it was patently obvious, given the state she was in, that it was possible she may not pull through. She wished Victoria well, she really did, but seeing James crying like he had at Victoria's side, begging her not to die, was simply awful. The truth was that he was not over her, not by any means, and the realisation hurt.

James looked away in an attempt to hide his emotions. 'We can only hope and pray,' he replied finally. He was certain Victoria had lost her babies, which would mean, if she did survive, she could be free of Robert, if she hadn't already married him, of course. She was Robert's wife now and there was no changing that. But the one thing Robert couldn't take away from him was the years James and Victoria had spent together, all the good times they had once shared. They would never be forgotten, in his heart Victoria would remain his forever.

'Is 'e goin' t' – t' - die?' Mrs Horner sobbed, still on her knees next to Alfie.

'Not if I can help it.' Coker fumbled around in his medical bag and pulled out a small plastic tube.

Eleanor wiped away her tears. 'Shouldn't we get 'im to 'ospital?' Tommy stood shaking and biting his finger nails nervously. He and

Alfie had always been close. They were the two youngest of the Horner brothers.

'No time I'm afraid. Alfie has a swelling on his brain – he needs help right now. I'm going to have to do a small emergency operation,' he said, fumbling around in his medical bag again.

'What do you mean - operation?' Mrs Horner looked at him with her tear-stained face and big wide eyes, watching him as he pulled out all sorts of weird instruments from his bag.

'Tommy - take your mother outside and Eleanor – you can wait here and give me a hand,' Coker instructed.

Tommy ushered his mother gently outside, doing as he was told. Mrs Horner was not happy about it, but was too tired and upset to argue. She had to trust Dr Coker, she had no choice.

Coker pulled the blanket away from Alfie. He needed Alfie's body temperature to lower quickly. A moment later, taking a small knife from his case, he made a tiny incision into Alfie's skull. 'Tube,' he ordered Eleanor, pointing to it on the floor. She handed it to him; feeling extremely queasy, and even more so once the cerebrospinal fluid began to drain away.

Tommy and Mrs Horner sat on the stone wall outside of the stables in silence. Suddenly that silence was broken by the noise of the rickety coach and the hooves of horses sounding on the stone path heading towards *Heron House*. Once parked, James stepped out of the coach with Sophie at his side and his arm bandaged in a sling and covered all over in cuts, burns and bruises. 'Mrs Horner?'

Tommy?' James croaked, still suffering from smoke inhalation. He walked towards them both, with Sophie right behind him.

'Captain 'Awkes - what 'appened t' you.' Tommy jumped down off the wall.

James waited for the noise of the coach and horses to die down as it left *Heron House*. 'Fire at the mill,' he said. 'Never mind me - what's happened - why are you here?'

'It's Alfie,' Mrs Horner blubbered, not at all interested in the fire at the mill, nothing mattered - only Alfie did.

Rose, John and Violet arrived at the hospital. Rose demanded to see her daughter at once but the nurse, a small chubby middle-aged woman with rosy cheeks, refused them entry and instead sat them all down and explained the situation – they had removed the still-born twins but Victoria was extremely weak and still in a critical condition.

Rose cried in John's arms. 'Those poor - poor babies – our poor daughter.'

'But she will survive?' Violet asked, clutching onto any amount of hope she could. She couldn't bear to lose her only sister.

'I can't answer that just now – but the more time that passes her chances of survival will increase. I'm so sorry. I wish I could give a more positive answer.' The nurse left the room.

Robert sat holding onto Victoria's hand. She looked so small and fragile. Losing the mill and money seemed trivial now. Why had she gone to the mill? This was his fault. If he had not played that stupid card game, gone home as usual. He had lost his babies, their babies, and he could also lose his wife.

The waiting room, if you could call it that, offered seating for only three people, it was airless with a tiny window up high that now let in some daylight, as the sun began to rise after what had seemed an endless night. The room was on the far wing of the hospital, away from the main entrance. John, Rose and Violet were not aware of the police having arrived at the hospital an hour ago.

John yawned and stood up. 'I need to see Robert,' he said. There were so many questions racing through his head. 'Why did she go to the mill so late?' he asked, with anger welling up inside. 'How had the fire started and where was Robert at the time? - For God's sake - he is her husband - he should have been there -- should have protected her.'

Rose let out another heartfelt sob into her handkerchief. Violet glanced at her mother with worry, then back at her father. 'Papa - I don't think now is a good time to be asking so many questions.'

'Now is as good a time as any,' John retorted angrily. My daughter – your sister - is fighting for her life.' A sob caught the back of his throat and without another word he marched out of the room.

He found the same nurse. She was getting ready to leave after her night shift and was busy writing notes at the little table situated outside Victoria's room. John walked right up to her. 'If you won't let me go in, at least tell my son-in-law to come out. I need to speak to him.'

'I'm sorry Mr Crawford, your son-in-law is not with your daughter,' she replied, looking up from her notes.

'Well where is he?' John frowned.

'Gone,' she replied flatly.

'Gone where?' John felt like he was in a middle of a bad dream, where nothing made sense. In a moment he would wake up and realise Victoria was safely at home and it had all been a terrible nightmare. The nurse seemed uncomfortable. 'I'm not sure it's my place to say,' she said.

'Not your place? For goodness sake woman, my daughter is in there in a critical condition. I need to know where my son-in-law is.' John looked as if he were about to explode with anger.

The nurse pursed her lips. What choice did she have but to tell him? The man was beside himself with worry. 'Police took 'im – 'e's been arrested,' she said.

'Arrested? - Arrested for what?' This was getting worse by the minute.

'They believe Mr 'Awkes might 'ave started fire,' she said quietly.

He stared back at her, lost for words. 'Started – started fire? Why would he do that - he owns the damn mill?'

The nurse shook her head. 'I don't know Sir – that's all I know.'

Alfie was now conscious. Everyone had helped to move him into the house and into the guest room. He moistened his lips and spoke for the first time. 'Me 'ead,' he groaned. Dr Coker grinned. 'You'll have a sore head for a while longer lad.'

'Blackie bolted - scared witless at thunder.' It was all coming back to him now.

Mrs Horner kissed his forehead. 'You gave us all a fright.'

Eleanor touched his hand. 'You're goin' t' be just fine,' she said softly. Seeing him badly hurt like that, knowing he could possibly have died, had scared her and made her realise she was, in fact, very fond of him after all.

'Thanks to Eleanor 'ere finding you and searchin' for 'elp,' said Mrs Horner. 'Saved your life - she's a good lass.'

Eleanor blushed. 'I did what anyone would 'ave done.'

It was noon the following day when James learned of Robert's arrest. Word had spread fast all over Whitby and Ruswarp. Jim had walked up to *Heron House* to find James.

'Do you think e's capable of startin' fire?' Jim asked, sitting in the parlour with James. James had insisted he sit down and have a cup of tea. Still shaken up from the fire and seeing the mill burn down like that, it had left its mark on Jim. He looked pale and drawn. His hand shook as he placed the cup back down into its saucer.

James sighed heavily. 'I'd like to say not – but,' James sighed, 'he can be ruthless at times. That temper of his, it's his own worst enemy.'

Jim nodded. 'Are you going t' see 'im?'

James lowered his head in thought. 'I don't know.' He rubbed his tired brow, and winced as his rough skinned finger tips caught an open wound from the fire. His whole body felt sore and ached from head to toe. He looked at Jim again. 'I'm not sure he'd want to see me.'

'He's your brother - all said and done,' Jim reminded him.

'Any news on Victoria?' James asked. He had contemplated going to the hospital, but didn't feel he should intrude, knowing full well the Crawfords would be there. It somehow didn't feel appropriate, although he was desperate to know she would be alright and perhaps it might be wise to offer help of some sort, given that Robert would not be there at her side.

'Word 'as it – there's no change,' Jim replied glumly.

'Jim,' James said thoughtfully, 'I'm going to give you a sum of money to be shared out between the millers. It's not much, but it will help put food on the table until we are up and running again.' He had lain awake in the night thinking about the workers and how they would survive. He had no idea how long it would take before the mill would be operational again, but fortunately, he had enough money to tide them over for the next few months at least.

Jim's face lit up at the news. 'Oh Captain 'Awkes, thank you so much – you don't know 'ow grateful I am – 'ow grateful all of us will be when I tell 'em.'

'No need to thank me - these are hard times Jim. I will get onto the builders just as soon as the police have finished. We should then have a fair idea of the time-scale we are looking at.'

'We can 'elp rebuild it and it will be much quicker - all of us can do it together.' His eyes lit up at the idea.

James looked thoughtful. 'There are certain things we need professionals for.'

'Of course - but I mean hard labour, brick-laying n'all.'

James agreed. 'Excellent idea, and like you rightly say, it will be much quicker.'

Sophie opened up the pub as normal, although everything was far from normal after last night's events. John Barrow was the first to walk in. 'Thank you for 'elping out last night,' she said with a small smile. He had cleared up the mess in the pub after everyone had gone home and closed up for her. He handed back the keys to her; she had used James's keys to get in that morning.

'Not a problem. 'Ow's Captain?'

'Cuts - burns - but he'll live.' She looked tired and in low spirits as she walked around the other side of the bar.

'Well you could look a bit more 'appier about it,' he said.

'I'm relieved 'e's alive - course I am - but with so much devastation its 'ard to be positive. Miss Crawf – Mrs 'Awkes - is in a terrible state in 'ospital and 'as lost her babies too.'

John screwed up his face with regret. 'Poor lass - I 'eard it was Captain 'Awkes who pulled her out of fire – you got a goodun there – one t' be proud of.'

She nodded and a tear trickled down her cheek.

'Hey - come lass - those tears will be of no 'elp.' He passed her a handkerchief and she accepted it.

'You should not 'ave opened up today - you're in no fit state.'

'He still loves 'er,' she said, unexpectedly, crying again.

John placed a comforting arm around her shoulders, realising she meant Victoria. 'She's not 'is t' love no more and she never will be now - now she's married to Mr 'Awkes – so you should not go gettin' yourself all in a state.'

She looked at him, unconvinced. Victoria maybe married to Robert, but that wouldn't stop her chasing after James when she got bored with Robert. And she knew full well, if that did happen, James would not turn Victoria away.

'Look what he did for you - this place,' he threw out his arm to show her the pub. 'The money 'e gave you - 'ow he stood by you at Nick's funeral. Captain 'Awkes is very fond of you - very fond indeed. It would not surprise me if 'e don't propose t' you soon – I feel it in me bones,' he smiled.

She looked at him with a forlorn expression. 'If she lives - Mrs 'Awkes that is - I don't know if can play second best.' She let out a small sob, not having listened to a word John had just said to her.

'Why don't you go upstairs and get some rest – you're dog tired. I'll look after this place.'

'I'll need to get back to James soon.'

'E can survive a while longer without you – 'e 'as maids you know.'

'One maid,' Sophie corrected him, 'and she's *no use nor ornament.*' She had never warmed to Eleanor, then again neither had Eleanor to Sophie.

She patted his hand. 'You're a good man John Barrow - Uncle Nick was right about you.' She got up and walked off upstairs to get some rest.

When James turned up at the hospital that afternoon, he was unprepared for the greeting he received from John Crawford, having found him in the waiting room alone.

'James! James my dear man – I - I can't thank you enough' he said, hugging him tightly, most uncharacteristically for such a reserved gentleman as John Crawford.

Rose and Violet had gone home to rest and were coming back later to stay the night again. They were taking bedside rituals in shifts. They were now permitted to enter the room, now that there was nothing more the doctors could do other than wait for Victoria to wake up. Contrary to what the doctors had first said, the danger was now, that the longer she stayed unconscious, the more likely it became she would not ever wake up. The medical team had prepared the family also for the fact that, should Victoria wake, it did not mean she was out of danger, far from it. There was a strong possibility that she could have brain damage, given the amount of time she had been unconscious. Each hour that passed became crucial. They talked to her, sang to her, kissed her and held her hand, but no life came from the limp body that lay in the bed like a rag doll showing no emotion at all.

'Thank me?' James felt embarrassed.

'You risked your life for my daughter. They told me you pulled her out of the fire,' John said.

'I did – but I fear it was not nearly enough. I should have found her earlier than I did – I should have been much quicker with my exit out of the building.' He fought hard to hold back his tears and John brushed away his own tears.'

'You did everything you could – a damn sight more than that brother of yours.' John's anger with Robert was still brewing. He had to blame someone and Robert seemed the obvious choice. The police would not have arrested Robert without reason.

'How is she now?' James asked, ignoring John's comment about Robert. He needed to know how Victoria was and had waited this long to find out.

John battled with his emotions, taking a large gulp, his eyes red and swollen from both crying and tiredness. 'She – she just lays there – I - I don't even know – even know if she can hear us.' He wiped his eyes with his handkerchief and gave a blow of his nose. James looked away, trying his best not to cry himself.

'They are just changing her bandages and then I must go back in again,' John said.

'I won't keep you. I came here also to speak to you about Robert. I know this is not the best of times but...'

'If he is responsible for the fire – the fire that has almost cost my daugh...,' John cleared his throat 'my daughter's life - and still could.' He took a moment to compose himself before continuing. 'I swear I will kill him with my own bare hands if I ever clap eyes on the man again.'

'I can understand your anger – I really can - but we have to presume he is innocent until proven guilty. What if he didn't start the fire?'

'Let the justice system work it out,' John said, sitting down on the chair behind them. James sat down next to him. 'As much as I dislike my brother – and God knows I do – he is family, and he is your family now too. What if they have got it wrong? Don't you owe it to Victoria to at least give him the benefit of the doubt? She needs to know her husband did not start this fire.'

He met John's pensive stare, their eyes locked for a moment, a moment that seemed to last a long while.

John sighed. 'I know a judge - a very good one - Samuel Turner - he's more than likely to be taking this case – he takes all the local big ones.' He took out a pen and found a piece of paper on the table in front of them and then scribbled an address down, handing James the paper. 'Speak to him and see what his chances are, say I sent you.'

'Thank you,' James glanced at the piece of paper. 'It's the right thing to do.'

'That's what makes you such a decent human being,' John said with admiration.

James forced a small, thankful smile.

The nurse poked her head around the corner of the door, 'Mr Crawford - come quickly!' John jumped up and followed the nurse, falling into step with her pace. James also followed behind, but waited discreetly outside of the room.

Victoria's eyes fluttered again, then opened fully. John cried with relief, looking down at her. 'Victoria?'

'Pa…Papa?' her voice was nothing more than a croaked whisper, but it was enough for John to see his daughter conscious again.

James watched through the glass door. He smiled and wiped away his tears, wishing more than anything that he could go in there and tell her just how much he loved her. Instead, with his head hung low, he walked away, knowing he did not have the right to express his love for her any more.

Chapter Eighteen

The house stood alone amidst the countryside. At a glance, and from a distance, to James it looked like a tatty old farmhouse, but upon arrival it became clear this was no tatty old farmhouse, but in fact a beautifully restored seventeenth Century home with stables and with much land attached.

James stepped down from his horse, tethered Blackie to a nearby tree and walked up to the main entrance door. Just as he arrived, the door opened before him, before he had even a chance to knock.

'Can I help you?' asked Samuel Turner's servant, a scrawny looking fellow with taut features and eyes that looked too close together.

'I've come to see Mr Turner.' James politely removed his hat.

'Is Mr Turner expecting you?' The servant gave a look of uncertainty.

James, thinking quickly on his feet for fear of being turned away, decided to tell a small white lie. 'Yes - we have a mutual acquaintance - Mr John Crawford - Mr Crawford has sent me.'

The servant looked momentarily impressed. 'And you are?' he enquired.

'Like I said - an acquaintance,' he replied, knowing full well if he gave his name, Samuel Tuner would, without doubt, link him to

Robert and probably not wish to speak with him. By now, everyone had heard about the fire and Robert Hawkes's arrest.

The servant eyed him suspiciously and then decided to give James the benefit of the doubt. After all, he did say John Crawford had sent him and he knew Samuel Turner was well acquainted with John Crawford.

The ceilings were high and impressive, James noticed, as they walked through the foyer. They stopped at the far end of a long corridor, the servant's hand poised on the door handle before he turned to face James again. 'Please wait - I'll ask if Mr Turner will see you now - he's not been feeling too well of late,' he added

'Of course,' James smiled courteously, hoping he would not be turned away. But he did not have to wait long to find out, a moment later the door opened again and James was beckoned in.

Mr Samuel Turner sat in a comfortable chair in front of a large fire, despite it still being very mild outside. He was a big man with a round face, the colour of light purple from over indulging in both rich food and drink. He placed a small glass of whisky down on the side table next to him and looked up at James as he entered the room.

'Mr Turner,' James addressed him before walking towards him to shake his hand. 'I'm sorry to intrude like this. I am Captain — Mr- Mr - Hawkes - and I am a close friend of Mr John Crawford's,' he hoped the name drop would soften his uninvited presence. Samuel remained seated and unaffected by the name. 'Well Captain

'– Mr- Mr Hawkes - you'll forgive me if I don't rise - trouble with the old foot,' he pointed down to his large swollen, purple and red foot caused by gout.

James grabbed Samuel's moist palm. It was unbearably hot and stuffy and the room smelt of stale food and liquor.

'Sit down,' Samuel gestured to a leather armchair.

James sat. 'My brother - Robert Hawkes…' James began.

Samuel was quick to interrupt. 'Your brother – *if* found guilty - is a foolish man.'

'Indeed.' James replied awkwardly. 'However, Mr Crawford…'

'Mr Crawford should know better than to send you here - to expect me to discuss a new case outside of court - especially with the suspect's brother.' Samuel's bushy eyebrows raised and he then gave a small throaty cough.

A sudden moment of awkward silence fell upon the room. The ticking of the clock on the mantelpiece sounded too loud, as did the crackling of the fire. James could feel the colour rise within his face, from both the heat and the shame, the shame Robert had brought upon him now that he was left to fight his corner. Nevertheless, he needed to continue, despite his discomfort. 'Mr Crawford's daughter – Victoria – as you are probably aware - was hurt very badly in the fire.'

'Yes I am aware – please offer my condolences to Mr Crawford and his lady wife.' Samuel sighed wistfully. 'In particular for the loss of their unborn grandchildren – tragic – tragic – shame,' he said shaking his head. 'The Crawfords are a well respected family and it saddens me that they should be caught up in this dreadful mess.'

'I agree,' said James, wiping his forehead with the palm of his hand. 'Which is precisely why I am here – you see, Miss Crawford has just woken from a state of unconsciousness – and – well - now wishes to know what will become of her husband.' Another small lie, or maybe not, he knew Victoria would soon be asking questions.

'As do you.' Their eyes met again in another uncomfortable stare.

'Yes,' James replied honestly.

Samuel moved his foot slightly with a small groan. 'And as I said before Mr Hawkes - I cannot discuss a new case outside of court.'

'And I respect that Sir - I really do - but all I wish to know is what chance does my brother have?'

'To get off the hook for - arson? Manslaughter? Murder of his unborn twins - that will be up to the jury to decide - not I Mr Hawkes.

James swallowed hard, his mouth now felt as dry as sandpaper, but he did not dare request a glass of water at such a time. 'He can't possibly be trialled for all of those crimes, surely?' he said.

'Your brother had motive to start the fire at the mill - that much is common knowledge – after your – *card games*,' he said with distaste, bringing further shame on James.

'But that does not mean to say he did do it – and if – if in the unlikely event he did – he would never have intentionally hurt his wife or his unborn children.'

'I dare say,' replied Samuel. 'But we cannot be certain of anything until the facts are examined.'

Samuel gave another disconcerting groan as he shifted his foot to yet another position on the stool it was resting on.

'Mr Hawkes - we should not be having this conversation and I would be most grateful if you would leave now.'

'Sir – if –If you may allow me to ask just one more thing?' James rose to his feet, ready to leave. Samuel looked annoyed. 'What is it, man? Make it quick.'

'You said before – murder – murder of his unborn twins - could he get trialled for murder?'

Samuel replied indignantly. 'Two unborn children were killed because of that fire.' He then shook his head. 'No – he would be looking at manslaughter, I should think.'

No matter what James thought of Robert, he still found it hard to comprehend the idea that Robert could be capable of starting the fire. He loved the mill, always had done. His nature would be to fight back, but surely not by setting fire to the mill out of spite? A sense of guilt washed over James again. Had he not taken everything from him, Robert would not be in this mess and, more importantly, maybe Victoria would not have been hurt and her children now dead. 'Please forgive me for my intrusion and I thank you humbly for your patience.' He stood up and bowed his head.

'Mr Hawkes,' Samuel rolled his eyes. 'If there is one thing I hate it is grovelling - your brother will get a fair trial just as any other man would - rest assured of that.'

James nodded with gratitude. As he reached the door Samuel said, 'Mr Hawkes - give my regards to Mr Crawford and his family. I hope the trial will be a swift resolve – for both parties,' he added.

Rose and Violet had arrived at the hospital as soon as they had received the news that Victoria had woken. They cried with joy at the news, but their happiness was somewhat tainted when they reached the hospital. The doctor, a handsome and charming man, who had been treating Victoria, took them all to one side for an update on her progress. 'The part of her brain that controls speech has been damaged,' he explained.

'Can it be corrected?' Rose asked.

'In time, I believe it will get better. She'll need help with her speech - which we can arrange.'

'What about her memory?' John asked, realising from speaking to her earlier that she had no recollection of the fire, or even seemed to know who Robert was, her own husband. In some ways it was a blessing that she had no memory of being pregnant, she just about recognised her own family and even with Violet, she frowned and struggled to remember her name at first. But dealing with the loss of her babies on top of her injuries would have made the situation far worse than it already was. They were thankful for small mercies.

'Victoria is suffering from what is known as *retrograde amnesia* - a loss of memory prior to the fire.'

'Will it come back?' Violet asked, feeling sick. She missed her sister dreadfully and it pained her so much when Victoria had hardly recognised her.

'Yes I'm confident it will - but in most cases like this - the memory returns like pieces of a jigsaw puzzle - randomly.' He gave a small sigh. 'Be patient with her and be prepared for a long road ahead to recovery.' He glanced at the papers in his hand and then back to the Crawfords again. 'The burns - most of them anyway - are superficial and will heal - but there will be some that will leave permanent scarring.'

'The one on the side of her face?' Rose dabbed her eyes. Her beautiful daughter, she couldn't bear to hear much more. 'Will that remain permanent?'

'Yes - more than likely, and a few on her breasts and stomach too.'

Violet covered her mouth. Victoria was beautiful inside and out, but she couldn't imagine how this would affect her sister psychologically. Her breasts in particular, it was as if Victoria had been stripped of her womanhood.

'The hardest part,' the doctor continued 'will be when Victoria sees herself in the mirror for the first time - after the bandaging is removed. We will have to do everything in our power to help regain her confidence.'

There was a stunned silence as each of them struggled with the news. The doctor left them alone. John embraced his wife and daughter. 'We should be thankful,' he said.

'Thankful?' they both said in unison.

He looked at them both. 'She is alive - we could have been burying her this week.'

When he said it like that, neither of them dare disagree. Yes, she was alive and, as the doctor said, it would be a long and difficult road ahead to recovery, but they were prepared to help her every step of the way.

Sophie sat down next to James. The pub had just closed and this had been the first time he had shown his face in days which, to be fair, she found to be perfectly acceptable given his injuries and everything that was happening, so Sophie had said nothing and welcomed him with open arms when he turned up. He did not embrace her but instead poured himself a drink. He sipped a small whisky at one end of the bar, lost in thought and seeming very down.

'James?' Sophie tapped him on the arm and gave a soft smile. He looked up at her with a forlorn expression; all she wanted to do was take him in her arms and comfort him, but he didn't seem to want her to touch him. She noticed his eyes were moist. 'Go and see 'im,' she said, sitting down next to him.

'It's my fault he's in there - why the hell would he want to see me?' He hated the sound of his angry and bitter tone, but he couldn't help it. Right now he loathed himself for causing so much havoc.

'It's not your fault,' she snapped. 'You didn't make 'im start a fire - you didn't tell Victoria to go inside mill that night - none of this is your fault.'

'We don't know that he did start the fire,' he replied with an angry tone. 'If I'd not played cards with him -won from him...' He hung his head low and wiped a tear, then took a deep breath before downing his whisky.

'If...if...if,' Sophie stood up straight. 'You can't change past and you did not start that fire - 'e did.'

'Why do you believe that he is guilty?' his voice was now raised in anger. 'You – you of all people I thought would stand by me – support me – support Robert – he's my family- God knows I've hardly got any left now!'

'And whose fault is that? 'Robert – 'e drove Lillian away – may I remind you. Folk in Whitby and in Ruswarp believe 'e did it and so do police. James you 'ave to face facts – it's likely 'e did do it - out of anger - out of spite - whatever reason - but none of this is your fault.'

'Isn't it?' he glared back at her and then got up and walked towards the door.

'Where you goin'?' she called out to him.

'Where do you think?' he shouted back, slamming the door behind him. She ran outside to find him halfway up the street.

'Wait! If you're goin' t' visit 'im I'll come with you – for support.'

He stopped and turned to face her.

'It's no place for a woman,' he replied harshly.

'I'll be judge of that,' she said defensively. 'They said public 'ouse were no place for a woman.'

'It isn't,' he shouted back, as he briskly walked off down the road.

She stared at his retreating back with disbelief. A tear trickled down her cheek as she turned and made her way back to the pub.

There was a noticeable change in the weather now as the feel of autumn set in. A cool northerly wind picked up and James pulled his coat tighter around himself against the wind, making his way from the train station in Scarborough towards the prison. He could see two looming brick turrets and a large archway with black wrought iron gates, resembling an old fort, or castle, before him.

A guard standing at the entrance with bad skin and a mean gaze eyed James up and down.

'I need to see my brother - Robert Hawkes,' James said.

The guard blinked and checked his watch. 'Tisn't visitin' time.'

'I don't care -open the door,' said James, he was not in the mood to argue with him.

The guard wiped his nose across his sleeve. 'Tisn't safe - there's been a breakout of fever.'

James watched him cautiously and decided he was probably bluffing. 'Open up.'

'You need authority.' He pushed his shoulders back and stood tall.

'Oh believe me I have authority - Samuel Turner sent me.' Another lie, what was Robert doing to him? He never lied - he hated lying, but *needs must in times like this*, he thought. 'And if you don't open that door and take me to my brother at once - I'll have you dismissed for neglecting your duties.'

The guard swallowed hard. 'Of course Sir - very sorry Sir - follow me.'

He led him through a maze of dimly lit corridors. There was a sudden burst of cries, moans, groans and animal like noises. The prisoners could hear them approaching. They turned right into an area of many cells that looked more like cages. A terrible stench of sweat and urine caught James off guard. He reached for a handkerchief in his coat pocket and placed it over his nose and mouth, trying not to give in to the desire to vomit right there and then.

They turned a corner and passed a cell with three men, one of which was chained to a wall, his wrists blue and purple, blood dripping down from the side of his face.

'These conditions are appalling,' James spoke out at last, now standing next to the guard.

'Their crimes are appalling,' the guard replied. 'That one's dangerous, 'e needs to be kept chained or 'e'll 'arm t'others.'

'You want to see your brother? 'E's over there,' he pointed to the end cell with five men, all huddled on the floor, barely room for them to lie down. Dressed in rags, they looked under-fed, exhausted and generally in a bad physical condition. Robert sat in the far corner, hardly recognisable, with a full beard and scruffy hair. He rose carefully to his feet, he swayed a little and winced at the pain in his ribs as he straightened his back and walked towards them.

'Get him out of the cell at once,' James demanded. The guard unlocked the cage and grabbed hold of Robert's arm, thrusting him forward. Robert pulled away from his grip and the guard stepped back, just enough to let them speak in private.

'Come to gloat,' Robert snarled.

James shook his head, full of remorse, not being able to bear seeing his own brother in such a terrible state. 'I never meant for any of this to happen – the mill - the money - you can have it all back.'

Robert said nothing, just stared at him with discontent.

'Robert - I'll get you out of here.'

Robert didn't react, he seemed to be staring right through him.

'I need you to tell me the truth - did you start the fire?'

Robert remained silent.

'For God's sake Robert - yes or no?'

'No!' Robert replied flatly.

'Right - alright, I believe you.'

'But I did pay Charlie Crouch to tell you that fancy woman of yours had gone into the mill.'

'You did what?' James stared at him incredulously. 'Why?'

'Why do you think? You had taken everything from me - I was angry.'

'So much so you wanted me to burn to death?'

Robert shook his head, this time he looked remorseful.

'I wasn't – I wasn't thinking straight – but - if I had not tricked you into that fire - you would not have saved Victoria.' Pearls of sweat trickled down Robert's face. He coughed, and then the tickle at the back of his throat turned into a raging coughing fit.

'Water! Give him water!' James called over to the guard. The guard laughed at him, then turned his back.

James ran over to him, placed a firm hand on his shoulder and forced him around as hard as he could. With anger burning in his eyes he said in a low precise voice. 'Get me water or I will report you for mistreating these men!'

Robert, still coughing and red in the face, fell to his knees.

'NOW!' James bellowed. With that the guard went to fetch some water.

James held out his hand for Robert and helped him to his feet, he then used the wall to steady himself.

'I sent you into a burning fire,' he croaked and coughed, 'And yet you still give me your hand - *Saint James* – always so decent – so correct.'

'I might despise you - but you are still my brother,' James said.

The guard returned with water and handed it to him. Robert guzzled it, spluttering and coughing in between.

'He needs to be seen by a doctor. Many of these men need to be seen by a medical professional,' James said, looking at the others in the cages behind.

'There's nowt wrong wi'em.'

'I thought you said they had a fever?' James said, calling the guard's bluff.

'Aye, those that 'ave – well they've been treated.'

James, despite the size of the guard, grabbed him by the neck and forced him up against the wall, taking him completely by surprise. 'I'm losing my patience with you - my brother is coughing violently and running a fever - get him a doctor now - or I will go straight to the top and sort this - one visit to judge Samuel Turner and you - you my friend….'

'Alright!' The guard put his hands up in the air, surrendering himself. Samuel Turner had a reputation for treating prisoners fairly and he knew the consequences would not be good if he failed to obey. 'This 'as all been a mis-understandin' that's all - course I'll get 'im a doctor.'

'Good,' James stepped away from him, pleased he had got through to him at last. 'And you'll get the doctor to take a look at the others too?' he pointed towards the cells behind them.

'Aye, of course.' He then dashed off.

Robert managed a small smile. 'That temper of yours – you really need to learn to control it.'

James raised an eyebrow, not amused.

'What happened Robert –when you left the stables - was the mill already on fire?'

Robert shook his head. 'No – I- I don't know - maybe it was - maybe it wasn't.'

'What do you mean - you don't know? You can hardly fail to see a burning building in front of you.'

'I didn't look at the mill - I was too angry to see anything. I rushed out of the stables and down to the river - next thing I knew folk were shouting and thick smoke filled the air......How's Victoria? They won't tell me anything.'

James sighed heavily, he wanted to believe him but there was a small doubt, a nagging feeling in the back of his mind that Robert may not be telling the truth. 'She's conscious now,' he replied.

'Thank goodness she's alive - I've been going out of my mind with worry.'

So much so he had waited only until now to ask after her, James noted. 'She has problems with her speech and memory - apparently.'

'I see,' Robert looked away, trying to hide his emotions. James wondered if Robert felt emotional through affection for Victoria, or guilt for what he might have done.

The doctor appeared with the guard. 'I'll take it from here.' He led Robert back into the cell. The guard turned to face James. 'I'll see you out Sir.' James looked over at Robert. 'I'll be back soon - I'll make some enquiries - see what I can do - I'll get you out of here.'

Robert shook his head. 'I wouldn't bother -they've got me banged to rights.'

'You are innocent - you said so yourself,' James replied. Robert didn't reply. He lifted up his shirt for the doctor to examine him.

'This way, Sir,' the guarded gestured, trying not to overstep the mark again, but make his point clear that it really was time for James to leave and before he had the chance to see the terrible bruising on Robert's ribs and back. He himself had been the one who had given them to him on his arrival.

Alfie sat up in bed to eat his soup and bread, served to him by Eleanor. He looked much better now. His eyes were bright and he had a twinkle in them. He seemed to be getting back to his old self again. Mrs Horner had visited that morning, as she did every morning, and so had Alfie's brothers and Becky too. They had gone now and Eleanor and Alfie were alone.

'You make a good nurse,' he said, dunking a wedge of bread into a thick vegetable soup.

'Glad you think so,' she smiled. She had been so worried about him and now she was relieved to see him on the mend.

'When I'm better,' he said, forcing the bread to one side of his mouth so that he could speak, 'would you come fishin' with me again?' he asked with hope.

She stood up and walked towards the window and turned her back to him.

'I promise not to try owt - no funny business - just as friends like,' he said, worried now that he might have upset her again. She was so easily offended, but he still liked her very much, more than liked her, he loved her, and on top of that she had saved his life.

She stared out at the sprawling land, the grass and weeds were getting high. She had missed watching Alfie out there, flexing his muscles, looking strong and handsome, and it suddenly dawned on her just how much she found him to be attractive as well as liked him. But how could she ever get over George? She had loved George dearly and he had broken her heart the day he left. She wondered where he was now. Would he ever come back to find her? Probably not.

'Maybe it was a bad idea - we don't 'ave to go fishin' - not if you don't want to.' He took a mouthful of soup, his eyes still fixed on her back. 'Bit nippy at this time of year any 'ow.'

She didn't reply.

'You – you don't trust me – after last time - I understand,' he said, with sadness in his eyes.

She turned to face him with a small smile. 'Of course I trust you - you great lump! Now eat your soup before it gets cold.'

He grinned happily at her and then slurped his soup. She rolled her eyes, smiled, and left him to it.

James returned to *Heron House* later that day, mentally and physically drained. His arm had been hurting for hours, having forgotten to take the painkillers the doctor had prescribed, and he could still smell the stench of the prison on his clothes. Eleanor, as if reading his mind, greeted him with a glass of water and his tablets.

'I know exactly why I hired you,' he said, taking them from her.

'A letter came for you today,' she walked over to the mantelpiece, picked up a small white envelope and handed it to him. He recognised the handwriting straight away. It was from Lillian.

'Supper normal time, Sir?' Eleanor enquired.

'Yes please, Eleanor.' He opened the letter.

'Will you be dining alone?' she asked cautiously, not knowing how his relationship was these days with Miss Dickens. He did not

- 270 -

seem to be spending as much time with her as before and she had not been to *Heron House* for more than a week now.

'Yes, alone' he answered. 'How's our patient?' he asked, as an afterthought.

Eleanor smiled brightly. 'Alfie is doin' just fine.' She left the room feeling pleased that, at last, some normality had resumed. Captain Hawkes was home, without Miss Dickens, and Alfie, dear sweet Alfie, was on the mend. She sighed with a smile and made her way towards the pantry.

James read Lillian's letter. She had no idea about the fire or Robert's arrest and he knew he must write to her and tell her everything; she had a right to know. But it seemed such a shame to spoil her happiness.

The wedding had been everything she had ever dreamt of and more, with no expense spared. The Beckwiths had really gone to town, and shown everyone how an English wedding in America should be done. After a beautiful church wedding the reception was held at the Waldorf Astoria Hotel, one of New York's finest hotels and, this was also where the Beckwiths had been staying. Lillian and Jack had moved into their New York penthouse, with views over the Hudson River, and although there was plenty of room for Jack's parents, Verity had insisted the young couple needed their own space. Verity had pulled out all the stops to make her daughter-in-law's day a special one, with her being so far away from home and with no family present. She had also taken her shopping, paid for her to be pampered at the beauty parlour and they had many lunches in fine restaurants. Lillian praised Verity no end in her letter, saying she was like a mother to her.

Lillian and Jack were blissfully happy and she loved New York, the way of life, the shops, parties; far more glamorous than Yorkshire. She ended the letter by announcing she was already pregnant and that she and Jack are delighted with the news. Verity and Lord Beckwith were now heading back to England and she missed them. *When will you come and see us James?'* she asked.

James folded the letter back into the envelope and leaned his head back on the chair, wearily, contemplating his reply. If truth be told, he could think of nothing better than getting on a boat to New York right now and leaving his troubles far behind.

Chapter Nineteen

The past four months had been difficult for everyone. Victoria had made little progress with regaining her memory, although her speech was significantly better. She could not remember Robert, let alone being married to him and still she could not remember that she had been expecting twins at the time of the fire. She felt sad, at times despondent and often frustrated. She felt no grief, not as a mother should have felt under such circumstances. It was if it had happened to someone else and she was on the outside looking in. Snippets of information came to her in sudden flashes, as the doctors had predicted, but often too quickly and she had no time to recall them properly. She had, strangely enough, recognised James when he had visited the Crawfords to update them on Robert and the impending trial. It was not clear to her exactly what she remembered, but there was a fondness to her smile whenever she saw him, something that both pleased and pained James while in her presence. He missed her and she seemed only a shell of the person he once knew.

Christmas had passed uneventfully. James had spent a quiet Christmas day with Sophie at *Heron House*. With Lillian in New York and Robert in prison, not to mention it being the first Christmas that Sophie had spent without Uncle Nick, it all felt strange and not right to celebrate. They had eaten a modest meal of fish and vegetables and had given Eleanor the best part of Christmas day off, which she was delighted about as it meant she could spend it with Alfie and the rest of the Horner family. This year they could afford a goose, which Mrs Horner cooked to perfection, it was all thanks to Alfie's employment at *Heron House* and the other boys also managing to find work and chip in with the cost of Christmas. They enjoyed a fine meal with plenty of festive fun and games.

Sophie seemed pensive and quieter than usual and James had been too pre-occupied with his own thoughts to even notice. She no longer knew what to say to him. Every time they spoke about Robert or the fire, James would shut her out. She no longer felt close to him, they were becoming more like acquaintances than friends or lovers. They were both lonely, both needed to draw comfort from somewhere, yet from each other no longer seemed to be enough.

The Crawfords had got together with the Beckwiths at *Bramblewick House* during Christmas, and this had helped lift Victoria's mood, in fact she was becoming far more positive and confident too, especially about her appearance. She had grown her hair longer and styled it so that her curls were fuller, hiding the scar on the side of her face. Apart from that one scar on her face, the others were not visible to the eye, as long as her dresses did not show too much cleavage. She found it mentally draining not remembering and having to ask her parents who people were and so forth, but they didn't mind. Violet was very patient and spent as much time as she could with her sister.

James had kept his word and had worked hard with Jim and the millers, in between regular visits to the prison, to get the mill rebuilt and operational again. The mill reopened at the end of January, 1912. To look at it now, you would never have known there had been a fire; it was as good as new and even boasted a new extension for a larger granary. The mill ran like clockwork once more, and despite feeling guilty for the way he had ended up in possession of the mill, James had to admit he enjoyed every minute of running it and the millers enjoyed having him as their new employer. However, he had every intention of handing it back to Robert, once Robert was a free man again. But not everyone believed Robert would be a free man any time soon. The workers had not forgiven their former employer for gambling with their future, although the outcome had been most agreeable, now that the Captain was in charge. '*Mr 'Awkes can rot in 'ell* – for all I care,' Mary had said, and the others agreed too. Jim, a little more lenient, said, '*bit harsh – Mary – to let 'im rot in 'ell - but a man who gambles on folks lives is not a man t' be reckoned with in my book.*' Charlie Crouch had said very little on the subject, but he had his reasons for keeping quiet.

On the morning of the trial, the 21st of February 1912, it began to snow in earnest. By nine o'clock, when the first fall of snow ceased, the fields and trees were already a blanket of white. Branches bowed and thick sheets of ice drifted down the River Esk. There was an unusually profound silence surrounding *Heron House*, and only the faint noise of a dog barking somewhere in the distance could be heard. Eleanor, Alfie and James had left over an hour ago for Scarborough.

Snow covered most of Scarborough, including the beach. Footprints embedded into the snow from early morning walkers were now being wiped away by gentle waves letting off a spray of white foam to match the snow. James sighed wistfully, watching a man playing with his young son and dog in the distance, all of them laughing, running and having fun.

Today was the big day, the day everyone had been waiting for. If found guilty, of starting the fire and manslaughter, Robert could face years in prison and if found not guilty, he could walk away a free man, but what did he have left to come home to? The workers at the mill did not want him back, his wife did not even know who he was any more, and the Crawfords were not ready to welcome him back into the family fold, even if he were to be acquitted. John Crawford had believed right from the start Robert was guilty and not only that, he would never forgive him for gambling the mill and taking the security of his daughter's future away, not to mention the loss of his unborn grandchildren. He wholeheartedly blamed Robert for everything, so much so he refused to go to the trial and forbade Rose and Victoria to go too. He had sent a note to the court, informing them that Victoria was not well enough to take the stand and would be of no use without any memory or the ability to speak properly.

Sophie had offered to come to give her support, but James had told her to open the pub and work as normal, he'd rather go alone.

The courtroom was gloomy at the best of times, but without even so much as a ray of sunshine through the dirty windows, and it being so bitterly cold inside and out, it felt worse than James had expected as he took a seat on a hard wooden bench. Eleanor and Alfie waited outside, Eleanor would be called to the witness stand later that morning. 'I'm a bag of nerves,' she admitted to Alfie.

'You're bound to be - which is why I said I'd come with you.' He took her hands and held them tightly; they were moist though cold. 'Just tell them what you remember - that's all they'll want.'

'That's exactly it - I don't remember - I was too worried about finding 'elp for you.'

'They must 'ave a reason for you to take witness stand - anything you can tell them will 'elp - I'm sure.'

She nodded. By rights she should be on trial herself for helping to dispose of a dead body, she thought, and then brushed the image of Bill Sanders' dead limp hand, hanging out of the bushes on that fateful night, from her mind. She needed to stay focused and she could not allow herself time to think of Bill or George now.

Cobwebs hung from the rafters in each corner, everywhere thick with dust and the room looked like it had not been cleaned in many a year. More and more people filed in through the wooden doors, taking their places. A clerk dropped his papers and bent down to pick them up, sniffing, as a droplet fell from his nose onto the papers, causing the ink to run. He took out his handkerchief, catching his sneeze just in time. James spotted the doctor who had treated Robert; he too possessed a bright red nose and looked unwell. James had visited Robert only two days ago, and found his brother not in a good state of health. He was suffering from a bad cold and a high fever, which was spreading like wild-fire around the prison.

The jury, men of all ages, took the bench and spectators above in the public gallery gathered for the trial in hope of a guilty outcome. It was a shame this crime did not carry a hanging sentence, as they would have preferred a "good hanging," rather than a prison sentence. Like vultures circling their prey, they chattered and jeered.

The prosecution and defence lawyers had arrived and then Robert was led into the box at the top of the courtroom, in full view of everyone. James looked up at him and their eyes met from across the room. Robert looked deathly pale, his beard long and scruffy and his face full of cuts and sores. He was extremely underweight and he seemed to be shaking as he sat down, more than likely from both fear and from being ill. James gave him a small, reassuring smile but Robert stared vacantly back at him, showing no emotion at all.

Samuel Turner, despite leaving his home in plenty of time that morning, was delayed owing to the snow blocking many of the small country lanes. Having abandoned his coach and horses, he walked the last half an hour of the journey with his walking cane in his hand, hobbling and wincing from the pain in his foot. He finally arrived, flung on his gown and wig, and with a flushed face and his wig skew- whiff, he threw open the doors from his office leading to the back of the court where he dropped down into his seat with a sigh of relief.

And so the proceedings began…

Robert sneezed into a handkerchief given to him by the clerk nearby. James watched him with concern. He looked like he needed to go to bed, not stand trial.

The first witness to take the stand was the prison doctor.

'Doctor, would you say that Mr Hawkes is well enough to stand trial?' Mr Thompson, a small stout man from the defence team asked.

Everyone looked at Robert. The prosecution presumed this was obviously the defence's tactic of delaying the case, giving them more time. Robert, on cue, sneezed into his handkerchief again. The doctor looked over at the same prison guard that James had threatened, standing at the back of the court. The guard flashed him a forewarning look and so the doctor composed himself with a small throat clearing cough and answered the question as he had been paid to.

'Yes - he's well enough. He is suffering from a common cold virus as many of us are right now - perfectly normal for this time of the year – you only have to look around this courtroom, to see for yourself.'

James stood up in protest. 'But my lord - you can clearly see my brother is extremely unwell.'

'Sit down Mr Hawkes,' if the court requires your opinion we will ask for it.

Victoria sat on the window-sill gazing out of the window. Two clouds separated, making way for the sun. It dazzled brilliantly, causing a brief thaw. Branches and bushes dripped and avalanches of snow began to slip from the roof and drop down onto the ground beneath the window. A robin hopped along, leaving a trail of its tiny prints in the thawing snow.

Downstairs Victoria had been listening to her parents talk about Robert's trial. It was like listening to an account of a terrible tale, a tale about someone she had never met. She had a deep sense of guilt. Even if she didn't remember him, he was still her husband; she must have loved him enough to marry him. Surely he could not be the monster they made him out to be. What if he really loved her, needed her to be there? By not going she was letting him down. Her eyes wandered to the direction of the mill and then, without warning, a memory came back again - a flashback. There was a church with many people, at the altar she stood in her wedding dress and a man with dark hair stood next to her. They were smiling, happy, and exchanged rings. She wiped a tear away from her eyes and rushed through the house to find Violet. Eventually she found her in the library, reading. She burst into the room taking Violet by surprise. 'Did I - I love him?'

'Who?' Violet asked.

'Robert. Did I lo- love him?' she asked again.

'I – oh – Victoria – it - it was complicated.' Violet put down her book and went over to her.

'How can it bah-be comp - complicated? I married him - I must have lo -loved him.' Her speech was slow, so much slower than her mind, which frustrated her further. Her eyes searched Violet's for an answer.

'I think you did learn to love him. You were happy the last time I saw you before – before the fire,' Violet said, wondering if she should tell her more. Her parents had avoided talking about Robert or the babies so as not to upset her.

'Why didn't I lo-love him from the st-start?' none of this made any sense.

Violet sighed and prompted her to sit down. She needed to tell her, it was unfair to keep the truth from her. She needed to tell her why she had married Robert.

'The court summons Miss Eleanor Jones to take the stand,' Samuel said, glancing at his notes, then expectantly at the stand, as Eleanor made her way there. She placed her right hand on the bible and swore in, - shaking. She looked over at Alfie who nodded encouragingly and then at James who managed a small smile.

Mr Thompson from the defence stood before her. 'Miss Jones, on the night of the twenty fifth of September 1911 - in your own words - please describe to us all what you saw that evening as you passed the mill?'

'I was in a big 'urry - didn't see much to be honest.' She swallowed hard and continued. 'Alfie – Alfie 'Orner that is,' she glanced over at him then back to the man questioning her, 'ad been 'urt badly by Captain 'Awkes's 'orse - kicked in 'ead to be precise. I thought he were gona die - so I ran for 'elp.'

'And running for help - did you pass the mill?' Mr Thompson asked, getting bored already and wanting her to get on with it.

'Yes.'

'Can you remember what time that was?'

'After eight o'clock - I think,' she seemed unsure.

'You think? How far after eight o'clock?'

He had briefed her outside of the courtroom and she seemed to have forgotten everything so far. He sighed.

'Can you please try to remember the time, Miss Jones?'

'Well it was gettin' late and I wasn't sure if Captain 'Awkes would be back for 'supper. I 'ad it ready for 'im before I left – s'pose it probably was more like nine come to think of it - by the time I found Alfie and I left for 'elp.

'Nine o'clock you say?' Mr Thompson asked, just to be sure.

'I recall 'earing the church bell ring – so yes- was later than eight and seeing as the church bell only rings on every hour - must 'ave been nine.'

'And was the mill on fire?'

'No. There was a light on in one of top rooms - rest of mill were in darkness – I remember that much.'

'Is there anything else you remember Miss Jones?'

'Lightnin' - it lit up sky like a great big light - loud crashes of thunder - and then I ran on to Mrs 'Orner's 'ouse – that's Alfie's 'ouse.

He seemed pleased, finally, with Eleanor's response. 'Thank you Miss Jones,' he replied. 'That will be all. No further questions my Lord.'

Mr Nesbitt then stood up, in preparation for his cross examination with Eleanor Jones.

'Victoria was shocked and grabbed a chair to sit down. 'And he was - was the fa-father – Robert? Not James?'

'Robert was the father. Vicky you did what was the right thing to do. You married the father of your babies.' Violet took Victoria's hands into her own and held them tightly. Victoria stared almost straight through her, trying to make sense of it all. How could she not remember something so important in her life? She suddenly stood up abruptly. 'I ha - have to go -to court – I - I have to see him.'

Violet looked panicked, 'No Vicky, you can't. Remember what Papa said - he doesn't want any of us to go.'

'I don't ca - ca- care. Are you com –coming - or will I – I go alone?'

'You can't go alone – it's too dangerous - with your memory.' She checked her watch. 'If we leave now we can catch the train to Scarborough on the hour. Get yourself ready and meet me at the back courtyard in ten minutes.'

Victoria agreed and dashed off.

'The defence calls Charlie Crouch to the stand.' The announcement took everyone by surprise. Charlie rose and made his way to the front, put his hand on the bible and swore in. Other than old Jim, no one else had bothered to turn up from the mill, not feeling it worth losing a day's wages over. Charlie had risked the others finding out that he would be defending Robert. They would not be happy if they knew one of their own men had betrayed them by defending Robert Hawkes.

'Mr Crouch - how long were you in the employ of Mr Robert Hawkes?' Mr Thompson asked.

Charlie glanced over at Robert, who again showed no emotion but was still shaking and sweating.

'Three years,' he replied.

'And how would you describe Mr Hawkes, as an employer?'

'Fair - 'onest – a good person - is Mr 'Awkes.'

'Was he ever violent to you, or anyone else at the mill, for that matter?'

Charlie shook his head defiantly. 'No never. Mr 'Awkes were always kind to everyone. He made sure no one went without.'

'Did everyone like Mr Hawkes at the mill?'

'Aye, they did. They said he was a goodun which is why I'm standin' 'ere today - don't care what they say about 'im now - at time they liked 'im….'

'Alright Mr Crouch, I think you've answered the question now,' Samuel Turner cut in.

'Would you say that Mr Hawkes - in your opinion - would be capable of starting the fire at the mill?'

'No, never.'

Murmurs rippled through the public gallery.

Samuel demanded order and then said, 'Mr Thompson, is any of this relevant? What Mr Crouch believes is neither here nor there.'

Mr Thompson looked at Samuel and said, 'The relevancy to my questioning – my lord – will soon become clear.'

'Where was Mr Hawkes when you came out of the stables - after the card game?'

'At riverside - I saw 'im run up bank when fire broke out.'

'How did he seem to you?'

'Devastated - he loves mill - it were 'is 'ole world.'

'Was he aware that his wife was in the building?'

'No - not at that moment.'

'So at that moment his devastation was based on seeing the mill on fire - his whole livelihood up in flames - before he even knew his wife was inside - is that what you are saying Mr Crouch?'

'Aye – yes.'

'So he didn't act like a man who had just started a fire himself?'

'Mr Thompson - don't put words into the witness's mouth,' Samuel Turner called out, he then winced at the pain in his foot. 'Members of the jury, I instruct you to disregard Mr Thompson's last comment.'

'Sorry my lord – I have no further questions for Mr Crouch.'

He sat down again, feeling pleased. So far he had shown the jury that the fire had not started before nine o'clock, which would be very significant later on, and he had shown them Robert was liked, respectable and of good character. It was a good start.

Violet had scribbled a note and left it in the hallway, saying that she and Victoria had quite fancied some fresh air and had gone to Whitby to watch the fishing boats coming in.

The train departed for Scarborough on time. Victoria reached out and held her sister's hand. 'Vi, I'm do - doing the right thing - aren't I?

'If your heart tells you to be there - then you must be,' Violet replied, although she had her doubts. It might be a disturbing scene for Victoria, especially if she remembered Robert when she saw him.

'The prosecution calls Lord Beckwith to the stand.' Heads turned, unaware that Lord Beckwith would even be there, let alone take the stand. James's forehead creased into a deep frown. What an earth would they want with Lord Beckwith? The double wooden doors opened and Lord Beckwith, very well tailored as usual, took oath and faced everyone. Robert, for the first time, showed some sort of emotion, an emotion which could be likened to fear. He possessed a terrible feeling in the pit of his stomach. The Beckwiths would not spare him after the way he had treated Jack.

Mr Nesbitt, a tall, broad man with almost black piercing eyes led the case for the prosecution. He had sat patiently throughout Mr Thompson's presentation of the case for the defence without saying a word, not at all worried by the opposition, he had plenty up his sleeve.

'Lord Beckwith - can I ask what your connection is with Mr Hawkes?'

'He is my daughter-in-law's brother,' Lord Beckwith replied, matter of fact, standing tall.

'Can you please tell the court, in your own words, what you claim Mr Hawkes did to your son - Jack Beckwith?'

Lord Beckwith looked up at Robert with distaste. He had only learned of the incident when he was in New York. Jack had been tipsy and had let slip why Lillian had been in a rush to leave for New York, and had agreed to marry in New York instead of Yorkshire.

'It seemed that Robert Hawkes did not agree with my son's proposal of marriage to his sister,' he said primly. 'And so he attacked him.'

'Where did the attack take place?'

'At *Somersby Hill* - my daughter-in-law's residence before moving to New York. Robert Hawkes beat my son so badly, and within an inch of his life - which is why I want this animal...'

'Thank you Lord Beckwith, please just stick to answering the questions,' Samuel called out, keeping him in check. 'May I remind the prosecution that Mr Hawkes is not on trial for allegedly beating Lord Beckwith's son.'

'When did this attack take place?' Mr Nesbitt continued.

'Early September. Jack stayed at *Somersby Hill* until he was well and then he and Lillian Hawkes left for America.'

'I see. And were there any witnesses to this attack?'

'Yes, Lillian and Victoria, and James too - In fact, I was told that Robert beat James too.'

'His own brother?' Mr Nesbitt turned to look at the jury. They showed no expression. James hung his head. This was so irrelevant now and he just wanted Robert to be free again.

'Yes, his own brother,' Lord Beckwith replied. 'It was, however, James Hawkes who looked after my son and nursed him back to health.' Lord Beckwith glanced over at James with gratitude.

'Why did your son and his fiancé choose to marry in America? Surely they would have wanted family and friends to be present, would they not?' Mr Nesbitt knew exactly where he was heading with the question.

'Because that man,' Lord Beckwith pointed up at Robert, 'bullied and scared them into leaving. His own sister is terrified of him.'

Samuel now stepped in, having heard more than enough. 'I'm sorry, but as interesting as this all is - I reiterate yet again that none of it is relevant to the case in hand – the fire.'

'I'm just getting to that my lord. I just wanted to show the jury and everyone in this courtroom the type of man Robert Hawkes really is,' Mr Nesbitt replied.

A sudden break out of murmurs and soft whispering sounded throughout the courtroom. Samuel banged the desk before him. 'Order!'

Silence then resumed.

Jim was called as the prosecution's next witness.

'You were there at the card game on the 25th September 1911, is that correct?'

'Yes - I was.'

'Whose idea was this card game in the first place?' Mr Nesbitt pushed back his shoulders and waited for Jim's reply.

'Captain 'Awkes.'

'Do you know why James Hawkes suggested this game?'

'Robert 'Awkes owed money to 'im – 'e set up the card game and said they could wipe slate clean if Robert won - and 'e did – win, that is.' Jim paused for breath and then continued. 'Then Captain 'Awkes suggested they play for 'igher stakes – money - mill n'all'

'And Robert Hawkes agreed to all of this? The chance of losing his mill?' Mr Nesbitt enquired incredulously.

'Yes - he even suggested they make it more interesting and they gamble share of Captain 'Awkes public 'ouse and *Somersby 'ill* too.'

'So - let me get this clear – as an employer of many people - who are dependent on the mill for a living – Mr Hawkes then decides to gamble with the workers' livelihood as well as his own?'

'Exactly - that's why we are all upset about it,' said Jim, avoiding looking over at Robert.

'I'm not surprised.' Mr Nesbitt turned to face the jury and raised an eyebrow. This time the jury did appear to be showing signs of siding with Nesbitt. He then returned to questioning Jim.

'And what happened next?'

'E lost everything and got very angry – did Mr 'Awkes. 'E threw table over and grabbed Captain 'Awkes by throat - we all 'ad to step in and save 'im from 'arms way – Mr 'Awkes 'as a vicious temper on 'im you see.'

'And what did Mr Hawkes do next?'

'He ran out of stables. Captain 'Awkes wanted to go after 'im like - but I suggested 'e let 'im calm down first - then Charlie Crouch ran back in and said there was fire at mill.'

'So how long would it have been between Mr Hawkes leaving the stables and then Charlie Crouch coming back in and saying there was a fire?'

Jim contemplated his answer. 'At least ten minutes - I'd say.'

'Plenty of time for Mr Hawkes to start a fire then?'

'Aye,' Jim replied, still avoiding eye contact with Robert.

Mr Nesbitt turned to face the jury. 'Does this sound like a man who is supposed to be,' he glanced at his notes made from the defence plea, 'A fair - honest and good person?' This man, he pointed up at Robert, 'beat his future brother-in-law to a pulp - also beat his own brother - bullied his sister into leaving the country - gambled with the future of his employees at the mill and had motive and time to seek revenge on his brother for winning the game and winning the mill. And how did he seek that revenge? - by burning it down. If he couldn't have the mill for himself, his brother certainly wasn't going to either. His own wife was pulled out of the fire and her unborn twins killed. This is a very serious crime, gentlemen, and a very dangerous man who has committed it.

'NO!' Robert stood up and then fell back in his seat, too weak to defend himself.

A note was handed from the clerk to Samuel Turner. He read it and then spoke, addressing the court and jury. 'Mrs Victoria Hawkes is still suffering from loss of memory and a speech disorder which is why she can not take the stand today. And given the fact that the defendant is so unwell, the court will now adjourn until the morning.' Robert looked relieved as he tried to focus beneath his drooping eyelids. His whole body ached from head to toe. The prison guard, once Samuel had his head turned, yanked Robert to his feet and pushed him down the stairs, away from the court.

As everyone filtered out of the court, Victoria and Violet arrived, rushing up the steps.

'Looks like we are too late,' said Violet, as they approached the main entrance. As they came through the doors, they collided with several people, one of them being James. He seemed utterly astonished to see Victoria standing there before him. 'Victoria?'

She blushed slightly, and forced a small smile, recognising him immediately. Violet spoke first. 'I fear we are too late - has Robert been sentenced?'

James shook his head. 'No - tomorrow it shall continue.' He eyed Victoria from head to toe, still confused but happy to see her, then turned his attention to Violet. 'I thought Victoria was too unwell to answer any questions.'

'She is too unwell, but she wanted to show Robert her support.'

'I am – I am here,' Victoria said, feeling annoyed that they were speaking about her if she was not.

'I'm sorry,' James apologised. 'Robert will be pleased to know you came - I'm sure,' he said with a pang of jealousy. Despite her loss of memory and obvious speech problems, she looked so well. Still as beautiful as ever, and the scar on her face hardly showed beneath her hair, and her stylish hat that matched her coat, showed how elegant she was. He could smell the familiar scent of her perfume from where he was standing and ached to hold her and kiss her again. He chided himself inwardly for being so foolish. Victoria was history now and she was married to his brother for goodness sake.

'We – we will co - come back tom -tomorrow.'

'We'll see how you feel tomorrow,' Violet said to her.

'We'll be – be here,' she sounded resolute.

James smiled, she was still as determined to get her own way. 'Good. Robert will be very pleased to see you.' An awkwardness took over the moment. 'You look well,' he said, addressing Victoria and kicking himself for saying something so ridiculous. How could she be well after everything she had just gone through?

'I – I.' She stopped, leaving them hanging on her every word. What she wanted to say was that she might look well but inside she felt terrible, not remembering anything, not knowing anything. It was as if she was trapped in someone else's life, remembering things that seemed like they happened to a stranger, and not to herself. She felt no emotion towards many people or even places for that matter, but, looking into James's eyes, she felt something, something she couldn't quite place, a feeling of happiness - perhaps because he had saved her from the fire. But she suspected it was something far deeper than that. 'Thank you – for –sa- saving my li- life.' she replied.

'You've already thanked me many times,' he said with a smile.

'It – it- will never b –be enough,' she replied shyly.

'We are all very grateful for what you did for Victoria,' Violet said.

'It's what anyone would have done, in my situation,' he replied modestly. 'I'll accompany you both back on the train - if you'll allow me to?' he said.

Violet nodded in agreement. She liked James. He had always been kind to her. If truth be told, she didn't like Robert very much at all and felt that her sister had most definitely married the wrong brother. Victoria, of course, had only done what was right, given the circumstances at the time.

'I – I'd like that,' Victoria smiled. With either sister each side of him, they took hold of his arms and huddled next to him against the cold, bitter wind and the snow now falling hard again, as they made their way to the railway station, each of them lost in thought. Victoria was confused about the man she was holding on to, and the husband who she didn't remember much at all about, now locked up and awaiting his fate. Victoria wondered what would become of Robert tomorrow, as did James, but he was also enjoying every moment of Victoria holding his arm and being close to her again.

They were glad when the train arrived and they could get inside, out of the extreme cold. They made idle chat, keeping off the subject of Robert and the fire. James told Victoria stories of their childhood and Violet remembered some of them too.

'I would – I wou- would never go scru - scrumping,' Victoria giggled.

'Oh yes you did - didn't she Violet?' James said with a humorous twinkle in his eye.

Violet laughed. 'Yes, and you made me hold the basket while you climbed up the tree with James.'

'It was all your idea,' James teased Victoria, nudging her. 'That old man - what was his name?'

Victoria looked blank of course, but Violet remembered. 'Mr English,' she blurted out in an enthusiastically loud voice as others in the carriage turned around and gave a look of distaste, which made them laugh even more.

'Oh yes - Mr English,' said James. 'He chased us out of the orchard - waving his stick furiously at us.'

'And you ripped your dress on the tree when you came down it,' Violet reminded Victoria.

'Oh no – wha - what did Ma -Mama say?'

'You don't want to know,' Violet chuckled. 'I gave the apples in the basket, with a blanket draped over the top of it, to James to hide.'

'Yes - and no sooner had I reached the end of the path,' said James, 'your father accosted me and asked me what was inside the basket?' I told him a stray kitten - and as he passed me I said *meow*. He turned and looked at me with a straight face and said '*that kitten's not right lad - best get rid*.' Victoria and Violet laughed hysterically, tears rolling down their cheeks, much to the dismay of the other passengers who were sitting quietly, watching the snow covered hills as they passed through the countryside.

Just for that short journey, that short period of time, all was well with the world, and it felt like the old days once more for James, and in an odd sort of way for Victoria too. She felt a strong fondness towards him and an overwhelming feeling of excitement being in his presence.

Chapter Twenty

At Sandsend the tide was out and huge waves leapt and roared in the distance. Ice and foam that had turned into a mucky brown and grey, mixed with sand, were now beginning to fade as a fresh lot of snow fell, covering the full length of the beach. In the distance a few fishing boats bobbed up and down erratically as they made their way back to Whitby. In Ruswarp, the snow was deeper. The steeple of St Bartholomew's Church peeked out from beneath its white covering, and across the way, the full moon reflected over the River Esk, as did the lights still burning brightly at the mill.

Up at *Heron House* a trail of small footprints led up to the stables and stopped at the door. Eleanor had taken Alfie a cup of tea to keep him warm while he attended to the horses.

'You're an angel sent down to look after me - I'm certain of that,' he grinned, accepting the mug from her and taking an appreciative sip.

'And just you remember that,' she chuckled. 'Are you nearly done? It's gettin' nippy out.' She rubbed her hands together to keep warm.

'Aye. They're all groomed and mucked out – and now I just 'ave to give 'em a last feed.'

'Doesn't it scare you - being in 'ere? I mean - with what 'appened.'

Alfie laughed. 'No - course not - might be a different case when a storm breaks out – but not when it's calm like tonight. Blackie only bolted cause he were scared – he knows me well – don't you lad?' He gave him an affectionate rub on the nose and Blackie replied with an appreciative snort.

''E's fond of you – even though 'e kicked your 'ead in,' Eleanor said with a small grin.

'You did good today - in court,' Alfie praised her.

She rolled her eyes. 'It were pointless me being there - I told 'em nothin' they didn't already know.'

'You don't know that for sure - any little detail can 'elp.' Alfie noticed her shiver. He put down his tea and picked up a small blanket from the barn floor, placing it around her shoulders. She smiled gratefully and their eyes locked in a meaningful stare.

'Eleanor?' he said, still standing close to her and with his hands on the blanket he had wrapped around her.

'Yes Alfie,' she replied expectantly.

'I…' He hesitated. Dare he say it?

'Go on - I won't bite,' she said, encouraging him. She knew what he wanted to say and, tonight, she felt like she needed to hear him say it.

'I love you,' he said at last and then kissed her. As much as she wanted him to kiss her, she still couldn't control the urge to pull away.

He looked at her with surprise and then disappointment grew in his eyes. 'I don't understand,' he said.

'You wouldn't - you couldn't.' She turned to walk away and he pulled her back by the arm. She looked down at his firm hand around her arm and he released his grip.

'I might understand if you told me,' he said, with a small, gentle smile.

She stared back at him. She wanted so much to tell him, share her burden with him, but could she really trust him?

'Whatever it is – I – look I just want to understand.' He put an arm around her and led her to sit down on a pile of hay. Much to his surprise she sat down and allowed him to sit next to her. He had expected her to run out on him, as she always did when things became tense between them.

'I'm scared to tell you,' she admitted.

'Scared? You don't need to be scared. Nowt'll shock me or – or- make me love you less.'

She searched his eyes. They were sincere, but she still didn't feel comfortable telling him. 'This will – I know it will.'

'You can tell me owt – promise – 'and on 'eart.' He placed his hand on his heart and smiled.

'I was in love - George Tanner was his name,' she began. By the time she had finished telling Alfie everything, Eleanor was crying openly. It was as if by telling someone, she could open the flood gates and let it all out at long last. Alfie said nothing when she finished, only looked at her in complete and utter astonishment. She felt ashamed and then worried by the expression on his face. Oh what had she done? He must hate her now. She helped get rid of a dead body, what must he think of her?

'I shouldn't 'ave told you,' she said, standing up quickly and throwing the blanket onto the straw.

Alfie stood up too. 'Yes you should've - you should've told me. 'Ow did you keep all this bottled up inside of you for so long?'

'What choice did I 'ave? I'm just as much to blame - I knew about Bill - I – I' she wiped her tears from her stinging eyes. 'I 'elped George get Bill's body on t' boat - I lied t' police.' She let out a small sob. 'What kind of person does that make me, Alfie?'

'A person who was dragged into a situation she couldn't avoid - a person who kept 'er loyalty t' someone she loved - enough not to tell police.' He took her hands into his own and looked deep in her eyes. 'El you need to let go of this now. You've shared it with me – and – and well now you have to let it go or it'll eat you up and destroy the rest of your life.'

'So you're not going t' police – to tell em what I did?'

'Course not.' He gave a look to the heavens and sighed. 'First off its nowt to do with me, and secondly I love you. Do you really think I'd let them cart you off and me never see you again - for somethin' that wasn't your fault?'

She looked relieved, and then she smiled through her tears. 'I love you too. Thank you Alfie.' She hugged him tightly.

'This George Tanner,' said Alfie stroking her hair. 'You know he's never comin' back and if 'e would - well e'd be caught - 'hung even for committing murder.'

She looked at him and nodded her head. She knew that, George had told her the very same thing on the night he left.

'You're not carrying a torch for 'im no more – are you?' he asked with worry.

She shook her head. 'No – not now – besides – even if I were, it'd do me no good. Like you said, he's never comin' back.'

'Police would be last of 'is problems – 'e would 'ave a fight on 'is 'ands if 'e wanted t' take you away from me.'

'You - you daft sod.' Eleanor punched him playfully and then he pulled her close and their lips touched, locking into a meaningful kiss. And this time she did not pull away.

Sophie waited up at *Heron House* for James. John Barrow had offered to look after the pub for a few hours. She had spent the whole day worrying about James, and wondering what had happened at court with Robert. Eleanor had made Sophie tea and warned her he could be a while and that he would probably be very tired when he returned home. Much to Eleanor's annoyance, this did not deter Sophie. Alfie had now gone home and Eleanor began preparing supper, enough for Sophie in case she stayed, although she hoped she wouldn't.

'James, 'ow did it go?' Sophie asked the moment James walked into the room. Eleanor had warned him of his visitor, and although he did not make it known to Eleanor, he was not pleased at the prospect of facing Sophie today, not after the court case and then having spent a wonderfully joyful journey back with Victoria.

'They will continue tomorrow.' James poured himself a brandy and flopped down on the sofa.

''Ow's Robert 'olding up?'

'Not good. He's ill, but the doctor insists he's well enough to stand trial.' He took a swig of brandy and closed his eyes, enjoying the harshness of it hitting the back of his throat.

'It's been busy today.' Sophie sat down next to him. He didn't answer her. 'I missed you. I thought I'd come up and surprise you - John's covering for me,' she said, in another attempt to gain his attention.

He stared at the brandy in his glass pensively, then turned to face her. 'Well, consider me surprised,' he said with sarcasm. She looked at him, not knowing what to say next. He had been so distant of late, not at all the James she met and fell in love with, or the man who had shown her so much support when her uncle had died – the man who had called himself her friend – the man who was so full of love and compassion towards her. She knew it could not be easy for him, with Robert on trial and the guilt he carried for organising the card game, then winning it. There was Victoria to think about too. She could not get the image out of her head, when he had rescued her from the fire, how distraught he was at the prospect of losing her. She realised now that he would never love her like he loved Victoria.

'Was Victoria there today?' she asked, in a less than subtle tone. He looked at her and took another gulp of brandy, finishing it completely.

'Yes,' he replied coolly.

''Ow is she?' she hated herself for asking, and her reason for asking was more than just polite conversation, she wanted to see his reaction when he spoke about her, gauge just how much he was still in love with her.

'Recovering well,' he replied, then placed his glass firmly on the table and rubbed his tired forehead. 'Sophie - forgive me - but I'm extremely weary and fear I shall not be good company this evening.'

She sighed. He didn't want her near him, it was written all over his face. She stood up straight and grabbed her cloak, thrown over the back of the sofa. 'I'll leave you in peace then.'

He attempted a small smile. 'Sorry.'

With her hand poised on the door handle she stopped. She had to say what was on her mind or she would never forgive herself for being so weak. 'James - I'm treadin' on egg shells not to upset you. I don't know what to do - what to say any more and you keep pushin' me away.'

He knew she was right. He was pushing her away, treating her abominably, but his head was all over the place with worrying about Robert and dealing with his emotions towards Victoria. He couldn't give Sophie what she needed right now, if ever. 'I'm sorry,' he said again, his expression full of regret. 'I need to get through this somehow, and I need to do it alone.'

She rushed towards him and knelt down before him. 'But you don't 'ave to do it alone. I'm 'ere for you. I want to be 'ere for you - like you were for me - I owe you that.'

'You shouldn't feel like you owe me anything,' he said, feeling uncomfortable with her kneeling at his feet. He stood up and walked across to the fireplace, resting his arm on the mantelpiece. 'You owe me nothing Sophie.' His tone was stern and business like. 'What I did for you was out of friendship. We are good friends and business partners.'

He might just as well have slapped her hard across the face, as the sting of his words hurt just the same. 'Good friends? Business partners? She repeated his words, her tone matching her expression of disbelief.

'Yes,' he replied, not really grasping why she seemed to be so upset. He would have thought that to be obvious.

She stood up and placed her cloak around her shoulders. 'So do you share your bed with all of your friends? All those you 'ave ever done business with?' She wiped away a stray tear. He suddenly felt guilty, grasping her meaning, and he walked towards her. 'Sophie – forgive me – I - I didn't mean to upset you.'

'Well you did.' She turned and stormed out of the room leaving him staring vacantly at the closed door she had just walked out of. In a burst of anger, he picked up the empty brandy glass on the table and threw it as hard as he could at the door. It shattered into tiny pieces as did he, as he fell back onto the sofa and cried for the first time in years.

The court resumed at eleven o'clock the following day. Victoria and Violet had met James at the railway station after making their excuses to Rose. Thankfully, John had a meeting with a business associate in Whitby and did not suspect a thing. Both her parents had completely bought their story of them going for a stroll to Whitby to watch the fishing boats come in. After Rose had scolded them both for walking around in the cold, she had to admit that Victoria did seem much happier for it and perhaps the fresh air and quality time with Violet had done her good.

The courtroom was packed with more spectators than the day before, despite it still being bitterly cold outside, even colder than yesterday. They all took their places, the same faces and new ones, many with red cheeks and dripping noses. Colds and flu were spreading like wildfire around Scarborough this winter.

Robert was escorted in once more, still looking deathly pale, coughing and sneezing, and if anything, he looked worse than yesterday. His eyes looked sunken and encompassed with dark circles. He suddenly noticed Victoria sitting on the other side of the room next to Violet and James. He smiled sorrowfully at her. She looked so pretty. She didn't deserve any of this, a husband like him. She would be better off without him. The best thing would be for him to be found guilty and locked up. Today he felt nothing other than self-pity, now seeing his wife sitting there before him. He hung his head in shame.

Domenico Cifaldi was the first person to be called in by the defence – Mr Thompson. Samuel Turner groaned as he stretched out his leg under the table, his gout was giving him much trouble today. He hoped that they would reach a resolution swiftly.

Domenico Cifaldi's big brown eyes glanced over at Robert. He didn't believe for one moment that Robert was capable of such a crime, and he had every reason not to believe it too.

Mr Thompson produced a brown envelope, containing a photograph. 'Mr Cifaldi, can you please confirm that you took this photograph of the mill yourself?' He held it up for him to see.

'Yes, I did,' he replied.

'What date and time was it taken?'

'Twenty fifth of September at-a five minutes past nine. I remember because-a the church clock of St Bartholomew – it-a chimed at-a nine – then five minutes after - I took-a the photograph, when the lightning struck-a the mill. It was incredible timing.'

Mr Thompson held the photograph up in full view. 'In deed it was. This remarkable photograph was taken after nine o'clock, showing lightning striking the mill,' he informed the court.

Victoria whispered something in Violet's ear and Violet suddenly looked startled. She crept across the bench and whispered in the ear of a gentleman on the defence team. People were now noticing, and Samuel banged the table for order, stopping Mr Thompson in mid-flow. 'Silence!' his voice boomed, echoing around the room.

'If Mr Robert Hawkes was still in the stables at the time the fire broke out…' Mr Thompson continued. Mr Nesbitt stood up in protest.

'There is no proof of Mr Hawkes being in the stables at this time. Not one person at the card games could decipher what time exactly it was when he left. A clerk handed a note to Samuel Turner and he read the paper and then called for silence again. 'We shall take a five minute interlude. No longer than five minutes,' he said, looking sternly at the defence.

The gentleman who had spoken with Violet now whispered something into Mr Thompson's ear. You could have heard a pin drop as everyone tried so hard to listen and fathom out was going on. Mr Thompson gestured to Victoria to come with him outside the courtroom, away from prying eyes and ears.

'What's happening?' James asked Violet, not having a clue what was going on.

'Victoria has remembered the night of the fire and what happened.'

Robert started another coughing fit. A clerk passed him a handkerchief. Robert grabbed it and put it before his mouth. He could taste blood, and when he opened the handkerchief he saw a small mess of blood soiled into the material. His head was pounding and he felt extremely dizzy.

A moment later Mr Thompson and Victoria walked back into the room. The room was full of whispers and soft chatter once more.

'Mrs Hawkes has regained her memory of that night and is now able to take the stand,' Mr Thompson said, addressing Samuel at the same time as the jury and everyone else. After a moment of whispering and chatter the room fell silent, as they waited to hear what Victoria had to say. She took the witness stand and swore in.

'Mrs Hawkes, can you please explain to the court what happened on the night of the fire, when you went in search of your husband.' Mr Thompson stepped back, feeling smug. Victoria was the answer to his prayers.

'I – I went to look for my husband. He was la-late ho-home.' She took a deep breath and glanced over at Robert. She could remember herself pacing up and down, wanting to go for an evening stroll with him. They had been trying hard to make their marriage work, she remembered it all now. 'I went to the m – mill.'

'At what time would you say that was?'

'I - I don't know - but I - I did hear the church be – bell ring – when – whe – I – I entered – the mill.'

'Was anyone at the mill?' Mr Thompson asked.

'No - they had all – all gone. I saw one li – light on upstairs. I thought it might bah- be Robert.'

'And was it?' Mr Thompson asked, knowing full well it would not have been.

'No. The room wa-was emp – emp…'

'Empty,' Mr Thompson said, finishing her word off for her. 'And so what did you do next?'

'Thunder – thunder,' she said, with tears now springing to her eyes. She could see it all so vividly.

'It was thundering outside?' he asked.

'Light- lightning too. It- it.' She started to cry. Mr Nesbitt stood up again in protest.

'My Lord, Mrs Hawkes is far too distressed and unwell to…'

Samuel intercepted. 'Mr Nesbitt, are you a medical professional?'

'No my Lord - but surely if she was not fit to take the stand yesterday, how can she be now?'

The chattering broke out again. Samuel's voice bellowed above everyone else's. 'Mrs Hawkes has regained her memory. Let her finish what she has to tell us. Please have the decency to be quiet.'

'I don't know if she is well enough,' Violet whispered, voicing her concerns to James, regretting telling the defence. She should have put her sister's welfare first, but looking at Robert, if he was innocent, she could not stand by and see him convicted, no more than James could. 'She'll be fine,' James said, 'you did the right thing. She is doing the right thing - speaking out.'

'Take your time Mrs Hawkes,' Samuel said softly. She looked at James and then at Robert. It was so painful to continue but she knew she had to, for Robert's sake, she owed him that at least, she was still his wife.

'Light – lightning stru- stuck a bah –beam above my head. Fire - I saw fire,' she cried.

'And then what happened?' Mr Thompson prompted, gently, in a low voice.

'Fire – beam fell- fell on me.' She felt her tummy and remembered the babies, the anguish now suddenly hitting her like a train at full speed. 'Oh – my- my babies!' she sobbed, almost falling to her knees, just about holding herself up. Mr Thompson rushed to help her. Robert stood up too, crying. 'Victoria!' His voice was nothing more than a weak croak that went unnoticed.

James rushed over towards the stand to help her.

Samuel took control once more. 'Thank you Mrs Hawkes, please be seated now. Someone fetch her a glass of water.' A clerk handed Victoria a glass of water. She took a sip and then allowed herself to be guided by James and Mr Thompson towards the bench. Robert watched her sit down and James touched her hand, to comfort her. This gesture did not go unnoticed by Robert. He looked away, it was all too painful, and for a moment he thought he might pass out, as the room spun and a sweat broke out on his forehead.

Samuel called for another interlude, something that wouldn't normally happen so soon after the last one, but then again there was nothing normal about this trial.

The court resumed once more and the case continued for a further one and a half hours before the jury went out to consider the facts. On their return, Samuel Turner asked if the jury had reached a verdict, to which their spokesman replied, *yes*. Samuel then asked Robert to stand up, which he did, swaying slightly as if he were drunk. He held onto the wooden shelf in front of him to steady himself.

'In light of new evidence,' Samuel began, addressing the jury, 'both photographic evidence and the account of Mrs Hawkes, how do you find the....'

Robert could no longer hear what Samuel was saying, it all muffled out into a blur as did his eyesight and he felt a strange sensation in his chest, as if his heart could no longer cope with pumping any more.

'*Not guilty!*' were the words that filled the court room, followed by a thud as Robert collapsed on the floor. 'Robert?' James shouted as he jumped up from the bench, followed by Victoria, then Violet and then the crowd.

Samuel heaved himself out of his chair and pushed them all back, making room for the doctor who had been waiting outside. The doctor knew just how serious Robert's condition was, and although he had accepted the bribe from the prison guard, his conscience had got the better of him and he had waited with medicine on standby for the moment the court had finished. He knelt down next to Robert and felt his neck, then his wrists. Everyone gathered round and spectators watched with glee. This was not a case that involved a hanging, but at least they had their drama.

The doctor stood up and announced in a low voice, 'he's dead.' Gasps rippled throughout the courtroom, followed by mayhem.

Chapter Twenty One

The news of Robert Hawkes's death had spread far and wide. Although not widely liked, and certainly not forgiven by the millers for gambling with their futures, there was an air of regret and sympathy.

Victoria had gone into hiding in her bedroom, not wishing to speak to anyone, not even Violet. She needed time to grieve, not just for Robert, but her twins too. The pain she now felt was not someone else's, but her own, and it was raw, very raw, as if she had lost her unborn babies on the very same day she had lost Robert.

'I'm worried about her,' Rose paced the parlour floor.

'For goodness sake sit down,' John groaned.

They had been livid that Victoria had gone behind their backs to court and also deeply concerned that, after everything she had been through, that she had to witness her husband dying like she did. The news of Robert's death had knocked them for six. The fact that the verdict was *not guilty* seemed not to matter. What mattered was he had been badly treated in prison and his illness neglected, causing his untimely death.

'The man was innocent and he didn't deserve to die like that,' John said. 'I'll speak with Samuel Turner, seek justice.'

'You've changed your tune,' Rose snapped.

'Alright, so I thought he started the fire - I was wrong. He shouldn't have gambled the mill though - and he shouldn't have had to die the way he did. With the right medicine, and proper bed rest, he could have recovered to full health, he was otherwise healthy. It was influenza - not the plague and now - now Victoria is left a young widow.'

'Alright! You don't have to spell it out,' Rose retorted, clearly irritated by him. Violet popped her head around the door. 'Mrs Darcy is asking if we should like supper soon.'

Rose shook her head. 'I can't even think about eating.'

'Speak for yourself - I'm famished,' John said, rising to his feet. Rose looked at him with contempt.

James had done nothing for the past two days, other than drink brandy and stare at a crackling fire spitting before him. Eleanor made him food regularly, but he refused to eat. Sophie had come to visit and pay her condolences, only to be told by Eleanor to go away and that James wished to be left alone. On one occasion she had bypassed Eleanor and marched right in, only to find him look straight through her as if she wasn't there and then he walked off into another room. She decided to give him the space he needed and went home.

He managed to write a short, brief, letter to Lillian, which he had written three times, because the first copy had got spoilt by his spilling brandy over it and the second had been stained by his tears.

The funeral was held at St Mary's in Whitby. There was not a huge turn-out, Robert was not the most popular of people. But despite their grievances, most of the millers turned up to pay their respects to the man who had been their employer for many years. Eleanor and Alfie also attended the funeral to show their support to James.

The Crawfords arrived by carriage, which pulled up outside of the church. Victoria's frame looked tiny beneath her black cloak, and her hat, embedded with tiny black and white flowers, perched on her head of dark curls, helped to shield her sad eyes. She linked arms with her father, while violet and Rose walked behind.

Sophie glanced up at the clock, her expression glum, as it had been for weeks now. John caught sight of her from the other side of the bar and walked over to her. 'I 'eard it's Robert 'Awkes's funeral today. Why are you not dressed for it?' he enquired.

'I'm not going,' she replied flatly.

'Why not?'

''E's made it perfectly clear 'e doesn't want me around.'

'When Nick died - Captain 'Awkes was a tower of strength to you.' He sat down on a stool in front of her. ''E's lashin' out because e's 'urt – upset – it's what we all do at times like this.'

Sophie looked at him with an air of guilt. 'I know – and - and you're right - but...'

'But nothing - if you love that man, you'll be there today when he needs you most.'

'And this place?' she put the cloth down she had been using to clean the bar with.

'Need you ask?' John smiled softly. 'Go on - be off with you – put a suitable frock on.'

She leaned over the bar and gave him a peck on the cheek, then dashed off upstairs to find something to wear. John was right, James needed her. He might not be aware of it, but he did, and she would not let him down in his hour of need.

James stood in the graveyard, not wishing to go inside the church just yet, even though the bitter wind whipped against him as he stood looking down at Whitby harbour. He needed some time to gather his thoughts. He wished, more than anything, that Lillian had been there today with him. He missed her. She had written back expressing her sorrow and deepest sympathy. The anger and heartache Robert had caused her and Jack seemed to be swept to one side for now, forgiven, but certainly not forgotten. She said, if she could have been there she would have, but apart from the obvious problem of not being able to get back from New York so soon, she was having a difficult pregnancy, with morning sickness that lasted all day long. She signed off by saying her thoughts and prayers would be with them all on this tragic day.

Big, dark, grey clouds loomed over Whitby, the mood depressing and cold. Victoria let go of her father's arm as they reached the church entrance. 'Go inside wi - with Mama and Violet - I'll –I'll be right there.' He followed her gaze over to where James stood. He patted her hand. 'Don't take long – it's cold.'

James stood with his back to the church; he did not notice the last of the mourners pass behind him and go inside. Neither did he hear Victoria approach him. 'You don't rea- realise how high up the - the church is until you sta- stand here looking down.'

He turned to face her with a ghost of a smile. 'How are you holding up?' There was so much tenderness in the way he asked, his eyes full of kindness and love towards her. He stroked the side of her face with affection. 'I'm griev- grieving for a man I married but didn't lo-love. Grieving for my –my unborn tw-twins that I- I didn't want at – at first. Nothing makes se-sense.'

'He was my brother. I didn't like him - I despised him- but I loved him - how does that any make sense?' Tears brimmed in his eyes and Victoria's too.

'Love is a str-strange thing.' She shivered from the cold and he pulled her close and held her in his arms, being careful not to knock her hat, although the wind was doing a good job of trying to blow it away, as she clutched hold of it with one of her hands. Her other hand she placed around James.

'I love you,' he whispered, holding her close, his voice lost in a gust of wind.

Sophie finally made it to the top of steps, panting and out of breath, still holding her skirts and cloak above her ankles so as not to trip. It might have been cold, but she was perspiring from rushing. The bells rang out mournful chimes that echoed around the graveyard, across to the abbey, and below in the village. As she regained her breath, steadying herself against the stone wall of the church, she saw him with *her* again. They turned around and walked towards the church, *her* clutching on to his arm like she owned him. Did she have no respect for her dead husband? Not even laid to rest yet and she was already latching on to James like a leach. And did he have no respect for the fact that she was his brother's wife? She wiped away her tears.

Flurries of snowflakes fell, leaving a light covering of white all around. Two grave diggers in the distance shovelled hard into the almost frozen ground, preparing Robert's grave.

She was still crying by the time she reached the bottom of the steps. There had been no point in staying, he obviously didn't need her. He had Victoria now.

The service was short, sombre and dignified. And by the time the coffin was carried out of the church and lowered into the prepared grave in the yard, a thin layer of snow covered the ground and the abbey, just as it did below over Whitby.

Chapter Twenty Two

Winter gave way to spring at last. A stunning array of pink and white blossom on the trees could be seen everywhere. Flowers in full bloom, butterflies and bees were also back, and bird-song filled the air again, saying *goodbye* to the cold weather and *hello* to the long awaited warmth of sunshine once more. Lambs stood next to their mothers in fields, and ducks swam with their young along the River Esk, while the sunshine created an illusion of tiny crystals sparkling on the water. Daffodils and crocuses seemed to have sprung up everywhere along the riverbank. What a difference spring made, it was almost as if Mother Nature meant spring to be a gift to all living beings, following the aftermath of a long, bleak winter.

Out of respect for Robert, and acting on the advice of Rose and John to avoid gossiping tongues, James and Victoria had kept their distance from each other since Robert's funeral. Although there were times they longed to see each other and seek comfort from one another, the time apart was doing them both good. Victoria needed time to come to terms with her loss and concentrate on her speech therapy, and James needed time not only to come to terms with losing his brother the way he had, but to focus on the mill and to think about the future ahead. He had spoken to Sophie soon after the funeral and done his best to justify his feelings towards Victoria, while explaining how he regretted hurting Sophie and his intention was never to upset her. Although heartbroken, Sophie stood with her head held high and said, in a dignified manner, 'James, your 'eart 'as only ever belonged to one woman - who am I to stand in the way of your 'appiness. I'm most grateful for the time we spent together.' As friends they parted, and by early June Sophie had raised enough money to buy James out, employing John Barrow to work alongside her.

On the tenth of June 1912 Verity Beckwith celebrated her fiftieth birthday by throwing another one of her elaborate parties at *Bramblewick House*. Both Victoria and James were of course invited, and this would be the first time since Robert's death that they would spend time in each other's company. Victoria looked stunning in an emerald green silk gown and her hair swept up high with curls framing her pretty face, her scar perfectly hidden under her hair.

'You look beautiful,' James kissed her hand.

She smiled coyly. 'Why, thank you Captain Hawkes.'

'Despite me leaving the navy more than a year ago now, my title still seems to stick,' he grinned. Everyone at the mill still called him Captain Hawkes, or rather Captain 'Awkes, as did Eleanor and Alfie.

Victoria smiled again. 'The title suits you.'

'It's good to see her smile,' said Rose, sitting next to Verity. Violet was chatting to a young, fair haired, handsome gentleman, a distant relative of Verity's, and she seemed quite smitten with him and he with her. 'Who? Violet or Victoria?' Verity asked.

Rose frowned, dragging her gaze back to Verity. 'Victoria of course. Her speech is so much better now – you would hardly know she had a problem. It's good to see her with James, they make such a lovely pair.'

Verity let out one of her infamous hoots, without humour. 'It was not that long ago you were saying James was not a good match for her, and how Robert was a far better suitor.'

Rose blushed. 'One can make a misjudgement now and again. Besides - circumstances have changed greatly.'

'Indeed they have,' said Verity, knocking back a glass of champagne.

'When are you going back to New York? asked Rose.

Verity laughed again. 'Why? Are you trying to get rid of me?'

Rose smiled sardonically. 'I meant, to see Lillian and Jack?'

'End of this month,' Verity replied. 'In time to be there when the baby is due in July.'

Eleanor and Alfie lay in bed, in Eleanor's small bed - both of them huddled together under a blanket, grabbing the opportunity while James was away for the evening.

'Alfie?' she lay on her side and propped her head up higher on the pillow.

'Yes,' he replied with a yawn.

'If you ever stop lovin' me…'

He turned to face her, alarmed at the idea. 'Now stop right there,' he touched her nose with the tip of his finger. 'That will never 'appen.'

'It might one day,' she continued, regardless of his protesting stare. 'And if it did - would you ever tell police about – you know - what I told you?'

He knew instantly that she was referring to George Tanner. 'No, of course not. I told you before - you weren't to blame - you didn't kill anyone – 'e did.'

'I 'elped 'im get rid of Bill's body,' her eyes glazed over with sadness again. She wondered if she would ever stop thinking about that night, the night George left with Bill Sanders body wrapped in a blanket, bundled into a rowing boat. She still had nightmares about it, still woke up crying quite often. She could see the blue and yellow boat in her mind every time she closed her eyes.

'Eleanor, you didn't go out to sea with 'im – 'e did that all on 'is own. As far as I'm concerned you got mixed up with the wrong person who dragged you into somethin' you shouldn't 'ave been dragged into.' He looked at her forlorn expression.

'What's brought all this on? Do you still love 'im? Wait for 'im to return?' he waited for her answer with baited breath.

'George Tanner? – No - course not- don't be daft.' She rolled on to her side, turning her back on Alfie, trying not to show her tears and praying silently he did not see through her lie. Try as she might, and she certainly had these past months, she still found it hard not to miss George. Alfie was lovely, but he wasn't George and never would be.

Alfie lay still looking up at the ceiling, deep in thought. He was no fool, he knew she still loved George Tanner and he hoped he would never return. But if he did dare show his face again, he would not get Eleanor back, he would see to that. He and his brothers could sort anything. Eleanor would remain his forever. He loved her too much to leave her in the clutches of a murderer, even though Eleanor claims it had been an accident.

The party was in full swing. A band on one side of the room played while guests mingled, ate lavish canapés, and drank champagne.

Lord Beckwith and John Crawford sat in a quiet corner, deep in conversation. 'I'd say you had a lucky escape,' said John.

'Thank goodness we decided to wait until June. April, we had originally planned for. I was going to surprise Verity - I thought we could combine it with going to the south for a few days and then catch the ship from Southampton to New York. Then business got in the way and Verity said perhaps we should wait until nearer the time – you know - when the baby is due.'

'I shudder to think what those poor people went through – terrible - terrible.' John took a sip of his drink, thoughtfully.

'Doesn't bear thinking about – I mean the Titanic - a brand new, luxurious and supposedly well made ship. From what I can gather, word is corners were cut in attempt to save money…'

James whispered in Victoria's ear. She followed him into the library as he had requested. They walked out of the room, but not at the same time and then met in the hallway, giggling and running hand in hand to the library, closing the doors behind them before anyone noticed they'd gone, like naughty children.

Once they had caught their breath, he said in all seriousness, 'I need to tell you something.'

'What is it?' she replied, with both concern and curiosity in her eyes.

'I don't want you to get upset - but…' he stepped back and eyed her up and down from head to toe. She watched with a deep frown.

'I'm no expert on ladies' fashion,' he said, 'and forgive me for saying this, but there is something terribly amiss with your gown.'

She glanced downwards, inspecting it to see what could possibly be so wrong. She looked back at him, trying not to be too offended that he appeared not to like what she was wearing. 'You don't like what I am wearing?' her tone was full of disappointment.

'Quite the contrary my dear - I love it! I just think it's missing something.' He then pulled out a little black satin pouch from his waistcoat pocket and handed it to her. He had waited a long time to give it to her, since arriving back from his voyage and finding out she was engaged to Robert.

Her delicate fingers opened the pouch and pulled out the hand crafted jet pendant. Her face broke into a beaming smile, which delighted him no end.

'Allow me,' he reached out and took it from her. He then stood behind her and placed it around her neck. The bare skin of her neck and the smell of her perfume, sent tingles down his spine. A small scar from the fire could be seen close to her shoulder, and he kissed it without warning. She knew exactly what he had done, she knew every single scar she possessed and she turned to face him with a look of surprise and torment.

'My body,' she said breathlessly. 'I – I have – many ugly scars.'

'They are not ugly - they tell a story - a story of survival. Would you love me any less if I were covered in wounds from a battle at war?'

With tears in her eyes, she said, 'how could you ask me such a question? Of course I would not love you any less.'

Their lips met in a long awaited kiss, a kiss of solidarity, love, compassion, an unbreakable chemistry that had always been there and always would be. And, had a herd of wildebeest passed them in a stampede at that precise moment, they would not have noticed, for they were wrapped up, consumed, in their very own magical blissfulness.

Chapter Twenty Three

At dawn the sky, a mix of delicate tones of orange and peach, met the sea on the horizon. The sea, calmer than it had been in days, lapped gently against the shore at Sandsend, bringing with it a shipwrecked blue and yellow rowing boat. There was not a soul to be seen along the sandy stretch of beach, framed by rugged cliff tops as the boat wedged into the sand. Sunrise soon faded into a glorious deep blue sky, with not a cloud in sight, and with it came a slight, early summer breeze. It promised to be a warm day ahead.

A young boy wearing ragged clothes, in bare feet, ran through the cobbled, winding streets of Whitby, stopping at a cottage with a blue door at the top end of Church Street. He banged his fist on the wood and a moment later, John Barrow opened it.

'I've got a letter for you, Mister,' the boy said, holding a sealed, cream envelope in his hand.

'Give's it 'ere then lad,' John replied.

'Not before I get paid,' the boy said, holding out his grubby, little palm.

John sighed and pulled out a coin and handed it to him. The boy looked back at John. 'Is that it? The woman what gave it t' me said it t' be right important.'

'Did she now.' John sighed and pulled out another coin. 'That's ye lot.'

The boy handed him the envelope then ran off down the street.

Intrigued, John ripped open the envelope right there on the doorstep. He recognised the handwriting, but couldn't remember who it belonged to and, as he started to read it, he soon realised it to be Sophie's. He did his best to make sense of the letter. Given the fact that John did not read well and Sophie did not write well, it was a difficult task, but in the end he managed to understand that Sophie had gone to visit a long lost aunt whom she had only recently discovered to still be alive. Her aunt, named Elsie, lived in the countryside close to the Scottish border. Sophie asked John to look after the pub while she was away. Although she did not know exactly how long she would be away for, she promised to be back before the end of the year.

'End of year!' John groaned, then went back inside and closed the front door.

The train chugged across the old stone viaduct bridge above the estuary and, in the distance, the seaside town of Berwick-upon-Tweed emerged. The sky, just as it was in Whitby that day, was a bright blue and the sun shone brilliantly over this busy little town.

The train whistled as it arrived into the station. A stout, middle-aged man wearing spectacles stood on the platform next to a well dressed elderly lady, they both waited eagerly for the passengers to disembark the train. Sophie walked along the platform and stopped at the station master's office under the clock. A moment later the man and lady, who had been waiting at the other end of the station, walked towards her. 'Miss Dickens?' the man enquired. She nodded her head and he picked up her suitcase. The elderly lady stepped forward. 'Sophie, my dear – I'm Elsie Pickering.' She stretched out her frail hand and Sophie shook it gently.

'Shall we?' Elsie Pickering gestured towards the entrance of the station. The man carrying Sophie's suitcase was already loading it onto the back of a carriage pulled by four horses. A couple of automobiles passed by, then more horses and carriages. It was a lively town, but this was not where Sophie would be staying. Elsie Pickering's home was in the countryside three miles away.

'Thank you for 'elping me like this,' Sophie said, as they walked slowly towards the waiting carriage.

'Any friend of Jenny's is a friend of mine. Her mother worked for me for many years before she moved to Yorkshire.'

'I worked with Jenny on market stall before me uncle got sick and I 'ad to 'elp out int' pub. She's kind – decent, and I know she won't tell a soul.'

'She won't - you need not worry,' Elsie reassured her. They stopped at the carriage and Elsie looked kindly at her. She was a sincere looking lady with rosy cheeks and soft, doe-like eyes. 'You'll be safe with me – you and the baby. I've brought up six of my own – I've plenty of experience,' she chuckled.

Sophie returned her smile and her hand instinctively glided over her small bump, the bump she had managed to keep hidden these last few months.

'You're in good hands,' Elsie said.

'I know, and I'm so grateful to you for takin' me in. I 'ad no idea what to do or who to turn to when I found out.'

'And the father – does he know?' Elsie asked attentively.

Sophie shook her head, fighting back her tears. 'No. And he must never know.'

James took the one hundred and ninety nine steps up to St Mary's church, with Victoria very much on his mind; in fact, he could think of nothing else, since the party and the kiss they had shared.

Robert's grave was full of flowers, newly placed, and James wondered who had brought them, Victoria perhaps? He stood next to the headstone, listening to the sound of a blackbird in full song, sitting on a nearby wall. There was no one around, other than the same two grave diggers, preparing for another funeral later that day.

He coughed to clear his throat and then spoke. 'I was never very good at speaking to you when you were alive,' he gave a small humourless chuckle. 'And I'm not much better now you are gone. I know you are not going to like what I am about to say - or maybe I'm wrong – maybe you would want this now that you are no longer here. You see - I love Victoria.' He sighed. 'I'm going to ask her to marry me.' He waited for a moment and then said, 'this is the part when you would have ripped into me and told me I was wrong and that she was *your* wife.'

The blackbird stopped singing and the sun disappeared behind a dark cloud that seemed to appear from nowhere. For a moment it felt cold and James gave a small disconcerting shiver. He glanced around the graveyard. An eerie silence filled the air, even the grave diggers had disappeared. He turned his attention back to the headstone. 'Are you objecting? She was my love before she was yours,' he said, justifying himself in annoyance. 'I had hoped to come here and ask you for your blessing – but - but even from beyond your grave you seem to...' Suddenly the blackbird cut in with song once more and the sun shone brightly, brighter than ever before. A stunning butterfly of many colours appeared and sat on the headstone, taking a well earned rest. It turned and faced James, he smiled knowingly. 'Thank you,' he said, with a soft smile. 'I knew you would understand.'

Looking down over Whitby harbour and the folk going about their business, James took a deep breath and inhaled the sweet summer air. If he could have turned back time, would he have? He had everything he could ever wish for now - Victoria, the mill, *Heron House, Somersby Hill,* but it had all come at a high price. He had inadvertently hurt people, Sophie included, and he regretted he could not give her what she wanted – the husband she deserved.

Yet, despite all of this, for the first time in as long as he could remember, he now had a future to really look forward to. He possessed a bitter sweet feeling of achievement. Should he feel guilty, or simply accept that one can not turn back time? Perhaps we all have to learn to live with the consequences of our actions, he thought, walking back down the steps, however hard that may be. For if we could not learn to live with them, learn to forgive ourselves for perceived wrongs, what would be the point of continuing our journey? A man's desire for a life full of happiness, love and good health cannot be frowned upon, surely not if he has learned from his own mistakes and promises not to make them again. And as he reached the bottom of the steps, two local fishermen greeted him. 'Mornin' Captain 'Awkes.'

'Morning gentlemen,' he replied, raising his hat to them.

He continued his stroll through the streets of Whitby. Familiar faces greeted him in much the same way as the fishermen had. *'Mornin' Captain 'Awkes! – Ayup Captain 'Awkes! - It's a fine day, Captain 'Awkes!'* He raised his hat to each and every one of them, but he did not stop to chat, he was too preoccupied with his thoughts as he continued on his way back towards Ruswarp. He would not have been aware of the talk on the streets in Whitby that same morning - talk about the rowing boat with two dead bodies washed up on Sandsend - talk of Sophie Dickens leaving *The Old Horseshoe* pub in the hands of John Barrow while she visited her *so called* long lost aunt. Who needed to know about tittle-tattle on the street on such a fine morning as this?

Author's Note

So many people have very kindly provided me with information and help for the research into writing this book, and I would like to say thank you to each and every one of them. Especially to **Mike Marshall**, for his stunning photograph of the *Stavros S Niarchos* ship, anchored in Runswick Bay at sunset, making a perfect front cover for the book. Also, thank you to **Andrew Dawson** for the superb photograph of the famous 199 steps in Whitby for the back cover.

Thank you also to **Ian Wilson** and the members of the ***Whitby Memories*** group, who answered so many of my questions and showed me so many wonderful photographs of Whitby during 1911 and 1912. Also, to **Bill Page** who kindly posted to me information and photographs of the Ruswarp mill when it was operational. As always, I owe so much to my editor **Alec Hawkes**, no relation to James Hawkes, I hasten to add, although his name did inspire me for the creation of James Hawkes! Alec has an incredible eye for detail, but I should emphasise that any inaccuracies in the book to do with the area are mine alone. Also I must not forget my good friend **Domenico Cifaldi**, who asked me to create a character based on him – Dom, you now have your fame!

I would also like to take this opportunity to point out to those of you who don't already know this - Ruswarp mill did, in fact, burn down on the twenty fifth of September 1911. The fire was caused by a freak strike of lightning. Of course, the story I created, and characters surrounding the fire, are totally fictional. Heron House, Crawford House, Somersby Hill, and any other properties mentioned in the book, are fictional, including the crown court in Scarborough and The Old Horseshoe Pub in Whitby. The parish church of St Bartholomew's Ruswarp, does exist and still stands today in the village, as does the mill, although it has now been turned into lovely flats and houses overlooking the River Esk.

Whitby and Ruswarp are rich with history, surrounded by stunning scenery and, for those of you who have never visited, I highly recommend you do! And should you walk along the winding streets of Whitby, or stand on the river bank in Ruswarp overlooking the River Esk, please spare a thought for Captain 'Awkes!

Claire Voet

Claire Voet is also the author of four other novels, these include *Whittington Manor,* (nominated and awarded third place at London's People's Book Prize Awards 2013) *Whittington Manor II – The Poppy Sunset, The Other Daddy - A World Away,* (Short Story) *A Helping Hand,* and Claire's bestselling novel *The Ghost of Bluebell Cottage.*

For more information about Claire Voet and her writing please visit www.clairevoet.com

Made in the USA
Charleston, SC
26 January 2016